Terror in Paradise

David Adams

Published by David Adams, 2023.

This is a work of fiction. Similarities to real people, places, or events are entirely coincidental.

TERROR IN PARADISE

First edition. December 29, 2023.

ISBN: 978-0645361186

Written by David Adams.

Also by David Adams

Terror in Our Homeland
The Other Stolen Generations
Terror in Paradise

I thank God for any gift, skills or creativity He has blessed me with.

Thank you to Broni my wife who travels with me into places that have a reputation for being dangerous. My companion through life as well, putting up with my being distracted when in her company and spending hours locked up in my office.

A huge thank you to my Beta Readers, who also include Broni (another demonstration of bravery).

On this novel I especially want to thank Prudence Bessant who contributed fearlessly and constantly in an attempt to make TERROR in PARADISE a much better book than it would have been.

More importantly, Prudence's input has I believe built on my writing skills and approaches especially in the area of character development.

TERROR in PARADISE

by DAVID ADAMS

This is a work of fiction.

Names, characters, places, brands, media, and incidents are either the product of the author's imagination or are used fictitiously. Any resemblance to actual events, locales, or persons, living or dead, is coincidental. This Book is licensed for your personal enjoyment only. This eBook may not be re-sold or given away to other people. If you would like to share this book with another person, please purchase another copy for each person you share with. Thank you for respecting the author's work.

Published by: DAVID ADAMS (REVISED VERSION DECEMBER 2023)

WHAT READERS FROM ALL AROUND THE WORLD ARE SAYING ABOUT;

TERROR IN PARADISE

JUDY from Florida USA

This is Judy writing. I just finished reading the book last Friday. Not only was it great to actually meet you and Broni on our cruise but it was exciting to read your book! I loved it. I was reading in the middle of the night, and woke up my husband to discuss that chapter where Ramone XXXXXXX. **Author has redacted this to preserve suspense.**

Your research for the book was amazing. I learned a lot about self defence, baddies, and international antiques smuggling.

WHAT READERS FROM ALL AROUND THE WORLD ARE SAYING ABOUT; TERROR IN PARADISE

PRUDENCE BESSANT from Qld. Australia

Terror in Paradise

A book with a hero in the essence of an Australian James Bond. This was a thrilling read with plenty of drama and suspense. A wonderful mystery to be solved and intrigue along the way. Exotic locations and interesting details about smuggling and ancient artefacts to inform the reader.

GUS HOUGH from Florida USA.

A terrific read! Can't wait for Adams' third novel. Both his books blur the line between fiction and (terrorist organization vs Australian security) non-fiction. Can't wait to see what operation Steve Wallace gets into next.

IVAN RUDOLPH (World renown Non-Fiction Author and Historian), Sunshine Coast Qld. Aust.

I had a fun day yesterday reading my first novel for many many years, and thoroughly enjoyed it. Well done! Each reader will see it differently, but for me it moved fast and had sufficient intrigue to balance the violence. I enjoyed the exotic settings and the way you moved the story forward from chapter to chapter. The potential for a sequel is obvious and I hope you are into it already.

OTHER ACTION THRILLERS by DAVID ADAMS

Available through all your favourite distributors.

TERROR IN OUR HOMELAND

All STEVE WALLACE wanted was to be left alone, but his war-torn past was about to catch up with him. Was he having yet another painful flashback, or were the two Taliban soldiers he had just killed really here in rural western Queensland? He had no way of knowing that he had just stumbled on one of the most sophisticated terror networks Australia had ever seen. For the first time since 1915, Australia is under attack by Islamic terrorists on Australian soil. Does Australia have the answers, the resources, and the resolve to fight against these attacks, or will more innocent men, women and children die? Can Steve Wallace convince the Australian National Security Centre that his discovery is not some Jack Daniel's fuelled PTSD hallucination? The reluctant hero finds himself drawn back into what he had worked so hard to escape.

TERROR IN PARADISE

STEVE WALLACE embarks on his most challenging mission so far !!!!!!

ISIS is funding its evil plans to dominate the world financed by selling stolen ancient artefacts. The CIA needs Australian Agent Steve Wallace to go undercover to collect vital Intelligence. He has to unravel the terrorist organisation's funding system. The money gained from these illicit sales is being used to buy missiles, guns, and ammunition and fund cells and terrorist attacks, including 9/11. Steve Wallace is ex-SAS and one of the best, but this undercover job calls for a James Bond or Jason Bourne. This time, he's way out of his depth. Can Wallace succeed out of his comfort zone? Tracking the smugglers all over the world while racking up a body count, he sends shock waves through the sophisticated organisation, all the way up to the third-generation New York Antique Dealer.

TERROR IN MY HEART, my latest novel in the Wallace sagas should be out early 2024.

Please note the Terror novels are not a series; however, they are in sequence, starting with TERROR in OUR HOMELAND.

CRIME NOVELS
THE OTHER STOLEN GENERATIONS

My first book in this genre takes the lid off the murky world of the Paedophile. This is a Fiction Novel. However, having worked in this field allows me to fill the book with real life cases, real paedophiles and victims and describe actual **Police** procedures. I have woven a story so authentic that it exposes the Reader to the truth about this topic that most people choose to avoid.

This book, while never condoning or excusing paedophilia, allows the Reader to listen in on conversations for the first time, providing shocking insight into their evil, selfish world and mindset. The book also depicts the multi-faceted challenges faced by Police.

The Reader also learns how the victim and those around them are impacted so powerfully by the damage as a result of the abuse. Not just when it occurs but for their entire life.

PROLOGUE

The immaculately dressed American sitting on the hotel suite's white leather lounge smiled at the small but muscular Middle Eastern man. "I don't care about all your Muslim bullshit. You can keep killing each other until there's no one left. As long as that money keeps flowing my way, you'll have all the guns, ammo, RPGs, even SAMS, whatever you want. High-quality goods, too, delivery services supported by high-level security. That means no worries for you, Hamza."

Of course, Hamza wasn't his real name. He had chosen it because he liked its Arab meaning, 'Name of the Lion resembling his nature and physique. Beneath the table, his fists clenched. The ISIS Officer was deeply offended by this corrupt infidel using the Holy Prophet's Name and a curse word side by side. He felt the beginnings of a smile start to touch the corners of his mouth as he imagined himself launching across the marble coffee table. Crossing the small space between the two men, Hamza would crush this infidel's skull like a gazelle caught in a lion's jaws. He didn't attempt to hide the contempt that seethed behind his dark, Obsidian-like eyes. They bored into this pretty boy's soft blue eyes until the arms dealer was forced to look down. He blew out a small breath between his teeth.

"You know, Mr Brooks, you have done extremely well from our transactions. To be fair, your quality and service so far has been outstanding. But we both know you are charging us a premium price on every delivery."

Of course, Brooks wasn't his real name either. He hated this smug Arab or whatever he was, and any contempt was mutual. And besides, the American hated comments that attempted to screw him on price. After all, he wasn't fuckin Walmart.

"Yeah, yeah, if you want to save a few bucks on your next deal, go down to McWeapons and get their weekly special. We both know you'll end up with old AKs, faulty ammo and late deliveries. Be back with me after one try. You know you only get what you pay for. Steak or hamburger, your choice. Speaking of money, your payment system is awesome. I have been playing this game for a while, and you seem to have sidestepped those slimy bankers. What's it called Hawala or something? Bayal, tell me, how come it works so well?"

This low life's prying into such a secret and sensitive area of the management systems of ISIS was inexcusable, but what could one expect from such a fool. Nearly enough for Bayal to draw his Glock and silence Brook forever. However, replacing such a weapons procurer, even one he despised, was not easy. He answered with a voice with a slight trembling caused by controlled anger. "Brooks, you know better than to go there. I will never discuss how our finances work. However, one of the reasons it's been so successful for thousands of years is its dependence on secrecy. A secrecy covered by the blood of the curious Mr Brooks. Hamza thought; O*ur age-old credit system, Hawala, has funded so many terrorist actions, even 9/11. I'm still amazed it remains effective even in the most modern settings, evading hi-tech surveillance. Hawala, these infidel pigs will never understand it or close it down.*

OFFICIAL DEFINITIONS

HAWALA– What does it mean.

The following are just a few definitions and explanations of the Hawala system. Please note keywords such as laundering, terrorist, used to pay jihadists.

INTERPOL DEFINITION

Hawala is a method of transferring money without actual movement. One definition from Interpol is that Hawala is a "money transfer without money movement." Hawala is an alternative remittance channel that exists outside of traditional banking systems.

Hawala – Treasury Department Definition

https://www.treasury.gov/resource-centre/terrorist-illicit.../FinCEN-Jawala-rpt.pdf

by PM Jost - Cited by 152 - Related articles

This paper presents a description of the hawala (also referred to as hundi) alternative remittance system. Hawala is an ancient system originating in South Asia; today, it is used around the world to conduct legitimate remittances. Like any other remittance system, hawala can and does play a role in money laundering.

Hawala: The Ancient Banking Practice Used to Finance Terror Groups

www.newsweek.com/underground-european-hawala-network-financing-middle-easter...

Feb 24, 2015 - Hawala A currency exchange trader counts money in his office in Islamabad. According to Spanish intelligence officials, Hawala's ancient banking practice has been used to pay jihadists' salaries. Washington this year has started attacking the Taliban's funding channels ahead of withdrawing most of its.

CHAPTER 1

CANBERRA
AUSTRALIAN CAPITAL TERRITORY
AUSTRALIA

After two commercial flights, I arrived at Canberra Airport, where a young Corporal met me. He saluted me as I was now on duty, and like an electric switch, I turned into Major Steve Wallace. I acknowledged his salute. I sometimes found it a little hard to comprehend living a dual existence. One day, I was an ordinary bloke living in sleepy Roma, Queensland, with my girlfriend, Chris. And, at any time, a phone call and off I go to our nation's Capital to be sent anywhere they needed my skill set. Once again, I am focused to travel the world on the next National Security Centre mission. After a successful career in the Army, I knew I had had enough. I was due to re-enlist but decided to retire, much to the shock of my Army mates and Superior Officers. I had bummed around in holiday mode for a while until I found a secluded spot where my Border Collie Jake and I could hunt and fish and generally avoid people. Jake and I shared a basic camp, but we wanted for nothing. We had settled into a simple subsistence life, occasionally helping my cattle farmer friend when needed. Just over a year ago, after a series of events near my camp, my world was on its head. But, that's another story for another time. I came out of retirement to work as an operative with the National Security Centre (N.S.C.), a combined anti-terrorist organisation answering only to the Prime Minister.

Taking my go bag and throwing it on the back seat, the Corporal said. "Welcome to sunny Canberra, Sir."

As he drove the well-designed streets of Canberra to H.Q., I thought he was far too cheerful, and Canberra, as usual, was cold, cloudy and grey. After a very brief welcome from Colonel Goodrich, the briefing began properly. Colonel Goodrich looked up from his desk.

"Steve, thanks for coming down so quickly. I hope you weren't busy when I called."

Smiling, I thought of how I was about to get busy when that damned phone rang. "No, Sir, not at all; to be really honest, I was still in bed."

My mind wandered back to our sunny bedroom. Was that only this morning? *I was lying next to Chris, my beautiful girlfriend. We had met amid the turmoil caused by my run-in with a terrorist group who had set up a training camp outside Roma. That other story. The insistent drumming of my phone on the bedside table intruded on the warm, sunny room. I grabbed the phone, mumbling to myself.*

"I hate frigging mobile phones. It was better out in the bush where I didn't have a frigging signal."

I gently got out of bed so as not to disturb Chris, and went into the lounge.

Gruffly, I answered. "Steve Wallace."

Ignoring my tone. "Steve, good to hear your voice. It's Pete Goodrich. Can you talk?" I smiled and adjusted my attitude; Colonel Goodrich was a Section Head at the National Security Centre (N.S.C.) Canberra. He had been instrumental in forwarding and supporting my concerns about the military activity I had observed in the neighbouring cattle property. Now he was my Boss. He was never a big conversationalist. "Mate, I need you wheels up ASAP. We have a job requiring your special skills."

"Roger that, Sir, what's the plan?" Goodrich answered succinctly. "Wait until you get to Canberra, and I'll brief you, see you tonight, OK?".

"All good, Sir, see you ASAP." I responded.

I knew what all this meant; the details would come later. Once I had accepted the job offer from N.S.C.'s Brigadier Dodds after the raid on the camp, they owned me. The arrangement was straightforward: I was to be on call to carry out covert operations, assassinations, reconnaissance, or anything else they needed. My life was to sit tight in domestic bliss until they beckoned. A strange mix of normalcy. I was living half my life with Chris in beautiful Roma, Australia and a few hours later in some war zone only a call away. As much as I enjoyed my new 'civilian' life in the back of my mind, I was always waiting for the call that could send me to the ends of the earth on another mission. I knew one way or another, someone's death would always be the outcome. I had also learned to avoid thinking that every assignment could mean my death. That said, if I was honest, hanging out with my dog I had missed the 'Rock and Roll'. The adventure and danger made for a great job.

Colonel Goodrich's raised voice brought my thoughts back to his office.

"STEVE, are you with me?"

Thinking it wasn't like me to daydream, I wondered if domestic bliss was dulling me. "Sorry, Sir, all good."

"OK, Steve, keep us informed of your loc as usual. Use your credit card, and we'll know where you are. Hopefully, it was you who used it."

Picking up on the undertone of his statement, I responded. "Yes, Sir, from what I can see in the briefing, it looks pretty good, hopefully, a quick in and out. If you see my card buying a massage, it'll be me, and I'm better than OK."

Laughing, Goodrich moved on. "Hilarious Major Wallace, good, the Corporal will take you to the Armoury. You choose the 'cutlery', and God willing, and if the creeks don't rise, I'll see you when you get back in a couple of days."

Smiling, I recognised the saying John Wayne quoted in numerous cowboy movies. However, it fitted rather well to my impending mission.

"Thanks, Sir, will do." I stood and shook hands with the Colonel and turned to leave his office.

Corporal Baldwin was waiting for me, and we automatically fell into step with each other as soldiers do. He chatted away as we walked along the hospital white corridor with numerous unmarked doors leading off.

"Sir, as the Boss probably told you, we are off to the Armoury. He asked me to steer towards the knives for this one. There's a nice collection of edged weapons down there for you to choose from." We took the lift down to what the Corporal called the dungeon and turned right after we exited. Arriving at a large steel door, Corporal Baldwin pressed a security pass to a wall-mounted digital reader.

A metallic voice asked. "Good morning, Corporal Baldwin. What is the purpose of your visit?" Baldwin replied. "Major Wallace here to be kitted ASAP."

A clunk followed a loud click, and the heavy Armoury door opened.

"Lurch, you wouldn't have met Major Wallace."

Turning to me, Corporal Baldwin smiled. "This is Sergeant Adams. Sir, we don't let him up into daylight very often. His nickname is Lurch."

Despite the informal introduction, Sergeant Adams saluted as he was wearing his beret. "Honour to meet you, Sir. Please have a look around. Any questions, ask."

I returned his salute. "Will do, Sergeant thanks for the welcome. Can you show me your knife collection first?"

We walked past walls covered in racks and display cabinets overflowing with weapons of every kind. To me, it was like Aladdin's cave. There were every conceivable killing tool, from my favourite Barrett 50 Cal Sniper rifle rocket launchers to several styles of Garrottes, for a quieter version of death. We got to the edged weapon section.

I recognised bayonets from virtually every part of the world, and the collection of civilian knives was impressive. It was from within this group I would make my choice.

My mission was relatively simple. Although, in my experience, it is often the ones that appear straightforward that blow up in your face. I was to fly to East Timor, where a local Mayor of a city called Lospalos, backed by Indonesian Islamic Fundamentalists, was agitating against the hard-won independence. He was encouraging and equipping young zealots to carry out attacks on Australian tourists and missionaries. So far, they had been responsible for several suicide bombings, violent muggings and rapes and the poisoning of copious large quantities of drugs and booze sold to tourists in Bali and Djakarta. I chose my weapon, a beautiful yet functional knife, and we headed back upstairs. My flight left in just under four hours, so the Corporal and I retraced our steps back to the Canberra airport. The crazy reality about air travel from Canberra to Sydney is it can often take you longer to get on the plane than you are in the plane.

Arriving at Sydney Domestic Terminal, I made my way over to International to await my flight. The Virgin Australian flight to East Timor was via Sydney; eventually, we took off from Kingsford-Smith International. I was already asleep. I awoke at some stage during the flight and pondered the more profound things in my life. I knew I loved Chris; she was good for me in many ways. But as much as that was true, I couldn't help but see it as an unplanned complication now I was back on duty. I had seen my first marriage self-destruct, and many of my S.A.S. mate's marriages break up due to lengthy training and deployments away from home. My fly-in, fly-out set-up should solve that. However, I also knew it placed an unfair burden on Chris waiting for a call to say I'd been killed or was missing. To be brutally frank, it was a new distraction to me. When I was on operations, it was one I could do without.

"Would you like something to drink, Sir?" I looked up to see a steward asking me.

"Jack on the rocks would be great, please."

EAST TIMOR

Eight-and-a-half hours later, the bang of the landing gear lowering woke me with a fright. It might be a while before I got any more sleep, so I was grateful for the rest. As I waited to exit the plane, I listened to a group of three missionaries chatting excitedly about the work they were about to begin. Although my work differed significantly from their mission, the thought crossed my mind: *they are braver than me in many ways.* Entering an unknown culture, staying at it for a year or more, and attempting to change age-old beliefs was a big job. My mission, all going well, was more straightforward. I would be back on a plane heading home in three days. My task was only to change the beliefs of one man permanently. I inserted myself between two of the missionaries as we got off the plane. I wasn't expecting anyone to be watching for me, but old habits die hard. My presence inferred that I was part of their group. As they turned towards the bus station, I headed for the Car Hire company. Using a different passport and driver's license than I had just travelled on, I hired a Toyota Hilux, as these were very common all over the island.

I recollected the details of the area from my Canberra briefing. Lospalos is an East Timorese city 248 kilometres east of Dili, the national Capital. The city's Mayor had influence and control over 17,000 city residents and a further 25,000 who lived in the surrounding Lautém Sub-District. He had no idea, but the region's influential Mayor was my Tango/Target. Knowing I had a five-hour trip ahead of me, I settled into a country drive. I cranked up the Hilux's air-conditioning, and it began fighting against the oppressive humidity that threatened to crush me. Arriving just before dark, I drove past the Tango's home. I had thought about parking a few blocks away from his house. Still, I figured a white face walking around would stick out where just another Toyota pickup would be virtually invisible. This Reece allowed me to confirm the Intel I had from my briefing.

I had studied the sat photos our local man had supplied, but I had learned long ago not to rely on other people's reconnaissance of my mission site. The target lived by himself but, from the reports, often had visitors. There were reports he preferred little boys and girls provided by several local pimps. The mission had priority, and my training prevented me from feeling significant emotion regarding the Tango. However, I'd be lying if I said his sick preferences hadn't motivated me even more. After the mission briefing, I had formed the beginnings of a plan. Initially, I had thought I might be able to ambush him in his driveway as he returned from his Mayoral duties. I didn't see the Tango as much of a defensive threat. By the end of the day, he would be more likely to be tired and not alert when he got home. Although I would have dealt with it, I was glad to note he didn't employ a bodyguard, a driver or even a maid. This lack of security may have been so he could be free to pursue his perversions. Even though he was publicly a Muslim, his file showed he had many vices, including drinking Western Scotch. Most people would be focused on their first drink and relaxing when they got home from another hard day. Combined with his age, fitness, and occupation, this should make his assassination quick and easy.

However, after closer inspection, his driveway was far too public and offered me no hiding place where I could wait in ambush. Although the Mayor lived in a relatively modern house, I was aware the building materials used in Timor were light on compared to the Western equivalents.

I decided I would enter the house while he was at work and wait for his return, dispatching him in the privacy of his own home. I was pleased to see as many as seven Hilux pickups parked on his street, confirming my choice of rentals and my plans. The target's house was on a corner block, so I parked on the side street and quickly jumped his six-foot-high wooden fence, instantly hidden from any neighbours or passers-by. There was no evidence in the yard of the Tango owning a dog, so I advanced to the back door. My credit card inserted around the tongue of the door lock gave me silent entry into the kitchen. I had plenty of time before I expected him to get home, so I had a good look around. I slipped on a pair of medical gloves and began to search the home. I couldn't help smiling when I found a notebook with heaps of phone and email contacts, including several that had Middle Eastern area codes and names.

The book was secreted in a hidden drawer under the coffee table, confirming to me that it was valuable. I would take these items back to N.S.C. Intel, hoping they might harvest some terrorist cells, financiers, or couriers. Typically, I would have photographed the numbers and returned to its hiding place. However, he would have no need for the book ever again or any other book for that matter. Smiling, I placed the notebook in my backpack. As I searched the house, I stumbled upon his porn collection; there were numerous professional DVDs. Sadly, there were other DVDs labelled with a name and date. These were real little girls and boys this low-life had brought to his home. The Mayor had then filmed his horrible acts with them. Considering the age of some of the children on the purchased DVD covers, it took all my self-control not to burn the lot right there and then. All going to plan, I would destroy the filth after I killed this animal. So much for objectivity, but I knew it wouldn't hinder me from successfully completing my mission. I also made a mental note to take his laptop. Because he had left it on the table near the front door, I couldn't touch it until later as he may have noticed its absence.

After thoroughly searching the house, I was sure how I would carry out my mission. I made my way through a sliding door into the small garage adjacent to the laundry. There it was, a step ladder leaning in the far corner caught my eye. As I moved towards it, I felt my body and mind change up a gear or two as the mission execution phase commenced. I had noticed a manhole halfway along the hall to provide access to the ceiling cavity. I set up the ladder, ready to use and walked around the house again. I double-checked I hadn't missed anything or moved or left anything out of place. Climbing to the top of the ladder, I pushed the square ceiling panel and climbed into the cavity. I had attached a rope to the ladder and drew it up into the ceiling; I then placed it away from where I would wait. As the trapped hot and humid air inside the roof cavity assaulted me, I was immediately saturated. The heat was overbearing, being this near the iron roof and without ventilation, scorching the back of my throat with every breath. My plan was simple. I figured the building's ceiling materials were much thinner and weaker than its Australian counterparts. I knew I couldn't open the ceiling access cover and jump through; it would make too much noise. So, I would have to drop through the hall ceiling between the rafters. As soon as the Mayor walks under me, silently, I'd jump down and cut his throat. Using a knife would make no noise during the assassination, so there was no need to leave the scene in a hurry.

As I waited, I patted my back pocket and felt the reassuring shape of my Kizlyar Gurza 2. Having to go through multiple airport security barriers, I could not carry any substantial weapons. However, no one cares if you have a sheath knife in your cargo luggage. Accordingly, I had chosen my favourite hunting knife from the vast array in the N.S.C. Armoury. I was careful not to select anything too big or military-looking if I was searched. I didn't want to look tactical in any way.

I learned from carrying out hundreds of ambushes that the targets don't always cooperate by sticking to the established timetable. They can do something at the same time, fifty events in a row, but the day or night of your ambush, they will arrive early or late. With this principle in mind, I had climbed into the ceiling an hour and a half before the target's 'usual' arrival time. I probably looked like I had just gotten out of a pool or shower. Sweat was running down my back in small creeks, making me feel like I was sitting in a warm puddle. Already, I could feel my legs starting to go a bit numb. Being mindful not to make any sound, I slowly stiffened and relaxed each major muscle group to ensure I would be mobile when the time came. I was starting to feel the effects of the heat and dehydration waiting in this oven, and the hot, stale air seemed to sap my energy by the minute. I was happy that my quarry proved my theory wrong when he arrived home within a few minutes of the time I had been told in the briefing to expect.

I heard the front door lock turn and then bang against the wall. There was a sound of bottles rattling, and I visualised the man, arms full of scotch and mixers, walking towards the kitchen and fridge. My guessing was confirmed when I heard another door gently hit a wall with a lot of rattling and clinking, the refrigerator. Once the noise ceased, I readied myself. I rubbed my hand against my slacks, attempting to dry my palms. It wasn't highly effective as my pants were soaked through. Picking up the knife I had earlier unsheathed, I controlled my breathing and waited. I had jammed the manhole cover open just enough to see the hallway. There he was, coming along the hall three more steps. He would be under my perch. I started to raise the weight of my haunches, ready to spring down. Just as I was about to leap on my prey, he turned to the left and headed into the toilet. I could hear him urinating loudly and then flush the toilet. Using the noise of the toilet refilling to cover my movement again, I took the weight from my haunches and prepared to spring down as he walked past. This time, he walked below, and the trap was sprung. As I jumped between the rafters, I tucked my arms in to ensure I got through the gap. The lightweight ceiling material gave way with no resistance at all. The fat Mayor screamed as my feet landed squarely on his shoulders, knocking him to the ground with a gush of air leaving his lungs.

In one action, I pulled back on the target's head and sliced his throat from one side to the other. The high-quality Russian-made knife was not all that pretty but exceptionally good at getting the job done. Its four and three-quarter-inch blade of razor-sharp high carbon steel worked perfectly.

With two major arteries cut, the blood spurted everywhere. I stood up to avoid the spray. The smell of copper filled the hall as his blood covered the polished wooden floor in a slow but steady wave.

I let his head sag forward and stood up; for the first time, I realised the man had not put his pants back on after going to the toilet.

At the National Security Centre (N.S.C.) briefing, we had discussed whether the hit was needed to look like an accident and decided it was unnecessary. I planned to be out of the country before the body had been discovered. However, it never hurts to cover your tracks. I was thankful I still had my gloves on when I grabbed the dead man's penis and cut it off in a single slice, drawing it away from his limp body. I then forced it into his open mouth. I was hoping this may suggest to authorities that his murder may be related to his paedophilia, perhaps some victim or victim's family seeking revenge for some previous abuse. Systematically, I retraced my steps around the house. I picked up the items I had identified earlier as possible Intel resources. I had an idea; I threw three horrible DVDs on the fat belly of the corpse to support my misdirection of the murder investigation. I was mindful of the problems the contents could cause me if I were arrested. I loaded my backpack with the selected items from the dead Mayor's home. Although this was highly unlikely, considering the airport security I had seen coming in. the risk of me being stopped was very low. However, the potential Intel value is very high.

The road trip back to Deli was uneventful. I stopped near a densely vegetated creek I had earmarked on my way towards the target location. Although I hated throwing away such a top knife as the Kizlyar, I couldn't have it in my possession if I got arrested, as the D.N.A. on it would have condemned me. I was confident no one would ever find it here. Two hours later, the suburbs and traffic increased as I approached the airport. I saw what I had been looking for an industrial area, stopping the 4WD in front of a putrid industrial bin. I Emptied the two shopping bags of revolting DVDs. I was hoping the stench would discourage anyone from going through the rubbish and retrieving them. After I returned the rental Hilux and checked in my bag, I waited in a coffee shop, ready to go to the departure gate when they were loading. I did this to avoid the Gate waiting areas, which came under too much scrutiny and were hard to escape if needed. I paid for my beer and sandwich with my credit card, informing Colonel Goodrich I was safely back in Deli and about to fly home.

A few minutes later, the announcement to board my flight went over the P.A. I was sitting in my assigned seat and relaxing. I was exhausted by a potent mix of adrenalin and dehydration and fell asleep before we had taken off. Arriving at Sydney airport, I awoke from a deep sleep and staggered to my connecting flight to Canberra. Exiting the terminal, I saw one of the Corporals I knew dressed in civvies. He waved to attract my attention and grabbed my bag. We were both silent during the short trip to the National Security Centre (N.S.C.), and he disappeared once we had passed through the security checkpoint just inside the entrance. The lift door opened, and after saluting, Sergeant Winatong held the door as I entered. "Welcome home, Major Wallace. The Boss wants to see you straight away if you please." He quickly ushered me to Colonel

Goodrich's office. After Sergeant Winatong knocked on the closed door, he left me there.

CHAPTER 2

Sitting in the bland office surrounded by shelves of books, the walls decorated with a few unit plaques and photos, I settled opposite my friend and Senior Officer, Colonel Peter Goodrich.

A man of few words, he began, "Good to see you, Steve. It looks like you'll be straight back out there, I'm afraid. This job has fallen into our laps out of nowhere, and the 'old man' has designated it as a Priority One. And it must be a Biggy because he very seldom interferes with Ops. But on this one, he demanded that you be assigned this mission." Colonel Goodrich said with a smile.

The Colonel and I had worked closely on life-and-death missions that had fostered camaraderie and trust despite the Rank difference.

"No worries, Sir, I was free anyway. I was going to head home now Timor is done." Goodrich looked annoyed for a second. "Ah, of course, Steve. I was so focused on this new job that I had moved on too quickly. How did it go? Were there any problems?"

Reaching into my backpack, I produced the items I had taken from the Mayor's house and laid them on the Colonel's desk.

"All good re the mission, and I may have picked up some Intel for your boys to work through. It might be useless, but who knows, especially how you Intelligence types cross-reference and share these days".

Goodrich's eyes lit up like he had just been given his Christmas gift, as any Intelligence Officer would do when offered information from the enemy. And who knows, maybe he had.

Reaching for his phone. "Sergeant, can you take some items into the Data Analysis Section and tell them to have a good look at them urgently and report any findings back to me?"

I couldn't hear the reply, but within seconds, there was a knock on the door, and the Sergeant entered.

I assumed he had already saluted the Colonel this morning, as he merely picked up the items for analysis and said.

"I'll put a rocket under 'em, Sir." With that, he disappeared, closing the solid door behind him.

The Colonel turned back to me. "So, you good to go, Steve, no injuries, you've had some sleep?"

"I'm fine, Sir. I sweated out a few Kilos waiting in the guy's ceiling, but I have been re-hydrating between a few beers at Deli Airport and water on the plane. And, of course, I slept all the way home."

The Colonel understood immediately. As a seasoned soldier, he knew you slept when the opportunity came your way; it was a given.

Smiling, he asked. "No time for that massage, hey?"

We both laughed a little; our work was serious, stressful and often dangerous, and like most soldiers, we used humour to lighten each other's load.

"OK then, down to this new business then. Of course, I'll give you a package, photos, articles, etc. What do you know about ancient artefacts?"

I let my breath out through closed teeth.

"Not a real lot, Sir, just a bit of reading and a few docos on T.V."

Goodrich was an excellent Officer, but with his approach to facts and authoritative tone, he could have made a good High School Teacher; without realising this, he continued.

"OK, I'll start with why we are suddenly interested in what you usually only see in museums or, as you said, on T.V."

"A good example that we can analyse is one that happened recently. A sarcophagus, an Egyptian coffin for want of a better description, is stolen from its resting place, dug up from under the sands deposited over two and half thousand years. Someone in Cairo or wherever cuts the coffin into four pieces and sends it to America, where an antique restoration expert puts the four pieces back together."

I was thinking, *I still can't see how this could have anything to do with National Security or even Australia, but I knew better than to interrupt. Maybe I just wasn't seeing it.*

The Colonel continued. "Well, anyway, thankfully, Intel led the Yankee Feds to know of the coffin's existence. They discovered it had been moved several times and now resides with some New York antique dealer."

Goodrich stood and walked over to a coffee machine on a small bench behind his desk.

"Want a cup?" I shook my head, knowing Army coffee was a health risk.

"Anyway, Steve, artefacts aren't like drugs or guns, which, for want of a better term, always remain 'dirty' as in illegal. These smuggled artefacts, some as big as a giant Buddha or as small as a necklace, become 'cleaner' each time they move through another set of hands. Eventually, the provenance gains momentum, resulting in highly reputable businesses such as well-known auction houses and antique dealers listing them."

I couldn't control myself any longer, taking an opportunity to interrupt as Colonel Goodrich paused to sip his coffee.

"Sir, surely this has been going on for thousands of years. What's it got to do with us?"

Goodrich looked up patiently. "Of course, you are right; apparently, some of the pyramids were robbed within days of burying the dignitary starting three thousand years ago. But it's only got worse. So bad, in fact, that an Egyptologist from the States has started using satellite images to track the extent of this grave robbing. She reckons at least 25% of the known Egyptian archaeological sites have been plundered and damaged. It's happening all over the world, wherever there is poverty. In China, teams of a hundred or more are systematically pillaging their sites. Industry and tourism crashed when the Global Financial Crisis hit Egypt, creating widespread poverty and unemployment. The result, many turned to this as an income. Then the 2011 revolution just multiplied the problem."

Colonel Goodrich sighed. "Now, like any antique or artefact, provenance is the issue. A documented chain of ownership multiplies an item's value. It immediately endows it with a sense of purity to be sold on to the next legitimate buyer. However, with most of this stuff, even the items collected legally don't have solid proof of ownership. The legitimate auctioneers, buyers, and even museum curators find themselves caught on the horns of a dilemma. This further enables the looters and several layers of smugglers to thrive. Even when an artefact is known to be contraband, no one can decide the best way to handle the item. Once the stuff is stolen and on the market, many scientists, museum curators and reputable dealers believe this confusion is good. It protects the artefact and facilitates its acceptance into the legitimate market system and, more importantly, the museum or official ownership and storage world. Hacking antiquities into pieces for transporting or having some grubby kid in the back streets of Cairo cleaning a priceless artefact with toilet cleaner is a constant danger to these priceless pieces. Not to mention that any smuggler would dump a shipment out of a truck or over the side of a boat if the authorities were about to pounce."

I respected the Colonel too much to ignore what he said, but it was a damn long story. I still couldn't see where I fit into any of this.

Goodrich's voice definitely reminded me of a school teacher. "The other perspective is if it is legitimised, then the piece will be on display for all rather than locked away in a private collection because it is contraband.

One big problem is that many priceless items are destroyed by impatient thieves working quickly by lamp light. They raid the site, break, cut their way in and take what they can, always ready to dump the artefact if some guard arrives."

Colonel Goodrich had built up a bit of a head of steam. "After years of training, archaeologists use soft toothbrushes. There have been cases where these modern-day tomb raiders have even used bulldozers to break in. You can only imagine the destruction. Once these thieves have the item, they believe they will get more money if they clean them up. There are places where chemicals such as caustic toilet cleaners are used to clean the item for sale. Any qualified restoration expert would be horrified to consider using these chemicals. Can you imagine cutting up a three-thousand-year-old sarcophagus? These people will do anything to turn a profit."

I nodded, encouraging the Colonel to continue. "Now I know you are still thinking, why us, why me? I wanted you to have a big picture of this industry because it has become massive, structured and organised. The different layers are the looters, the organisers of those crews, and the sub-bosses paying the robbers. Then they sell up the line to small-time smugglers and then onto the exporters. Now, they exit Egypt through over fifty different ports, airports, and roads. Dubai is the main destination of ex-Egypt. Then, after passing through even more individuals and groups, the items end up in places like high-end antique shops in London and New York. Sometimes on the books, other times a 'private sale.' OK, that's some background. There is a lot more detail in your briefing file there." He pointed to an overfull standard-size manilla folder on his desk. It held only information readily available on Google or found in magazines, so it required no security classification. It could be carried and read in a public area, such as on board a plane.

This suited me as time didn't allow the number of documents to be studied in the H.Q. building. The Colonel started up again. "Now, Steve, this isn't in the file, and not many people know this is happening. That plague ISIS has swept across many areas holding archaeological sites containing treasures. As you probably know, they have no respect for anything but their own raving ideology."

Goodrich seemed frustrated as he explained further. "They have made a public statement, a spectacle of destroying statues and reliefs that are thousands of years old. They demonstrated their power, non-conforming attitudes, and, of course, by a total lack of respect for the past glories. However, less publicly, they are not beyond getting involved in the illegal trading of the antiquities that aren't destroyed."

Pausing a moment, I followed Goodrich's eyes as he looked out the office window, taking in the grassy quadrangle provided for staff to have a bit of sun or maybe a smoke.

"Steve, just like tomb-robbing, this is not new either. The Khmer Rouge in the Cambodian civil war-controlled groups of looters robbing and destroying ancient sites and selling the artefacts to fund weapons and supplies."

"Of course, the poppy business has funded the Afghan resistance and Al Qaeda forever, blood diamonds in Africa, illegal trades funding wars. Not only do they publicly destroy artefacts, but they profit from them as well. Today, all across Syria and elsewhere, ISIS is profiting from the illegal looting and destruction of irreplaceable ancient sites. For a fee, ISIS also issues a type of license to these local lords to raid the tombs and sites.

Some local families have grown wealthy and powerful, guarding their territory with their own private militia. Steve, you have probably worked out that the transportation of the artefacts out of these countries uses the same illegal routes as the drug trade and the weapons trade back into the country."

He handed me a different file, this one red and marked TOP SECRET. "This is a report on a U.S. Special Forces raid back in May last year. Read it fully while you're here. The mission's main objective was to get the Head of the ISIS Division of Natural Resources, Abu Sayyaf, which they did. Only he was killed in the fire-fight."

"But what we are interested in is the Intel they found. They discovered that away from their public claims, ISIS coordinates and finances the systematic looting of several ancient burial sites. This robbing of antiquities, in turn, funds its operations with the immense profits from the contraband sales."

"Steve, what do you know about Hawala?"

"Not a lot, Sir. From memory, they believe 9/11 was funded using it. I must admit I don't understand much about it, but it's some sort of ancient Arab banking system, I think."

Scrubbing his face with his hands, the Colonel responded. "You're spot on, Steve. Basically, it is an arrangement where money may not be physically transferred. Through an agent's trust, the buying power of this money can be used elsewhere. It's used for laundering money. There is evidence that jihadists and other terrorist groups have been funded this way, as you said, including links with 9/11.

Finally, we were getting to the part I was interested in. The Colonel seemed to sense this and continued. "Now, you won't need to understand much more than you just quoted, but be assured this mission is interwoven with Hawala. Everybody is banking on it, pardon the pun."

Shifting in my chair, I moved forward as a sign of interest. "Once we can track the smuggled artefacts, to the transport, then the sales, we should be able to identify the bankers and perhaps the trusted Hawala agents. And then, hopefully, we can unravel the Hawala part of it all. That should then lead to the ISIS representatives, and best outcome, it all gets closed down forever."

I quickly gathered that this mission was very different from my regular assignments. I shook my head slowly. "It all sounds so vague it'll be like chasing the wind, Sir, not like the usual identified Tango followed by an action. This time, there is nothing solid."

The Colonel went on to explain, which confirmed my assessment. "Steve, you may be right about chasing the wind, but it's the Wind of Hawala, so it's worth a try. I'm hoping once you get cracking solid, Tangos (targets) will pop up like on a range."

Finishing his coffee with a loud slurp, he finally got to the details of the mission.

"Steve the C.I.A. has requested our help as part of a covert mission to locate, identify and target the middle to upper tiers of this grave-robbing smuggling international enterprise. One John Greet, AKA Jack Greet, was arrested three days ago by U.S. Customs while trying to smuggle a sea container full of Egyptian artefacts as old as three thousand years ago. The plan was to try and take his place with one of their operatives. They specifically want an Aussie because they don't believe an American can infiltrate these secret groups. This character, Greet, is from Sydney initially and, by all reports, hasn't lost his Australian accent. Now, we're happy to cooperate with our U.S. brothers in arms. They have assured me Greet's arrest was low profile and without witnesses. It will still be risky, but at least there is little or no chance anyone knows the real Greet has been taken off the board."

Still trying to fully understand my role in all this, I asked. "So, I'm going to be Jack Greet for a while?"

The Colonel nodded. "Yeah, your mission is to collect detailed Intel on contacts, locations, operating procedures, like I said, on as many levels as it takes. You'll make first contact in Jordan. However, my money is on you, accumulating frequent flyer points travelling wherever this wind blows you. Greet has a meeting booked at Petra in Jordan. The plan is for you to attend that meet and play it from there."

Again, I shook my head in wonder. This was very different to my usual missions and, if I was honest, even my skill set.

Smiling, the Colonel continued. "Spend the rest of today studying your new identity and everything else you need to know. You'll start off from Thailand to fit into the smuggler cover. So, your new passport, other aged papers, and air tickets will be waiting with Sergeant Winatong when you are ready. All the best, Steve. None of your missions are free of danger, but I don't need to tell you that being undercover is always a higher risk than others. Be careful, and I'll talk to you soon. As per the comms schedule in your pack, you report to me. I will pass any Intel onto the States."

We shook hands, and I left the Colonel's office and moved into a nearby lounge area to study the material he had given me. There was a knock on the door, and without waiting for my permission to enter, Sergeant Winatong walked in with a small satchel and handed it to me.

"Major Wallace, I figured the sooner you got a look at this stuff, the better, and you can start owning your new identity."

I wasn't surprised. Whatever the rank of the National Security Centre (N.S.C.) staff, they were all knowledgeable, highly trained, and motivated. Winatong was no different, showing initiative and making a lot of sense.

"Thanks, Sergeant. Good work, a pretty unusual name they stuck me with?"

Winatong laughed. "Surname Greet, John is his first name, but he goes by Jack Greet." Humour was a tried and trusted friend to help you get through this type of work. With a smile, I said. "Not too bad, it could be a hell of a lot worse, hey, like Bond, James Bond?"

Both of us laughed.

"Thanks again. See you when I hand some of this back in."

"Pleasure, Sir, I mean Mr. Greet."

With that, Sergeant Winatong spun on the heel of his highly polished dress uniform shoe and was gone. Three hours later, a driver took me to the airport and, with a "good luck, Sir", dropped me off at Departures.

BANGKOK
THAILAND

As usual, security checks coming into Bangkok International were light. As I moved through the duty-free shops and overpriced cafes. As usual, they monitored my credit card usage to minimise the danger of communicating directly with the N.S.C. So, my buying some magazines at an airport store would inform them I had arrived safely in Thailand. I had the cab drop me at a low-key, fewer-star hotel than I was booked into. It was probably unnecessary, but it was worth the effort just in case I had picked up a tail or even some random interest in me, as my new identity was that of a well-known smuggler. And it was a given people in this sort of business always have contacts, either criminals or law enforcement of some kind, looking for them for one reason or another. It's probably how Jack Greet got arrested.

I slept incredibly well, dreaming of warm days hunting and camping back on a Roma cattle property with my dog Jake without a care in the world. The cold air-conditioning woke me, but knowing this would be the last cool air I would be in for some time, I wasn't about to complain. I brushed my teeth, making sure to use the bottled water the hotel supplied. Breakfast was too Asian for my liking, so I had two strong coffees and headed for the airport. I was hoping, or more like kidding myself, that there would be something edible on the plane to Amman, Jordan. The taxi left the hotel and wove in and out of the chaotic traffic. And not for the first time, I was amazed to see workmen scurrying up and down bamboo scaffolding on the many high-rise buildings being erected.

CHAPTER 3

AMMAN, JORDAN

On the flight, I re-read my info file, deciding to flush it down an airport toilet when I arrived at Queen Alia International Airport. As I exited the plane, the heat assaulted my face and throat like a punch from the fires of hell. I could feel myself sweating immediately, causing my clothes to cling to me as I crossed the shimmering tarmac to the terminal building. Once, I was through customs and passport control. Being acquainted with the controls and handling capabilities, just in case I needed to push its limits for some reason, I hired a Toyota Landcruiser 4WD sedan. The one hundred- and eighty-kilometre journey should take me about two to three hours. I was expecting to get to my hotel close at 1800 Hours. Most people call into the Dead Sea for a look and maybe a swim in the famous salt water where a bather cannot sink. But I was there for other reasons, so I kept going past all the resort billboards, trying to woo the constant passing tourist trade. Although I should have realised how close we were, I was surprised to see a road sign for the turnoff to Baghdad, Iraq, which borders Jordan.

In a way, depending on your point of view, Jordan was lucky. It has no oil or much of anything other than famous archaeological and historical sites and lots of sand. So, on the surface, it appears neutral and never involved in the conflicts surrounding it on its many borders. The country has gotten into trouble over the years, accused of allowing one lot of neighbours to cross its borders to attack or infiltrate the other neighbour, but the nation survives. It has gained a reputation for housing terrorists who cannot return home. This status has made Jordan the launch pad for some of the worst terrorist attacks. No one actually invades Jordan because there is nothing to take. However, like its international delinquencies, it is very involved in facilitating or, at the very least, unofficially allowing the transit of many forms of contraband and people to traverse its narrow territories.

PETRA
JORDAN

I pulled up outside the Movenpick Resort Petra; this time, I had allowed myself a bit of luxury to hide out in the open. A four-and-a-half-star hotel with the address of Tourism Road Petra, straight across from the famous ruins, made a lot of sense. I would disappear with all the other foreigners awaiting their tours into the world-famous site. The CIA had informed Colonel Goodrich that Greet would meet at the Petra site with an illegal artefact dealer in Jordan. As with many of these covert ops, someone in Canberra, Washington or Virginia, it doesn't matter, comes up with these grand plans.

There are always so many unknowns; I have learned the hard way. Often, the smallest detail sends the plan pear-shaped, and the mug in the Middle, me, must make the best of it.

The first 'Biggy' was I hoped the dealer had never met the real Greet. I would be lucky to get out of there alive if he had. In my room, several brochures entice tourists to visit the ancient sites rich with Roman and other culture's artefacts.

The reason I was here was to infiltrate the tomb robber's organisation. The irony of the meeting place was not lost on me. I was to wait at the famous temple of Al Khazneh, used in the 1989 Indiana Jones movie The Last Crusade, with the follow-up movie Raiders of the Lost Ark. I was thinking about this irony, and what fate awaited me the next day. I went downstairs to dinner, where I enjoyed the buffet of a mixture of Western and Middle Eastern cuisine. And, of course, a couple of Jack Daniels. I skipped dessert and headed for the hotel bar just outside the busy restaurant. The bar was decorated with colourful wall hangings and subdued lighting from imitation oil lamps highlighting the curved scimitars and several other different types of Arab daggers, including jewel-decorated Kanjars and Janbiyas. As I was about to finish my drink I stood up to leave, a flashy-dressed Middle Eastern woman approached my end of the bar, taking the stool beside me.

In good English, carried on a Jordanian accent, her voice was as alluring as she was. “Would you have a light please?” She produced a long cigarette held in her perfectly manicured fingers. The fact she also turned on her bar stool toward me, showing me her short dress. This was not missed by my highly developed powers of observation. Stuttering like a schoolboy, I blurted out. “I'm sorry, but I don't smoke.”

She smiled. “That's OK. I am sure you have other ‘vices’ we can share. Are you staying in the hotel?”

I wasn't blind, but I wasn't interested.

I decided to let her move on to the next tourist or businessman, where she might do better.

“Listen, honey, you're a knock-out, but I'm not looking for any company right now, thanks anyway.”

As they say, this wasn't her first rodeo. With a shrug, she left without another word heading for an overweight sales rep sweating over a goat curry sitting by himself over at a corner table. I decided to stay a little longer. I had two more Jacks and called it a night. I headed for the lift and pushed the button for the third floor. My door was open when I arrived, and there was no service trolley in the hall. And besides, it was too late for a cleaner to be working. Travelling internationally, I was unarmed. Ready for anything, I entered the dark room. The curtains were as I had left them with a crack, letting in some light from the floodlights illuminating the car park below. When I flicked the main lights on, I saw my room had been thoroughly tossed. All my possessions had been strewn over the bed and floor. I didn't really have anything of value to steal. I was carrying all my credit cards, money, and passport. I couldn't see anything else was missing. So, I was pretty sure I was being checked out rather than robbed. Whoever did it probably wanted me to think it was just a burglary. But I could tell by the thoroughness that it was a professional job.

I picked up my Oman Air used ticket stubs from Bangkok to Amman off the floor and the rental papers for the Landcruiser, all of which were in John Greet's name, supporting my cover identity. I sat on the bed and thought through the options: an attempted theft was unlikely but possible. Had I been compromised already? Was my cover blown, or were the people I was to meet in the morning merely being careful? I decided it was probably the latter, as so few people knew of my mission. Quite bluntly, if the wrong people knew I wasn't Jack Greet, the smuggler, they would probably have knifed me coming up in the lift. My thoughts turned to my interlude with the beautiful woman in the bar downstairs. There are times when my powers of deduction are just extraordinary. Just when I thought my lady friend from the bar couldn't resist my animal magnetism, I realised she may well have had the task of delaying me long enough to allow sufficient time for my room to be tossed.

Egos aside, if that was the case, it showed they were organised and professional, whoever they were and whatever their reason.

PETRA ARCHAEOLOGICAL PARK

As any good tourist would, I had researched the system as far as visiting the archaeological site and found it was a twenty-minute walk from the site's entrance to my meeting place. However, talking to the barman, I found the walk usually took twice that long due to tourist traffic and the unrelenting heat. The barman advised me to hire a horse. As I walked under the banner entrance to the site, I saw a group of skinny men with even thinner horses over to the left. I walked up to a man holding the reins of two smallish horses whose bored faces were only matched by the young man's. As I approached, his face cracked with a broad grin that didn't quite make it to his dark eyes. Something about him worried me. I wasn't entirely sure if he was just a garden-variety thug or something more serious. My friendly barman had warned me about the horsemen. They were men of the Wadi Musa—a tribe with a reputation for mistreating their horses and overcharging tourists. In contrast, the Bedouin men handled the camel hire and always treasured and looked after their camels as they had for millenniums. However, I didn't have the time for a camel ride or the motivation to haggle over the price.

After the shortest negotiating the horseman had probably ever seen, I mounted the nearest dirty, smelly pony and headed downhill. We dodged the tide of tourists on horses, camels and on foot, making their way down or up the two-kilometre stone canyon that meanders its way to the numerous archaeological sites. Petra, initially named Raqmu, had been the impressive capital of the Nabataean kingdom from around the 6th century BC. In AD 106, the Roman Empire occupied the region and continued to expand the city. An important centre for trade and commerce, Petra continued to flourish until a catastrophic earthquake around AD 663 destroyed buildings and vital water management systems. After Saladin's conquest of the Middle East in 1189, Petra was finally abandoned. The memory of its grandeur was lost to the West as much of the once great city was buried under the unrelenting sands of centuries. The ruins remained hidden from most of the world until the Swiss explorer Johann Ludwig Burckhardt, disguised as an Arab scholar, infiltrated the Bedouin-occupied city in 1812.

Burckhardt's accounts of his travels inspired other Western explorers and historians to explore the ancient city further. The most famous was David Roberts, a Scottish artist who created accurate and detailed illustrations of the city in 1839. There are still teams of archaeologists with their students from all parts of the world patiently brushing away the sand accumulated for over two thousand five hundred years.

The ride down took me past ancient carvings, burial chambers and impressive stone archways providing temporary respite from the blazing sunshine reflecting off the canyon walls. As my horse knew the way from treading the route so many times before, I could maintain a constant state of alertness. Being in such a foreign country, I was naturally on edge. However, the whole area was so rich in history and unusual sites that it took effort to stay focused. I noticed there were armed, uniformed Police on large, well-kept horses travelling both downhill with me and uphill back towards the entrance. These were Tourist Police primarily there to ensure tourists were not mugged or worse by the many unsavoury types standing around smoking in nearly every shady nook. As the path narrowed in shadow, a burst of cool air hit me, only to be chased away as a wave of hot air that could have come straight from a furnace. There before me, in part shadow, was the famous and impressive al-Khazneh, an incredible two-level stone temple with carved pillars, just as it was in the movies. I dismounted, tied my horse to the well-worn hitching rail, and looked around.

Three men were leaning against a rock wall to my left, and two more over on the temple's right side. Two mounted Tourist Police rode in from the right and stopped in the shade before climbing back up to the site entrance. I noticed two men smoking and talking went quiet and turned ever so slightly away from the Police, making sure they didn't get a good look at them. Alarm bells sounded in the back of my brain, but I still wasn't sure if their actions were related to me or just because they were petty criminals. An overweight American tourist wearing a cruise ship tee-shirt and sweating profusely asked in a loud Texan drawl for the Police to smile while he took their photos. Of course, they obeyed this request but then bent down from their mounts with their hands out, looking for a tip or a fee. Once the tourist had slipped them some notes, they gently kicked their mounts and headed up the hill. I could still hear the sound of the Tourist Police horse's shod hooves clip-clopping, echoing off the canyon walls. The two men who had avoided the Police moved towards me; both of them reached beneath their robes.

Happy with his photo, the American moved further along the stone road, passing the two other men leaning in the shade. There was a slight lull in the tourist traffic, and we found ourselves alone, now five of them, one of me. The other three, perhaps not armed, were ready but hesitated, probably planning to join in if needed. It was apparent I was their target as they had ignored the fat American entirely. I figured their main trade would be rolling tourists. So, they had probably expected me to run, enabling them to shoot me down and earn their fee without much effort. I wasn't a tourist, but still, with five-to-one odds, I was in big trouble. I was sure of one thing: I wouldn't make it easy for them. To their surprise, I ran flat out towards them instead of running away. This move allowed me to close in on them quicker than they had expected. Their local dress of flowing robes didn't make for a quick draw either.

As the bigger man drew a semi-automatic handgun, I heard him flick the safety off as I grabbed the weapon. Turning his hand away from me and towards his accomplice, his finger was committed to firing. He pulled the trigger twice, involuntarily sending two slugs into his friend's chest with soft thuds. I continued to twist his gun and hand. I was rewarded by several cracking sounds. As his fingers broke, he let go of the handgun. I simultaneously elbowed him in the throat, silencing his screams.

I released his hand as the handgun came free and, in one motion, shot him once in the forehead as he fell to the sandy rock canyon floor. I heard a swish behind me and was surprised that two men who had waited had drawn long curved swords and were advancing on me. Now, Indiana Jones may have been more sporting, but this wasn't a movie, and I wasn't him. I fired four shots, hitting one of the running assailants twice and the other once, my stray bullet ricocheting off the stone steps of the temple with a whine. I looked for the last of the band of five and saw him disappearing into the canyon, heading towards the main entrance. I couldn't risk shooting as there were tourists behind him. I lost him in the crowd. People were shouting, camels and horses were running everywhere, he was gone. There was nothing to be gained by his capture, so I didn't bother chasing him. I couldn't interrogate him in such a busy place. In any case, he may not have spoken any English, and I was a bit low on whatever his native tongue may be. Once again, there are more questions than answers.

I had no idea who these men were. I don't believe in coincidences, so I thought it was related to me or, at the very least, Jack Greet. I had to get out of there to avoid being questioned by the Police, but I figured I had a few minutes. I quickly searched each dead assailant, each with empty pockets except for cigarettes and matches, no ID of any sort, and no phones. These weren't hitmen, their lack of possessions reflecting their poverty more than preparation for the attack, local thugs hired locally. I walked over to my trusty steed, patiently standing at the hitch rail. I grabbed the reins and was about to swing up into the saddle when I heard a soft moan coming from the back of a vast man-made cavern opposite the temple.

Walking out of the bright sunlight, my eyes fought to adjust to the darkness of the square cave, causing me to nearly fall into one of the grave-shaped holes carved out of the stone floor.

It appeared I had entered an enormous burial chamber with stone graves cut in rows along the floor and into the walls. These graves were empty. I assumed they had been plundered by tomb robbers hundreds if not thousands of years before I visited the cold stone room. Another softer moan led me deeper into the tomb to one of the graves at the rear of this chamber. Looking down into the stone coffin, I saw a small man dressed in Western clothes, although he was clearly of Middle Eastern origin. His head was covered with blood from what appeared to be a recent wound on the top of his skull. I wasn't concerned as head wounds bleed profusely but are often far less severe than they look. At least, that was what I hoped because here was someone who may be able to answer my questions. I was still mindful of the Tourist Police arriving outside the cavern to investigate the shooting. However, I guessed that this man must have been who I was to meet at the temple opposite us, now littered with four bodies.

Lying on his back, looking up at me from the stone grave, he smiled. "Ah, you must be Mr. Greet. I am so glad those scum did not prevail."

I looked down at him, still lying on his back in the stone coffin, and I couldn't help smiling as well.

"And who might you be? I heard you moan. Are you OK?"

He looked up and pleaded.

"My friend, I will be much better when I am not lying in someone else's grave and away from this place."

I was still being cautious, so I asked. "Sorry, I still didn't get your name."

He quickly replied. "You may call me Almahdi, my rescuer."

This was the name I had been given as a contact.

"Jack Greet, Mr. Almahdi. Now, let's get the hell away from here."

Wiping more blood from his eyes with his coat sleeve, he stood up, staggered backward, and leaned on the grave's stone wall.

"Now we know who we are, Mr. Greet. I will need your assistance to climb out of this hole."

Almahdi recovered quickly, grateful not to have died at the assailant's hands. By the nature of his business, he was used to surviving harsh conditions, living by his wits, and making every opportunity count.

He moved on without a glance backward, both figuratively and physically. As we made our way from the battle scene, he deftly shouldered me into a crevice as six Police on horseback rode past the hooves, thundering and skating on the stone floor. As soon as the threat had passed, he gently guided me on wards along the well-worn path towards the entrance.

I asked. "Almahdi, one of those rats, got away by now. He has reported in, and another crew will be coming our way."

Breathing heavily, Almahdi continued. "Yes, Jack, may I call you Jack? Once we get a bit closer to the entrance gates, we will take the vendor's side track to where I parked my 4WD. This should prevent us from bumping into his friends."

Puffing from the exertion of the climb, he panted. "They will be watching your room, of course, so I think leaving Jordan as soon as you can appears to be our only option. I assume you are carrying everything you need to do that."

Subconsciously patting my pocket, which held my passport and air tickets, I nodded. "Yeah, you are right. Can we have our meeting as you drive me to the airport, yes?"

The blood had started to dry on his forehead, but the front of his shirt and jacket were blood-soaked, giving him a macabre appearance. He noticed me looking.

"Fortunately, I have a change of clothes in the 4WD. Roadblocks may have probably been set up, so we need to look like a squeaky-clean tourist returning from Petra with me his local guide. Of course, we are understandably confused and upset by the unexplained shooting at the site."

I had only known this man a short time, but my respect for him grew by the moment. Brave, skilled in evaluating the fluid situation and creatively preparing for every contingency. After Almahdi changed his clothes, we climbed into his 4WD. It was old but started well and felt OK even on the dirt road we followed until we got back onto the highway to Amman.

We had gone about sixty klicks, and he had not stopped talking. I had already learned a lot about the local smuggling operations without having to ask a single question.

"Now, Jack, with my connections and local knowledge and your contacts with drugs and guns, we should make a heap of ... how you say big bucks, hey? And you know what is the most important thing, Jack? And I am not kidding, you know, (a question in his voice) well, I tell you, my new friend, it's TRUST." He spelled the word to add emphasis.

I felt slightly guilty; this bloke was a nice guy with qualities many 'honest' people I'd come across lacked.

I don't think he had taken a deep breath since we left Petra.

"You see, Jack, you know for sure I had nothing to do with all that back there, and I know three things. One, I already sort of knew that Jack Greet had upset the local family smuggling cartel by ignoring their efforts to form some sort of partnership with them. The final straw broke the camel's back, as you would say".

At this, he laughed so hard he began to cry and pull the steering wheel left and right.

Wiping tears away from his eyes, he continued.

"Sorry, my friend, in a land of camels, it is a very funny saying, no?"

Almahdi started laughing again, and I felt even more guilty. He really was a nice bloke. A smuggler, yes, but a good man just the same.

He finally continued. "Anyway, Jack, it seems that when they found out you and I were to meet today, well, that was just too much for them. The second thing is you saved my life. Those camel-dung-eating scum would have come back after killing you and would have finished me off."

I chimed in. "My pleasure, mate; what's the third? I am starting to feel like Superman."

"Ah, Jack, you Australians talk strangely. The third reason is although I did not see how you killed four out of five of those assassins all by yourself, you did. I can see you are a man who can look after things, you, our business, and hopefully me. You know, Jack, when we form a partnership, we call it a 'musahim'. In a way, the trust between us would typically take many months and many deals. What we have just gone through, what has happened in those few minutes, we are now a strong musahim. Watch out; we are going to make it big time."

Still not stopping to take a breath, he kept talking. "Now, Jack, your main secure route is through Egypt. Like I was saying, I have used the same man for years. He is good, but don't trust him as far as you can throw him, my friend. And if you meet him, you will understand what I am saying, OK. Our contact in Cairo is one brilliant man. He has bus-loads of tourists visiting his factory. Out the back, he has his other business. Thousands of tourists flock to his place, paying crazy prices for papyrus prints of Pharaohs in chariots and Nile River scenes. He nearly makes more from them than his 'other' enterprises."

I enjoyed the scenery, the beautiful flat desert, the occasional goatherd, and the small farm or village. Almahdi finally seemed to take a breath. "Some of his illegitimate stock items make it into America marked as papyrus prints ordered by tourists and dispatched worldwide daily. The factory is called Pharaoh's Papyrus and is just off the Ring Road near the pyramids in the Giza Region".

Amazed by how much new Intel I collected with little or no effort, I hardly had to do more than nod my head occasionally. Trying to kill me and beating up my new partner, the smugglers, had opened a door I could only have dreamt about.

"Almahdi, I really appreciate your help. I can see things are going to work just fine. I hope our partnership, what did you call it mushin?"

"No Jack, a musahim."

"Anyway, I was going to say I hope our musahim can grow into friendship."

"Jack, that would be my heart's............". His words were cut off as his chest exploded a small hole surrounded by a glistening spider's web in the windscreen explaining what had just happened.

The old 4WD swung dangerously to the left side as Almahdi's dead hands clenched the wheel, and his limp body slumped to the left. His foot was jammed hard into the accelerator. The vehicle flew off the highway, landing nose down and eventually ending up on its side after slamming into the ditch beside the road. Luckily, I was wearing my seat belt; the sudden stop still threw me forward so hard it felt like my head nearly flew off. I didn't move. I figured the sniper was still out there somewhere, waiting for me to poke my head up. I played possum, looking like the crash had killed me or at least knocked me out. I was hoping the gunman who had murdered Almahdi would come down and check to make sure.

I slowly took one of the handguns I had taken from the would-be assassins back in Petra out of my jacket and clicked the safety off. The adrenalin that had flooded my body after the 4WD crashed into the ditch started to ebb. Every muscle in my body began complaining about being held back, hanging by the seat belts, fighting all those Gs created by the vehicle resting on its doors below me. I hoped the guy up on that small hill wouldn't wait too long. I knew I wouldn't if I was in his place. The heat was intense as the sun bore down on the wrecked vehicle, with the cinder-hot wind blowing through the open windows, making it hotter. Then, the flies sensing Almahdi's blood arrived in numbers. I now realised if he didn't come soon, I would have to move or suffer heat stroke or worse.

I heard a vehicle pull up behind our wreck, its tyres skidding on the gravel. The sniper was a pro; I could tell straight away there was no rushing in like I had hoped for. He came from behind slowly and patiently, stopping several times to listen and to look carefully for any sign of life. Of course, I couldn't see any of this, but I could hear him. I would do the same if I were in his place. He moved in close, and I could hear him breathing. He must have felt safe when he saw me hanging in my seat.

There was a screeching grating noise as he forced open my damaged door. I figured he was planning to finish me off, to make sure by shooting me. Without any movement and still holding my breath to encourage him to believe I was dead and no threat, I opened my eyes the smallest amount I could. In Jordan, they drive on the right-hand side of the road; this placed me in the right front seat, which meant I had to hold my gun in my left hand away from the open door.

I am fractionally faster shooting with my right side, but I can still handle any weapon with my left hand. It wasn't natural for me, but I had practised using my left hand to overcome that weakness. My best plan was to capture the man standing less than a meter away from me. To do this, I was counting on him still having a rifle. For close work like this, the length of the barrel would make him slow and ungainly. However, unbeknown to me, the sniper had changed his rifle for a semi-auto handgun. Yep, he was a pro.

Hanging on my trapeze, I opened my eyes only to find a 9mm Glock pointing at me. All that saved me was him not expecting me to have a handgun ready and especially have it levelled to shoot anything in front of me. There was no time to work through my options. There was only one. Plan A was gone, survival replacing it it in a millisecond. I fired my handgun twice and saw two wet red circles on the man's neck and chest. He fell to the ground with a loud sigh.

He hadn't got a shot away, thank God. But I was annoyed that I could not subdue and interrogate him. After climbing out of the wreck, I searched him for any ID or anything that might help. He travelled light as a pro, unlike those thugs back at the Petra site who were just poor. He had nothing on him; even the labels on his clothing had been removed. I noted that the serial numbers had been filed off his handgun, and the rifle slung over his shoulder. His wallet contained some local currency, and as I went to discard the wallet, some firmness in the leather caught my attention. Taking my folding knife from my pocket, I cut open the soft leather, exposing some cardboard, which I thought was probably just there for support. I pulled on it, and the cardboard came away. It wasn't blank at all; it was a business card.

My temper boiled; it was from the Pharaoh's Papyrus factory. It looked like Almahdi had upset more than just the local competition. The hit appeared to have been arranged by Almahdi's partner/smuggler in Cairo. Clearly, he was right not to trust him. I figured others may be looking for Almahdi's 4WD, and I was unsure about any damage. I walked towards the sniper's Landcruiser, planning to abandon it once I got to Queen Alia Airport at Amman. My head was filled with a seething mix of anger at these attacks and grief for the near-stranger but likeable Almahdi. I was wondering what was waiting for me in Cairo. Then everything went black: no pain, no noise, just nothing.

I came to with a splitting headache, and blood caked over the right side of my face. I forced myself to remember what had happened back at the ambush. I didn't have to be Sherlock to conclude the sniper must have had an accomplice hiding behind the 4WD after I shot his partner. Whoever had hit me had waited until I was about to enter the sniper's Landcruiser, and by the quality of the headache, he must have walloped me. Grimacing, I could feel the dried blood splitting on my face, the metallic scent mixing with the smell of the Hessian bag tied over my head. I could see some light but nothing else. I systematically flexed and relaxed all my limbs, checking for injuries. It all seemed OK, but I quickly discovered I was securely bound. I was lying on the floor of what must have been a pickup or truck, every bump causing my aching head to hit the wooden tray.

There was a strong farm smell of sheep, probably the previous passengers. I didn't know whether a guard was in the back with me, so I acted as if I were still unconscious, allowing the truck to jerk and throw me around, not bracing to protect myself. I wanted the element of surprise on my side for whoever took this bag from my head or cut the ropes on my wrists.

The truck slowed, and when the driver hit the brakes hard, I couldn't stop myself from being thrown forward, my shoulder crashing into the front board of the tray. I could smell diesel and hear a pump running, so I figured we must be at a service station. After a little while, two doors slammed, and we took off again. I was unsure if I was alone in the back because I hadn't heard a single sound or smelt anyone eating or smoking. But there could have been ten people there with me. But I couldn't have felt more alone than I did right then. I kept thinking *if they were going to kill me, I'd be dead already; that was a good thing, right? Not necessarily. Torture was an option. Was my cover intact? It probably meant they wanted to find out how much I knew of their operation. Or if they knew I wasn't Greet,* whether I had passed any of the Intel onto my superiors. We travelled at what felt like highway speeds for what my body clock guessed to be close to an hour or so. Then the truck broke hard again and veered off to the left, throwing me against the opposite side.

Immediately, the ride became slower and quieter. I guessed we had turned off the highway and onto a sand road to who knows where. Two hours later, we stopped, and I heard shouting and laughing. They were probably planning what they would do to me and looking forward to my pain, providing them with a night's entertainment. I heard what I figured was someone removing the tailgate pins. With a crash as the gate fell on its hinges, rough hands grabbed my ankles and unceremoniously dragged me out of the truck. My shoulder banged against the pickup floor, and then I fell out. I automatically raised my head in that direction, hoping to save my face or head from hitting the floor. By taking this evasive action, I was alerting my captors if they were observant, but I couldn't risk any more injuries. Although trussed up, I did my best to fall feet first. Rough hands caught me as I hit the sand and lifted me effortlessly to my feet.

Now, strong arms under mine, a man on each side carrying me along, my bound feet dragging in the deep sand. I couldn't help, and I couldn't resist. I just let them take me to wherever they were heading. I felt some heavy material brush against my head and shoulders, and then I was thrown forward by the two men carrying me. For a split second, I didn't know if we were standing near a cliff or in front of an oncoming truck. I thought; well, this is it, and I began to pray. Unexpectedly and mercifully, after an extremely short flight, I landed on something soft. I still had no idea where I was, but it could have been cushions or even a bed. My hands and feet were still bound tightly, and the blindfold bag pulled on my blood matted hair. However, I knew to get through this I needed to rest, not knowing what was coming. Exhausted as I was, I was far too vulnerable for sleep. So, I attempted to relax and use the time to assess my situation.

There was less light filtering through the bag over my head. I still had no idea whether it was day or night or if I was in a cellar or cave. Occasionally, I heard metallic sounds like saucepans or cans being banged together and voices not clear enough to tell what language was being spoken. After a while, there was a heavy swishing sound and a blaze of light that was so bright I could see it even through the

Hessian bag. Shadows crossed over the light, and I felt someone grab my boots and lift them from the soft base I had been reclining on. Released, my legs flew apart as the unseen man cut the bonds holding my feet together. He pulled me to my feet; I could stand unassisted this time. I was a bit stiff but happy to be free of my bonds.

Then the sweat and blood-soaked bag were roughly dragged off, tearing the caked hair from my face and head. I was surprised to find myself in a tent made of heavy, black, coarse Hessian material. A pattern of red lines sown horizontally around all four sides of the tent at about chest height. The front flap had been opened, explaining the instant increase in the light I had seen through the blindfold. As I blinked and rubbed my eyes to improve my sight, I noticed I was in a sort of Bedouin tent. I then realised I had been lying on a Western-style bed covered with a bedspread of the standard Bedu colours of black with a bit of red. There was a chair, some throw cushions, and a small desk / table on the left of the tent entrance. Although it was not switched on, an electric light hung from the tent's ceiling and a small lamp on the table. I found this mix bizarre. Was I in a Bedouin camp?

The man before me was dressed in a traditional Bedouin Thobe covered by the colourful Kibr, a leather belt, and shoulder straps. I noted he also had a 1911 model Colt 45 in his belt on the right side and a silver Khanja dagger on his left. He had a well-kept grey beard, and his hair was invisible under his Kufeya or headdress held in place by an Igal of black twisted camel wool. His black eyes shone like chips of onyx when his dark, weather-beaten face split into a white-toothed smile.

"Ah, you are back with us, my friend. I know you will have many questions, but I must tell you that you are not here for that. I will ask the questions, and if you answer honestly, it will go well for you, yes?"

I had seen all this before and was thinking, sure; *I am a nice guy who doesn't want to hurt you, but this is up to you. Then, when you don't tell them what they want, the nice ones turn nasty.*

Meanwhile, I was focusing on adjusting and adapting to my new environment. I still didn't know what would happen, but I knew every clue, every detail, however seemingly valueless, may be crucial if I could escape this tent prison. The Bedouin's deep voice interrupted my thoughts.

"I am Abu al Khayr, which means the one who does good. Now, you must understand what's good for me may not be as good for you, so you need to be totally honest with me, yes?"

This was where James Bond would remember what gadget Q had given him and escape this danger. The trouble was I wasn't James Bond, and the only Q I had was the FAR Q. Yeah, I was in big trouble.

He started again in his deep, heavily accented voice.

"I am a Bedu, and for thousands of years, we have always lived where others can't. Living in the hardest places on earth teaches you many things; one is patience. So, my friend, be assured that eventually, you will tell me what I need to know. It is up to you. But I will be waiting. Now, whether *you* can wait, that is another thing I think, no? Now, have you heard of a place called Wadi Rum? You may have heard of this if you are a student of history. The famous English Lawrence of Arabia operated in this area."

I was pleased he may have just given me a clue as to where we were by mentioning Wadi Rum, my captor continued.

He continued as though reading my mind.

"Now, escape will be impossible partly due to my skilled brothers guarding this camp. But you must not try, my friend. Because we are in the Middle of 720 square miles of nothing but desert, sand dunes, rocks, and sun. All that means death to everyone but the Bedu Tribes."

The lamps flickered and reflected a warm red light off the tent walls, and he started smiling again. "Anyway, enough of this unpleasantness. It is soon time for dinner; you must be starving, but first, I think you may want to have a shower and clean up a bit. As my valued guest, we will enjoy a good dinner and a good sleep and talk more tomorrow. How does that sound? How do you say, OK?"

I was very parched, but the truth was I was at a loss for words. I nodded weakly as my friendly kidnapper stood and exited the tent. A guard dressed in similar but much more subdued colours to Abu al Khayr had stayed with me when his Commander left my tent. Using gestures, the guard encouraged me to go outside. I found myself in a large quadrangle of tents identical to mine. Followed by my silent guard, we entered another black tent. I was surprised that this tent was well-lit and several times bigger than my accommodation. Along both sides were wash basins and mirrors at first and then shower cubicles. After a wonderful hot shower, I came out to find a complete set of Bedouin clothes awaiting me. I felt strange in these, but my other clothes were filthy and covered in my blood, '*when in Rome*.'

Once I'd dressed, we walked past my tent, passing through the accommodation quadrangle and entered another large tent. Around all four sides were large black and red cushions with gold cords and tassels. We would probably describe them in the West as bean bags. Small low tables were spaced along three of the walls of this tent. There were little booths as though the shelter could accommodate maybe thirty couples sitting in their own small lounge. At what appeared to be the kitchen end, there was one long Western-height table covered in plates and condiments. My guard gestured for me to sit on the cushions nearest this table. By the time I had sat down, I had already noted that there was not a single knife anywhere in sight, no forks either. A wonderful Middle Eastern banquet of herb-coated lamb, grilled chicken and couscous was served, accompanied by plenty of flatbread. Pots of aromatic mint tea were brought as another was emptied. I could have nearly forgotten I was a prisoner. One who had no idea what tomorrow held for me. Nearly.

Making a sweeping movement with my hand, I secreted a skewer up my sleeve and thought; *if this is all I have to escape with, I am still in trouble, but you have to try.* I enjoyed what was before me while simultaneously probing and evaluating the quality and numbers of guards, cooking staff exits and where vehicles may be parked. My captor joined me, bringing a carafe of wine from which he poured me a cup.

"Ah, my new friend, Mr. Greet, or can I call you Jack? How are you enjoying your dinner? I hope everything is to your liking."

Before I could answer, he continued. Did this guy ever stop smiling? "You look good in that Thobe. Of course, I would never drink too much of this wine, but if I did, I could easily think I was sitting next to Lawrence of Arabia himself. I imagine you have many questions about this place."

I had figured out how this guy was going to torture me. He was going to annoy the hell out of me by being so nice.

Deciding to concentrate on the realities of my plight, I replied. "Thanks, but I've already got an excellent dog back home, so I don't need a new friend. And, yeah, dinner was fucking great, so can I go now?"

The slightest flicker in his dark eyes meant I had scored at least a minor hit, but he didn't miss a beat. He continued, his smile a little less bright. "This is a tourist camp set up to appear as close as possible to a Bedouin camp but with the level of comfort demanded and expected by Western visitors. Hence all those accommodation tents, the bathroom you have seen and of course this dining tent. All this is fully occupied in the year's cooler months, but not now. This time of year, it's far too hot for tourists wishing to experience a Bedu lifestyle for a few days and drive to Lawrence of Arabia's old camp.

I was losing my patience. "Yeah, very nice; I'll come back for a holiday next year."

He seemed to be trying to demonstrate the Bedu patience he had bragged about. "Oh, Jack, my dear, I hope you are more relaxed and cooperative after a good night's sleep. Abbudin will take you back to your tent. Please, my friend, do not think about escaping. I know you have been observing our security measures, seeking any weakness since your arrival. But there are many armed guards, and you have only seen a small part of our force".

With that, he stood and gestured to Abbudin, my guard, who was standing nearby. I got up from the cushions to follow him towards my tent when Abu al Khayr touched my chest.

"Now, Jack, you are outstanding but not good enough." Smiling like a hungry lion, he removed his hand from my chest and placed it in front of me, palm up.

"Even the brother who cleans the dishes is trained to count the skewers just in case a tourist like you might take a souvenir and hurt themselves. I would hate to see you accidentally stab yourself." Looking down at his outstretched palm, I handed him the skewer I had hidden up my right sleeve and headed towards my tent. Credit where credit is due. These were slick operators.

I had been in hundreds of firefights and lots of other sorts of fights as well and endured extended periods in horrendous conditions, but being a prisoner was new to me. I have done two different SERE (Survival Evasion Resistance and Escape) courses, and the first thing you are told is that eventually, everyone cracks under torture. I knew the interrogation was coming tomorrow, and it wouldn't be friendly in any way. I was about as scared as I had ever been. Many people think brave people such as Soldiers, Police or Fire Service personnel don't get afraid. They do. The difference is what they do to manage that fear. I was totally alone, so as they say, if it was going to be, it was up to me. Doing something, letting your training kick in, stops you from thinking about fear. I systematically felt every inch of the tent in the inky darkness, especially where it met the sand, hoping to find a place to crawl under. I discovered that the bottom of each tent wall was secured firmly to some hard object buried in the sand.

I lifted the front tent flap a little so i could look out. I saw the area outside was still well-lit, and several armed men were standing at each corner of the courtyard. As Abu al Khayr had bragged, these men were well trained and disciplined, not standing together talking, no one smoking. I could see they randomly searched the entire 360 degrees, not concentrating on the outside and ignoring what might be behind them coming from the inside. I hadn't seen Abbudin as he was standing in a shadow beside my tent. However, he had seen me and made a very soft cough to alert me of his presence. I stepped back and let the tent flap fall back into place. I sat on the bed and went through the various scenarios that may present themselves. I eventually came to the realisation I might as well grab some rest.

All I could hope for as we walked to the interrogation in the morning, was an opportunity to disarm a guard and get a rifle. If so, it may be my only chance to escape. For once, I couldn't sleep. My body rested, lying there, relaxing my muscles and breathing deeply. I tried to think of Chris, remembering her smell and the warmth and softness of her body. I thought about hunting with my dog Jake and could see a scene so familiar that I could smell the gum trees. I finally fell asleep. A few hours later, something, maybe a noise, perhaps one of those gut feelings, woke me from my dream. I lay there for a few seconds listening when the front tent flap lifted slightly. I sprang off the bed and then stood statue still.

I could see an unmistakable silhouette of Abbudin and the menacing curved magazine of his AK 47. Probably, he had routinely come in to check on me, not expecting I would wake. My launching off the bed must have frightened him into thinking I was attacking.

As he raised the AK47 to his shoulder. With no choice I launched towards him. Timing was paramount if I was to survive the next two seconds. I dived onto the sand floor, knowing when fired, that most automatic weapon's barrel moved upward. It was a desperate move, but it was all I had. As a burst of at least twenty shots tore through the tent wall behind me, I sprung from the floor.

I figured I had two choices, neither named good or better. I could fight my angry guard or make a run for it. I chose a mixture of the two strategies. Grabbing the hot barrel of the AK47, I slammed the butt into his face. He expected me to continue my assault, and then to escape through the open tent flap. With this in mind, he attempted to draw me outside the tent where the other guards could help him. Capitalising on him reeling backward instead of following him, I let go. He fell out of the tent. I turned and threw myself against the black and red tent wall, where I could see the moonlight shining through a spray of bullet holes. Weakened by the burst of machine gun fire, the course hessian tent wall tore enough for me to fall through it onto the cool sand below. I was counting on them expecting me to run away from the camp immediately, so once again, I did the opposite. I ran along the line of tourist tents towards what I hoped to be the front entrance.

I was rewarded by the presence of a Landcruiser seven-seater, the moon reflecting off its dusty white roof. The tents were in rows, sharing common side walls. I had run past the back wall of at least ten tents in the row. For Abbudin and his fellow guards to catch up, they either had to go through the same hole in the canvas I had. Alternatively, they could run down the same row of tents but on their front side before getting to the front of the camp. They would have been unsure which way I had run, so hopefully, this gave me a little time. However, after hearing his twenty-round burst, the rest of the camp would be on high alert.

Praying the keys were in the vehicle, as I had no time to hot-wire the ignition, I sprinted towards the 4WD. As I approached the driver's door, a figure stepped out of the vehicle's shadow, swinging an AK in my direction. I threw myself sideways and hit his legs with my full weight and the force of my running. Sweeping him off his feet, he fell sideways, slamming his head into the side of the 4WD, with me ending up under him.

Even so, he had the presence of mind to swing the machine gun down onto my back. I rolled to the left and kicked him in the throat. He grabbed his windpipe, trying to open it from the outside, then still silently clawing at his crushed larynx, his eyes glazed over. He fell on his back, looking up but not seeing the incredible canopy of desert stars. Pushing him aside, I grabbed his weapon and checked his pockets for spare mags. None, so I jumped into the Landcruiser. No, the keys weren't in the ignition. It was worth a try. I pulled down the sun visor and laughed when the keys tumbled into my open hand. The big diesel caught the first time, and I took off. Not knowing where I was heading, I saw the 4WD had a Satnav, so I would work that out later.

As the vehicle fishtailed under acceleration in the soft sand, something moved on the passenger seat beside me. You little beauty, another AK47. However, my joy was short-lived as I saw three sets of lights coming fast around the kitchen end corner of the camp. I was at a considerable disadvantage, outnumbered by both vehicles and armed men. And wherever I headed, they all knew every wadi, rock, and canyon. All I could do was run blind. I had spent lots of time driving Military vehicles in giant sand boxes like this one, but at night, I also knew I could quickly come flying over a small ridge and drop fifty meters without warning. That said, I kept the gas pedal flat to the floor, trying to stretch my lead but knowing a confrontation was inevitable.

One of the chasers came alongside me and sidled over towards me. I realised I had an element of surprise; they probably didn't know I was armed. As I picked up the AK47, there was a soft metallic clinking on the passenger's seat. My luck was holding, I put the gun down. I felt around, finding three spare curved mags for my machine gun. They were holding back for some reason, maybe hoping I would buckle under such a pressure chase and surrender. I acted as though that was what was happening. I slowed slightly, they came closer. The two 4WDs driving parallel to each other must have looked like cars on a highway. I waited until I could clearly see the occupants in the high-beam lights of the vehicles still behind us.

As I picked up the weapon, I flicked off the safety and rested the barrel on the window sill in one quick motion. Not giving my pursuers a chance to realise the immediate danger, I fired half a mag into the Landcruiser's cabin. The window glass shattered, and the cabin filled with red. The 4WD with a dead driver behind the wheel careened off to the right, hitting a small rocky outcrop and rolling several times. One down, two to go. I accelerated again. The others had seen what had happened and probably heard the shots. They would be more cautious from now on. In the rear vision mirror, I saw them separate, and I immediately knew their plan: they were herding me like a team of sheepdogs moves a mob of sheep through a gate. I didn't know what gate they were aiming for, but I had to keep the pace up. They kept just enough pressure on me to keep me moving. I saw we had gently swung to my left towards what looked like a prominent rocky ridge.

I had been an avid student of military history and a big fan of Lawrence of Arabia. In the moonlight, I guessed this feature to be the famous Tooth Hill. If I was right, that meant that Lawrence's lost camp, which had only been discovered in March 2014, must have been near our present location. It was no time to appreciate being at such a significant military history site I would typically drool over.

But now, at least, I knew roughly where I was. If I beat these guys, that would help my escape. The scary part was that I still had no detailed local knowledge of topography.

For all I knew, there could have been a thousand-foot straight drop somewhere in the dark just in front of my speeding vehicle. I felt increasingly trapped as the two vehicles behind me hit me with their spotlights. Even turning the mirror down, the inside of the Landcruiser was brighter than daylight. I couldn't see much at all. I guessed they had timed that for a reason.

As I struggled to see in front of me, I decided to slow a little and pulled down hard right. This caused my chasers to do the same, but it had only bought me a little time. I slowed some more, hoping one of the 4WDs following me would lose their position. It didn't matter which side. I was trying to get them to think I had become disoriented in the intense glare of their powerful lights, like a deer or kangaroo on the road. They would have been pretty close to the truth. One of the drivers eased up beside me. Now I had slowed down I put all my money on them, not shooting me to shreds, preferring to re-capture me. I could see the Landcruiser pickup had two men in the front and three more in the back. I wanted them to relax, thinking they had beaten me into submission. So, trying to look like I was driving to the local store instead of being chased by heavily armed Bedouins, I put my elbow on the Landcruiser's windowsill and smiled at them. Although initially, their spotlights had blinded me, I had noticed as I changed the angle of the pursuit that their lights were working in my favour. Up ahead, I could see a dark shadow, and I was hoping this was some sort of canyon or hole.

Whatever my attackers believed they hadn't bothered shooting, probably because they thought they were driving me towards certain death. Or they were still hoping to capture me. It appeared they had bought my relaxed charade, and it had distracted them. They were probably confident that I would plunge to my death in this sandy, rocky grave. I was pulling all the tricks I could muster, so I reached over and turned the radio on, praying it had reception. It didn't, but even better, it must have had a CD inserted. The music was some Arabian male voice; as much as I would rather have had Toby Keith, but it did the trick. All five Bedouins started laughing. I looked over and waved as my ultimate bait distraction. As I stood on the brakes, all the occupants, including the driver, were watching me, not where they were headed. Their pickup sailed off the cliff top, then the screaming started.

The three Bedouins in the tray seemed to hang there momentarily as the heavier pickup fell faster than they did. I lost sight of the vehicle except for two flashes of light, probably from its high beams, as the 4WD rolled end for end, descending to the canyon floor. I couldn't see how deep it was, but it had to have been deep enough to kill most of them or, at the very least, the ones in the back. I had been super lucky so far. One to go. My thoughts were shattered by someone hammering rapidly on the Landcruiser's roof; clang, clang, clang as the 50 Cal projectiles zippered the steel with three uniform-sized holes down the passenger side. The third chase vehicle had seen what had happened to the other two 4WDs and had decided to end this quickly. I may have been clever in luring the pickup over the cliff, but now I was trapped between the last chasers and the same canyon.

I stabbed my foot through the gas pedal and let the vehicle swerve to the right under hard acceleration. I was in trouble, and I knew it. The Landcruiser lost traction in the deep sand, sliding sideways towards the cliff. I corrected before inadvertently following the pickup into the black canyon, taking the 4WD parallel to the dark snaking valley. I was thinking; *I've gotta get away from that edge before they arrive and push me in it as well.* I threw the vehicle around a rocky outcrop and killed the lights, keeping the power on the 4WD. I headed back in the direction our deadly convoy had just come. Knowing my tactic was only a stalling ploy, I tried to distance myself and my chasers as much as possible. I was doing well until, in the darkness, I found myself heading up a vast sand dune; I changed down twice, slowly pulling up the steep incline. Cresting it, I became airborne, my head and the contents of the 4WD flying to the ceiling as the vehicle descended. The AK hit my elbow painfully as it fell.

Being careful not to hit the brakes and go end for end down the dune, I allowed the vehicle's weight and gravity to land me safely and start rolling again. My pursuers must have known about the incredible dune, combined with having their lights on, they came over the crest more slowly. As they turned, I watched their progress and saw them slide sideways, totally under control, working all the way to the bottom like a rattlesnake might. I had gone straight down the face of the dune way too fast once my 4WD had eventually landed. But now I found I had lost any lead I'd gained. They lived and breathed this stuff, correcting quickly. They were on to me again. The Bedouins in the remaining Landcruiser opened up the 50 again. I swerved, ducked, and dived as much as possible, reducing their opportunity to get a good aim on me. However, deep down, anyone shooting from a sliding speeding vehicle knew it was impossible to aim properly. I had tried it often enough and knew you had to be lucky to hit anything on sand or dirt. It was desperate stuff I could just as easily zig or zag into the path of the onslaught.

However, the more the Bedouin fired on full auto, the higher the chance they might get lucky. But theories are one thing; fear is another. I kept zigzagging. The back window had shattered long ago, and now a burst whistled past my ear and took out the windscreen. So far, I had done well, and I certainly wasn't going to chuck it in now.

But a dark feeling was slowly descending over me. It was only a matter of time, and I was pretty sure my time was running out. Bouncing along, after two fumbled attempts, I put a fresh mag into the AK and prepared to make a stand. Slowly, I eased the Landcruiser to the side a little and took up the machine gun. I could see the chaser's 4WD coming closer and closer. I needed to make every shot count. Capitalising on them descending on me, once again, I rested the barrel on the window sill, pointing uphill as they rushed toward me. Intending to empty the fresh mag, I squeezed the trigger. I kept the pressure on until the gun fell silent, out of ammo.

Their Landcruiser exploded in a ball of flame, flying into the air several meters and falling into the sand to send out sparks and smoke. I have been around weapons all my life, so I knew something was very wrong. Happy as I was to see such a spectacular result, unless that Landcruiser was packed to the roof with C4, there was no way my shots had done that. Then, over to my right, three distinct pairs of lights came on, and a sound I would recognise anywhere shattered the cold desert air. Three US Marine Corps Humvees rumbled towards me.

As they got closer, one broke off and headed to the wrecked Landcruiser. I figured they went to make sure all the Bedouins were dead. Marines jumped out of the vehicles, and I noted all but one faced outwards, setting up an instant perimeter around their Humvees and my 4WD. The breeze must have swung around and brought the smell of burnt rubber and flesh from the smouldering Bedouin 4WD. They were all equipped with Night Vision Gear (NVG). As the one approached my 4WD, I climbed out of the Landcruiser, and he flipped his NVG up his forehead.

"You Greet?" The hard-faced Marine Lieutenant said with a total lack of warmth, nothing but business. Dressed in desert cams and pointing a Heckler and Koch HK416 towards the sandy desert floor, he was the real deal and then some.

"Yeah, I'm Greet. Thanks for that, mate." I pointed over to the wrecked Landcruiser. "Fucking good work; who are you"?

"LT Sam Richards USMC, let's get your ass out of here, hey?"

Richards touched his throat mike. "All call signs package in hand. Let's go, guys." He said something I couldn't hear, and then, without another word, the perimeter folded down in a staged sequence.

We drove towards the burning 4WD; as we got closer, I saw several twisted bodies strewn across the blackened sand in the light of the flames. A corporal handed Lt Richards a vehicle-mounted mike. I figured this was to reach his HQ.

"Sir, we have the package."

A voice of apparent authority from a hidden speaker commanded. "Report on return, ASAP out."

The Marine Lieutenant handed the mike back to the Corporal, and that was the last word spoken until we arrived at the US. Embassy. I was relieved to be safe and utterly exhausted. Sitting in the Humvee, as I had been trained to do, I took a stock-take of my battle readiness. All I had to show for my little adventure was some lacerations from being peppered with shattering glass and a sliced arm when the AK47 fell on me. A Medic had put a field dressing on it before we left the burning wreck and instructed me to get stitched up once we got to HQ. Within seconds, we were moving at breakneck speed across the sand. They were navigating by Mil Satnav. There were no roads and no threat of Improvised Explosive Devices (IEDs) compared to most places these guys had served.

They made the best of it, maintaining this speed until we hit the highway. It was only forty Klicks into Aqaba; that was a surprise to me.

The Bedouin leader, the late crisp and crunchy Abu al Khayr, had lied to me about being hundreds of miles away from civilisation, probably to discourage any attempts to escape. We passed through Aqaba at the speed of light, except to screech to a stop for a herd of goats crossing the highway. In Jordan, they always have the right of way. Three and a half hours or so after we had left Wadi Rum, we could see the outskirts of Amman, the Capital of Jordan. The small Military convoy meandered our way through a mix of ancient and new settlements, eventually finding ourselves in an avenue occupied by several Embassies. As we got to the US Embassy, steel bollards disappeared into the driveway as our vehicles rushed through the heavily guarded gates high, the compound surrounded by a razor wire-topped fence. We headed around the back of the buildings. Two young Jar Heads escorted me to an office on the second floor. There were no signs or names on the door. One of the Marines keyed in a pass-code, turning the red digits to green and unlocking the grey steel door.

CHAPTER 4

The office had been decorated with a minimalist theme, or maybe no theme at all: three uncomfortable looking office chairs and a small desk, its top scratched by years of service. I sat in the one facing the door as anyone trained and experienced would do every time. After five minutes, the door opened, and a man who looked like he was about to have a heart attack entered the office. His face was red and sweaty, his hair was thinning, and he seemed generally unhealthy. His shirt armpits were damp with sweat, and his nose had that venal look of a drinker. As he walked past me, there was a strong scent of a blend of recent tobacco and stale sweat.

"My name is Agent Smith, CIA. We don't always say what team we play for, but we are all on the same side here, aren't we? I knew I wasn't expected to reply, "I didn't expect you to be dressed in that gear, but I suppose there is some reason. We'll find you something a bit better in a while, hey?"

You look OK, but looks can be deceptive. You need Medical at all? He didn't ooze compassion. I figured he didn't care but was just covering his arse. "No, I am fine. I might need some stitches in my arm." I held up the offending appendage. The Bedus looked after me well, although I think that was about to change this morning. Yeah, I had totally forgotten about these clothes."

"Yes, well, we weren't sure what they had planned for you. Saw you get snatched on the Petra road from a drone we had keeping an eye on you. Then we followed you to that tourist camp, and well, here we are".

I was tired and sounded it. "Agent Smith or whoever you really are, thanks for rescuing me. But why did you wait so long before you sent in the Cavalry? I had no idea you were following me, but I sure am glad".

He shrugged off my thanks. "Yeah, well, we didn't want to spoil your mission; it was an acceptable risk."

I thought; *Some things never change. Apparently, with no surprise, the risk was acceptable. I was expendable.*

The CIA Agent continued. "Now, if you are fit, we need you to keep going. You're racking up a bit of a body count, but that only means you are on the right track. The good news is all this friction confirms your cover is still in one piece. Where are you heading next?"

I wondered about security, but this guy seemed to be in the loop. "Cairo, I got a lead that I think might help."

Smiling with tobacco-stained teeth, Smith continued. "We've decided you might need some help, and it might even strengthen your cover."

He touched a number on his phone and whispered into it. Seconds later, the office door opened, and an attractive woman about my age walked in. Now, while I haven't got a clue about women's clothes. But, even I could tell she was expensively dressed, and there was no doubt she was definitely hot. Agent stained-teeth, I had decided I would nickname him that, waved her to a chair next to me.

It seemed strange that he introduced me to my new partner under my alias, but it was his call. "Mr. Greet, meet Agent Julia Ramone, Ramone; this is Greet. Now, you guys will be travelling together as a couple to make it look good. There is no reason to suspect Greet's cover is blown, so having a partner won't hurt. You seem to attract trouble, so having some backup can't do you any harm".

I was used to working independently, and springing a partner on me wasn't part of the plan. "Now hang on, Smith. I work alone, and I travel better alone, and besides, my mum used to warn me about talking to strange women."

Smith looked dead set bored. "This isn't negotiable. Greet, we are glad to have rescued you, but now we want our own people on-site. Ramone here speaks Arabic and four other languages, and your mom *should* have warned you about her. She can kill you from a mile away."

He continued. "Now I know how your Military types think, so here's a printout from a Colonel Goodrich basically ordering you to be happily married to Ramone here, at least for the duration of this mission."

He was right about what I was thinking. But, I was a soldier first and last. "Yeah, OK, like you said, what the Colonel wants, the Colonel gets, but let the record show I am not happy about it."

Laughing to himself, Smith smiled. "That's fine, Greet, but we all know there isn't any record anyway. So you two have a great honeymoon."

I couldn't help myself. "Yeah, well, with incredible respect Fuck you and your honeymoon."

Smith was still smiling with his stained teeth and annoying me even more. He continued like I hadn't spoken.

"We have new paperwork, the whole package under the names Robert and Laura Johnson, so congrats, Mr. and Mrs. Johnson. Now we figure it makes sense for smuggler Greet to travel under another alias, so it's all good."

I learned long ago that picking your battles kept you alive just as much as being good in a fight, so I gave in. Ramone didn't look any happier about the situation than I did, but we were all under orders. Half an hour later, I was back in Western-style clothes and had grabbed a few extras in my carry-on.

For me, checking in at the airport should be quick as I had so little luggage. By now, some Movenpick Hotel cleaner's husband was probably enjoying the things I had left in my room in Petra. When the Marines rescued me, I kept a handgun in my pocket just in case there was another attempt on my life. Agent Smith had a driver put me in a low-profile local car to avoid anyone seeing me arrive at the airport with a Marine escort. Local taxis were also avoided as they reported all traffic from foreign embassies. Driving to the airport, I gave the handgun to the driver, explaining what it was. Even my knife wouldn't get through in my carry-on. Maybe here they would have let me take a knife on board, but I didn't want to test it and be caught up in a scene. So, I made a mental note to put it in Ramone's check in a suitcase when she got to the airport.

Ramone arrived looking every bit of the tourist. Immediately, she rushed up to me, throwing her arms around my neck, and kissed me passionately.

I understood she was in character in case anyone was watching, so I acted as if I enjoyed it. But it still felt so wrong.

Picking up our carry-on luggage, I smiled. "Ramone, I mean Laura, let's wander around for a while. We were about to be checked in, and I'm always alert, to ensure I don't have any tails."

With a condescending smile, she responded. "Rob, my love, I may be new to you, but I'm not new to the work. Let's settle it now; no more explanations, or you trying to train me, OK? Equal partners, OK?"

I thought, *I'm sick of being married already, I am already in trouble.* "OK, Laura, sorry, you might have to allow me a short period of adjustment, but I'll try to remember."

Ramone glared at me, whispering the first four words and then getting louder at the end of the sentence. "Shut the fuck up, 'sweetheart.'"

Dragging Laura's suitcase close to me, I slipped my knife into it, and we walked into the check-in area. I was pleased Ramone didn't query this, clearly she understood why I had done so. Then, without approaching the counter, we walked away. We swung in and out of two sets of restrooms until we were satisfied that we were alone. Returning to the check-in counter, we put Ramone's bag in and got our boarding passes. Realising that we hadn't eaten since early that morning, we grabbed some food and a coffee and waited for boarding. It was a strange set up, but we were both professionals and to the casual observer, we would have just been another couple talking and occasionally laughing as we waited for our flight. We were not over the moon with the arrangement but knew enough to make the best of it.

CAIRO
EGYPT

As we touched down in Cairo, an unexplained shiver passed through me, warning me I was probably walking into another mess. I had no choice but to follow the Intel; it was my only live lead. We got into the old taxi and quickly realised I didn't speak Egyptian, and the grey-bearded driver didn't speak English. But his wrinkled eyes twinkled Ramone spoke a sentence in rapid Egyptian Arabic as if she was a local. He was delighted to hear a beautiful foreigner speak his native tongue. I had kept the card I had found in the dead sniper's wallet lining and handed it to him. I thought this *tired, weathered old man would have looked more at home behind the reins of an ancient donkey cart.* He glanced at the Papyrus factory card and nodded vigorously. With a crunch of gears, he took off with a jerk, probably motivated by the kickback he would receive for bringing some tourists to the factory/shop.

I knew the factory was off the ring road, so when I saw the sign showing we were circling the city's outskirts, I was assured we were on track. The heat in the taxi was stifling, not to mention the pungent smell of stale sweat and cheap tobacco. So we wound down the window and were immediately overpowered by the smell of rotting garbage interspersed with putrid smoke where someone had attempted to burn the piled-up bags of rubbish. The city administration had been in shambles since the revolution, and services such as rubbish removal were non-existent. As we ran along a canal connected to the Nile River, I saw bloated donkeys and dogs floating towards the once majestic icon.

We passed ancient wooden carts overloaded with straw driven by wizened, fez-wearing old men whipping sad-looking, scrawny donkeys. On the roadside, fruit and vegetable sellers threw handfuls of canal water over their produce to remove the dust and keep their stock looking fresh. I made a note to avoid such fruit, knowing what I had just seen floating in the only water source the merchants probably accessed. Good tradecraft would have had me stop a block earlier than the address on the card, but that may have attracted unwanted attention from our happy driver. I paid the old man and thanked him, which exhausted my knowledge of the local dialect. "Shukran."

I had already noticed Ramone's sarcastic sense of humour; she didn't disappoint me. "Very impressive, Jack."

We closed the cab doors and moved away from the old taxi. "Very funny not, Ramone." I had decided to keep calling her Ramone to help me distance myself from this incredibly attractive woman. *I mean agent.* It wasn't working, but I was trying.

The old driver smiled; we could see him say something but couldn't hear or understand him. With a metallic meshing noise of gears that had seen better times off, he went in a cloud of engine smoke. I had been thinking about how I would approach this next phase. I had to assume the Staff at the papyrus factory were used to Western tourists arriving all the time. Of course, I had no way of knowing whether the legitimate operation ran independently of the other enterprises or whether the people in the store would recognise me on sight. I hoped this was highly unlikely. I was counting on the hitman from Jordan, who had Almahdi's picture and vehicle description, not to have had mine as well. Hopefully, he would have expected Almahdi plus one, but without any detail. Or maybe after sending the hit team at Petra and the hitmen on the highway they wouldn't expect anyone at all.

That would have made sense. If I was totally wrong about this, I was about to enter the enemy's camp and probably an ambush. All we could do was go in and wait for some reaction. I hated the idea but figured I had little or no choice. We walked through the dirty concrete car and bus parking area. Ramone took my hand and looked lovingly into my eyes. A faded sign that hung over the wide front doors would have been impressive twenty years ago and heralded the building as housing the Royal Papyrus Factory. Just before the steps began to ascend, there was a long, rough wooden table with benches on both sides. It was shaded with an ancient grape vine weaving in and out of the lattice sides and roof. Several bored male tourists had swapped the shopping inside for the heat outside for a while, enjoying a cold drink beneath the vine.

Walking up the seven or eight steps, we pushed through the double glass doors and found ourselves in a wonderfully cool, air-conditioned showroom. I had never been much of a tourist, although I had seen much of the world. It was usually flying in a noisy green machine on a mission. I put on my best-interested look, and we walked along rows upon rows of beautifully framed papyrus pictures of every scene imaginable.

Lots of chariots in hunting scenes using spears or bows and arrows. A lot had a black background, with overlays of gold, silver, and Pharaoh's favourite colour, blue. Often, a block of hieroglyphics was present. Ramone looked like she had just stepped off the bus with all the other tourists and was already cruising in shopping mode.

I couldn't help being impressed by the quality while still knowing it was a façade to provide tourists with an ancient memory that may have been created the day before. Two beautifully dressed women circulated, offering mint tea to the potential shoppers. I had learned to like this tea in other parts of the world and happily accepted the small glass tumbler. A man dressed in brilliant white robes raised his voice to attract the attention of the group of tourists, and it had the same effect on me.

As one, we all turned to see what he was doing or wanting.

After a welcome and a short history of the factory, the man demonstrated what papyrus looks like when it is growing on the banks of the Nile. Then he processed the reed until we could all see that after enough pressing, the one-time plant had become a sheet of paper-like material. After he had finished, he encouraged the group to continue inspecting the extensive display.

He also explained they offered free shipping to anywhere in the world. The elderly group of tourists clapped as the man finished his presentation and then eagerly returned to selecting the papyrus prints that would one day adorn their lounges and dining rooms all over the world. I could see the tour guide licking his lips in anticipation of the fat commission he would receive. Hiding out in the open, Ramone and I stood in amongst the bus load of hungry shoppers. We were younger than most of the group but still Western and, therefore, not noticeable. Nodding to Ramone, I worked my way to the rear of the showroom, heading for a grey door marked Staff Only. Moving to it, I looked for security cameras or guards, and finding neither, I turned the handle and discovered it was unlocked. Going through the doorway quickly, I found myself in a small warehouse. As I walked along the aisle, I saw large crates of each of the prints I had just seen out on display. Behind the pallet racking was another door. I hoped this one was also unlocked and would get me away from the retail end of the business. I ran to this door, crouching down as I got to it. Once again, I twisted the filthy handle and was rewarded by the door opening, the noisy complaints of the rusted hinges.

I took two steps in and, still crouching low, took shelter in the shadow of another row of shelving. I couldn't believe that no one had heard the door. But, after two long minutes, I was still alone, no noises, no alarms. As I moved further into this back part of the warehouse, I couldn't understand it, but I could smell a strong scent of toilet cleaner. Turning a corner, I found myself in a very primitive wooden walled workshop. It was well-lit, with several benches along the three walls; no one was working at these workstations. On one of these benches were several Plaster of Paris moulds. I could see several small figures in different stages of painting, most looking like ancient Egyptian women and animals. As these newly moulded figurines progressed along the bench, they appeared to become slightly damaged or worn.

I knew that making new furniture look older was called stressing. The latest piece would be hit with a wooden mallet, sometimes with nails or screws embedded in the hammer. After staining and polishing, the resultant furniture looked hundreds of years older than it was. The little statues were made to look worn and slightly faded to give the appearance of being hundreds or thousands of years old, even though some had been manufactured just hours before.

It wasn't these fakes I was worried about; however, it did confirm I was probably in the right place. What I was interested in was that some authentic artefacts may be shipped out to the UK and the USA amongst these imitations.

This was going through my mind when I vaguely heard a whirring sound. Turning to hear better, I suddenly saw two large horizontal steel blades coming straight for my head. The forklift was electric, which explained the whirring and the fact that I hadn't heard it coming. Unlike petrol or gas-powered forklifts, these were super quiet. All I could do was turn completely sideways, which placed me between the two forks as they slammed into the bricks, embedding the prongs deep into the cinder block wall. I thanked

God the iron spears were now in the bricks, not my head. Without waiting, I placed a hand on each fork and vaulted my legs up and over the forklift's control panel, hitting the driver square in the face. I was rewarded by the sight of his hawk-like nose spreading across his dark, weathered dial, his blood covering his greasy overalls. He was out for the count and slowly slumped in his seat.

Letting gravity take my weight, I swung back a little to where I had been standing and let go of the rusty steel forks. Landing on the smooth concrete floor, I looked around to get my bearings, only to be hit from behind. The piece of wood broke across my back and sent the two halves of the board flying either side of me. Staggering momentarily, I willed myself to fall to the right. By the attack's direction, I knew his momentum would naturally take him to my left. This ploy worked well enough for me to regain my balance with only an instant to spare. A large man dressed in loose grey overalls appeared to my left.

I swung my elbow backward and caught him in the side of his sweaty bald head. He grunted angrily but recovered quickly, coming at me, crouching more like a wrestler than a boxer. Instead of backing away, I stood my ground. He smiled, causing his bushy moustache to curl up. Coming for me, I attempted an Ashi Barai, trying to sweep him off his feet. He avoided it well for a man of his bulk. Perhaps his wrestling had trained him to avoid this attack. I was thinking furiously: *Just a little further, come on.* My right leg lashed out with a Kekomi thrust kick when he was in range. My foot slammed solidly into his balls, evoking a high-pitched scream as he grabbed his injured groin. I smiled as I thought; *I hope you enjoyed that big fella.* I knew I had really enjoyed taking the smile off his grubby face.

But you could tell he had been fighting all his life and was used to winning. A look of rage and determination crossed his face, overpowering what must have been intense pain, and like a bull, he came at me again. He was big, and he was tough but not the sharpest knife in the draw. Coming at me the same way and now in anger, I was sure he had used this tactic many times before. Probably, in past fights, his intended victims may well have turned and run. But, I was sick of this guy and wanted this over with. Not me. I ran towards him and was pleased to note the smile disappeared, replaced by a look of surprise.

Like a bullfighter, I stepped to the side just as he reached me and allowed his momentum to carry him past me. I stuck my foot out, tripping him in full flight. I pivoted and punched him where his skull joined his neck. He was incredibly muscled around his neck, but I was rewarded by a loud crack as his vertebrae separated. The dying giant continued falling to the dusty floor and was dead before his unprotected face ploughed into the concrete. I stood panting, trying to catch my breath and listening.

During a fight, the adrenaline coursing through your system causes everything is magnified and heightened, including sounds. I wasn't sure if the dead brute and I had made as much noise as it had seemed. I hoped I might have gotten away with this as no one had come to investigate the scene or kill or capture me. I threw a dirty old tarp over him and moved on.

Moving deeper into the old wooden warehouse, I came to yet another door; however, this one had a large padlock securing the bolt. I always carried my pick set, camouflaged to look more like a manicure kit if anyone ever searched me.

The padlock was big and strong to discourage cutting or hitting but was quickly opened by the gentle approach. It sprang open in under a minute. Quickly, I opened the door to this new area and, once inside, I quietly closed it behind me. This section contained several benches, each with two dark-haired children standing on wooden boxes so they could reach the plastic tub in front of them. Beside each child worker was a pile of what appeared to be pottery and coins. This was the work area I had been searching for. Where the authentic antiquities were cleaned and prepared for overseas markets.

Undetected, I watched as these youngsters picked up an item from these piles and placed it into a tub of unidentified liquid in front of them. After soaking for a little while, the object was retrieved, and the worker scrubbed it ferociously with what appeared to be a toothbrush. I had read in my briefing papers many artefacts were cleaned with toilet cleaner, which explained the smell I had detected earlier. Any museum curator or a real archaeologist trained in the restoration and preservation techniques would take hours painstakingly dusting the debris deposited over centuries. These child workers had neither the respect nor the knowledge to protect the history before them. Naturally, the children's masters were no better. They only wanted to make the item saleable and presentable, and using toilet cleaner was quick and cheap.

I took a few minutes to observe the structured approach of this enterprise. I started wondering: *what difference would it really make if I were sneak back tonight and blow this factory sky high. The discouraging truth was there may well be no impact at all. Another factory just like this one would spring up while this place was still smoking.* This thought had been nagging me since I left Colonel Goodrich's office back in Canberra. It was one thing to collect Intel about this artefact smuggling business. However, by its very nature, just like any part of the process, you closed one operation down, and a new one would start within a short day. I was happy with the progress of my mission so far. However, I was unsure about what the final outcome may be. I would keep chasing the wind and let smarter people than me work out the bigger picture.

Looking past the children cleaning the coins and jewellery, I saw a reflection. I wasn't sure what it was, but as I moved a little closer, I could see it was the glass wall of an office. Unlike the old wooden warehouse I had seen so far, this room was a modern set-up.

It appeared to be a cube sealed off from the dirt and smells of the factory floor. I edged forward and began systematically searching every wall and ceiling for security cameras. Thankfully, I couldn't locate a single one. The glass-walled office allowed the manager or owner to keep an eye on his operation in air-conditioned comfort. But it was glass, not a mirror like you see in the Police interview rooms. This meant I could also see inside without breaching the office and stumbling into a situation I couldn't survive. I could see a large man sitting at the desk, absorbed by whatever was on his computer monitor. He was dressed in a traditional white Muslim Thobe or robe, the shape reminiscent of a polar bear. His round head was covered with a red and white check Ghutra with a black rope Egal holding it in place.

He was very, very fat, so big he nearly filled his entire side of the desk. The longer I stayed outside, the more likely one of the child workers or someone else may discover me. I walked quickly up to the glass and chrome door and stormed into the office.

The round white shape looked up slowly. He had probably expected to see a staff member or something mundane, such as his tea arriving. Shock registered on the mahogany face. The deep cracks around his eyes stretched open in surprise, and then it changed to anger. Without taking my eyes off the huge man, I locked the door behind me. My progress from the front door to this point had shown me this operation felt secure from any threat. They believed they had no need for any real security. There was no technical security such as strong locks or CCTV, and minimal human protection except for my wrestling partner, who had met his demise earlier. That being true, this man still must have remembered he was in a dirty and dangerous trade. With a speed that defied his size, he grabbed for a Glock 42, Semi-Automatic.380 ACP. Lax security or not, I didn't want to get shot or alert any other personnel.

I slashed downwards with the edge of my hand and connected just as his chubby fingers touched the trigger guard on the lethal black handgun. He sputtered something in Arab that didn't sound very polite as the pistol flew from his grip. I backhanded him to establish who was in charge, causing a steady stream of blood from his long hawk-like nose. A vivid crimson stain appeared on his white Thobe as he whimpered and wiped away the blood cascading from his nose with the back of his hand.

Thankfully, in English but with a strong Arab accent, the fat man spat out the words. "I don't know what you think you can steal from me, infidel, but you won't see the next sunrise. I promise you that."

I laughed. "That's not very friendly," I said sarcastically. I closed the vertical blinds to ensure our conversation would be private.

"I am not here to rob you, fat boy. I want information, and I'm not leaving until I get it." I noticed I couldn't hear any sound outside this glass office, so it figured the outside world couldn't hear any noise from inside either. I saw a flicker in his eyes. He had just realised something, but what?

Having to fly limited my ability to be well-equipped or armed to intimidate my temporary prisoner. I didn't even have a decent knife. My Gurza was still in Ramone's bag. Then I noticed a beautiful gold and precious gem-encrusted Janbiya hanging on the wall. I took the dagger down, and, making sure he saw what I was doing, I slowly drew the razor-sharp weapon out of the decorated scabbard. I was grateful that it was authentic and not the blunt tourist version. His eyes grew larger as I pulled the blade across his meaty stomach parting the fine white cloth like a surgical incision.

He attempted to be brave by stifling a cry. I grabbed his hair through the Ghutra and bent his head back. This was too much even for a brave man. He thought I was about to cut his throat. he began to squirm and moan, and although it was impossible, he attempted to escape the menacing blade.

"Please, I have money, what do want? Anything, it's yours, please." He pleaded.

I made out I was moving the dagger towards his exposed throat and then stopped.

"I don't want money. I want to know everything you can tell me about your smuggling operations both ways into here and then to all parts of the world. I want names, emails, and phone numbers and have no time to waste. I want to know who your freight forwarding companies are and which ports are paid for to allow your trade. But let's start with something easy first. What's your name?"

The fat man wasn't used to things being out of his control. He attempted to regain some composure by threatening me.

"My name is Ali Ben Adham. I am not a man to attack without consequences."

My silence worried him more than a threatening response. Looking into my eyes, I could see the recognition that he could tell I was committed to hurting him some more if needed. He had probably been a strong, tough guy in his youth before setting up this operation and getting comfortable. But he was now arrogant and soft from sitting in his glass castle counting his ill-gotten gains. Reluctantly, a look of defeated acceptance I had seen many times before flowed across his face, and he began to speak.

"You Americans are ruining me. Just last month, wonderful items I had worked extremely hard to procure and dispatch were taken by you. You stumble over the shipment and impound my goods, my goods, young man, bought and paid for and now stolen by you American pigs."

He spat these words with venom. "I've had to find new conduits, new ways of avoiding your Police, all out of my profit."

I smiled, but it didn't mean I pitied him. "You're breaking my heart, fat man; someone stole the fucking things first, did they not, stole them from your own country forever? We're on the same side of the law, mate. That's why I need you to teach me your secrets. I need more ways to move my product too."

For the sake of my cover, I corrected his assumption. "I am Australian, not an American."

With spit flying from his angry lips, he continued. "American, Australian, you are all infidels to us, no difference, huh! "

He was angry and scared, not prepared to give much ground.

"Just words. Maybe stole them from people who died thousands of years ago so some of us can live today. What do you think? Not different to you, I think. The simple facts are once they were mine, and now they are gone. You are disruptive to my personal economy and a small part of my country's economy. I employ many people you know."

This went on for nearly half an hour, with me asking for details or clarification here and there. The fat smuggler was tougher than he looked and needed the occasional encouragement, but in dribs and drabs, he spilled it all. Somebody approached the office twice, but I had him wave them away. This appeared to be a regular activity when he had visitors; the Staff just knocked and then went away. I had collected more Intel in the last few days than I had expected to find in weeks. I thought; *Was my mission complete, or was this just another step in the journey?* I searched every part of the office and found some interesting-looking USBs and freight dockets.

I pointed and asked. "Hand me that mobile, will you?" His face looked confused. "Your cell phone, where I come from, we call 'em mobiles."

He acted like he was handing it over, suddenly hauling it back and throwing it at my head. I ducked in time to let it go past, only to find the fat man nearly on top of me, using his bulk as a battering ram, hoping to pin me and knock the air from my lungs.

Distracting me momentarily with the flying phone he nearly made it by, he hit me much harder than he could have hoped in any other scenario. I slid my left foot to the rear, allowing him to slide past. I grabbed a flabby arm as he went. I twisted it up his back until I heard a loud pop as his shoulder dislocated. He had failed in his second attack and would now pay the price.

He screamed as I continued to push his dislocated shoulder further up his chubby back. He was outraged, unused to not having his own way and probably with himself for finally giving in.

He may have been telling me just enough while he waited to make his play, confident I wouldn't leave his office alive. Having now lost his physical prowess, he now deployed his last weapon. His intellect and his mouth kicked in as he attempted to rile me into making an emotionally based mistake.

"You know, he was my best man, the one I sent to kill that scum Almahdi. He was supposed to get you as well. You have caused me a lot of grief. You killed my man. But then I got a call from my Bedouin friends. They have you. I was so happy and thrilled that night I sleep like a baby. I look forward to the morning, finding out what you know. Then I hear absolutely nothing, I'm tired again, I'm worried again. You make me worried. I couldn't even eat." He annoyed me, and I wanted to get out of there. "I know you're scared, but could you shut up? Just answer my questions.

He seemed to enjoy my annoyance. "Did the rat Almahdi suffer, I hope so? He was always over-ambitious that one. The fool thought to have you as a partner was going to be better for him, discarding me like last week's whore."

Even though I could feel the rage building within me, I looked bored, as he continued. "Did the fool think I would just give him my blessing? Yes, Almahdi my friend ditch me and go with Allah's blessing to become my competition. Well, he got what was coming to him. I am only sorry I couldn't see it happen."

I had heard enough. He was pushing me, and it was working. I was looking forward to knocking him out of his chair big time. I would be out of the country by the time he came to. Ali Ben Adham started laughing, his colossal belly rising up and down. He enjoyed talking about my short-term friend Almahdi, who he had ordered killed. I remembered poor old Almahdi laughing away at my silly camel saying, and the anger began to boil within me.

I was still going to knock this prick out, but now, the way he was laughing, I thought I might have to hit him more than once to make sure. I thought of the happy, friendly man that the sniper had killed beside me.

"You know, Almahdi said I couldn't trust you as far as I could throw you. Now, I understand, it's a saying made especially for you.

I was angry, but not enough to miss the subtle change in the fat man's eyes that betrayed his thoughts by a millisecond. From under his desk, he drew an identical twin of the Glock 42 he had pointed at me when I had first entered the office. Leaping to the right, his shot nearly missed me, slicing a small nick in my left ear. The fat man had finally succeeded. He had pushed me just a little bit too far. Enough was enough.

Obviously, he hadn't noticed me pocket the first Glock 42. I fired 3 rapid shots, one in his head and two in his chest. His stark white Thobe turned crimson as he slowly fell forward onto his desk.

Shaking a little and I spoke to the very dead Egyptian through my teeth, hardly opening my lips.

"You know, in my country, we would call Almahdi a good bloke. He didn't deserve to die on the orders of scum like you".

I could feel a righteous anger rage drain from me. I left the office without even a glance back. Walking slowly past the child workers, it was clear they hadn't heard or seen anything. I exited the building through a side door and walked along the side of the factory warehouse and around to the shop entrance. I went into the shaded area at the front of the Papyrus factory and sat next to two elderly men who were probably off the tourist bus parked nearby. I looked at my watch and shook my head. They smiled and nodded understanding about our wives and shopping. I sent a quick text to Ramone to meet me out front.

CHAPTER 5

Well, Cairo had been fun. My credit card expenditures kept the boys back at the National Security Centre Australia well informed and Ramon happy with her purchases. But it was time to check in and pass it on to the analysts back in Canberra. Then I remembered I had 'help.' Ramone walked up to where I sat in the shade of the ancient grapevine. The two older men had only just left when their wives had come down the cement stairs laden with shopping bags and joined the bus-load of happy tourists.

"Jack, was that successful? You sure were in there a while?"

The irony was not lost on my 'wife'. who was smiling

"Let's hit the road and talk on the way; it might cost me a lot to hang around here."

We started to walk away from the factory, and I answered her question.

"If you call having to kill two or three more scum and collecting a heap of freight documents and Intel a success, yes, it was," I said sarcastically.

Ramone ignored me; it was starting to feel like marriage more and more.

"Sorry about that, I enjoyed that place. You sound like it was pretty heavy going in there. Are you all good? I just noticed your cut ear."

"Yeah, I'm fine except for a few more cuts and bruises."

Ramone wanted to bring the conversation back to centre. "That Intel sounds great. So where are we off to now?"

I knew my irritation was due to the letdown as my body purged the adrenalin accumulated while I was in the factory and tried to lighten up a bit.

"I'll give you a hint: your language skills will be invaluable, and I hope you love sand."

"Awesome, I always wanted to go to Australia and the Gold Coast."

She understood humour took the stress out of situations.

"Very funny; I'll save you guessing we are heading for Abu Dhabi and then Dubai; it should be fun. Now, Ramone, I want to flick a report to H.Q. before we go. Can you organise the flight and book us into the Shangri-La Hotel? It's a long story and classified, so don't ask for details, OK? All I can tell you is a high-level terrorist we closed down stayed there, so I figure if it's good enough for him, it must be good enough for our honeymoon. What do you say?

I was too busy to give it much thought, but I figured Ramone couldn't help but notice I was keeping my distance. I smiled as I thought: *She probably thinks I'm gay, maybe married or have someone back home. That was so sweet. I can tell she's the romantic type.*

My thoughts were interrupted by Ramone's Yankee accent. She obviously enjoyed stirring me up.

"I knew love would bloom eventually, a honeymoon. Wooh Hoo, Abu Dhabi, can't wait."

"This is another reason I work alone. A few jokes and a bit of fun, then you'll start asking about what I've left back home or how did I get into this business?"

Ramone glared. "Don't get carried away; I just like my partners to relax around me. And, let's face it, if someone checks us, we need to look like we at least like each other".

"OK, Ramone, but we both need to focus without added distractions."

"Fuck me, Jack, you think you're Brad Pitt or something? I wasn't sure. But now I'm certain you're scared of me. Did we just have our first lover's tiff? We did, didn't we." The C.I.A. Agent said with a smile.

I was sick of this already.

"OK,OK, that's it, give it a break,"

I wanted to end the demand with a 'darling' to lighten the moment, but the bullshit would have gone on forever.

We flagged down a taxi that seemed even older than the last one we used; it took us straight to Cairo International Airport. Poor old Egypt didn't even have enough confidence and pride to name its airport after someone significant like nearly every other international airport in the world. We were checking in using our new passports as Mr and Mrs Johnson we made our way through the security barriers and checks. Now we were in the public areas, it was time to start using our new cover names.

"Laura, I need to find an internet café to let our families back home know how we're doing."

Ramone went seamlessly into character. "There's one up ahead. I'll get us a coffee, honey; you hungry?"

I thought I had been a bit hard on her before and knew we had to look happy and in love, so I smiled and squeezed her hand.

"That'd be great," I whispered because she didn't know my tastes or habits. "Flat White double shot, no sugar. You know I'm sweet enough, baby."

She rolled her eyes and headed for the cashier. I got onto a computer over in a corner cubicle and used the protocol and encryption sent in my report.

Ramone came over. "Baby, here's your coffee, and I got you a toasted sandwich as well."

Maybe being married was OK after all. I was too easy, a sandwich, and I was convinced. How sad was I?

"Thanks, Laura, we have enough time to enjoy this; wheels up isn't for nearly two hours."

Enjoying the coffee, we chatted about what we'd be doing when we arrived in Abu Dhabi, as any honeymooners would be, excited by the upcoming adventure. Ramone dispatched her report to her Control as we chatted. After our flight was called, we boarded like every married couple, having a short fight about who got the window, and then we settled in. We flew through the night, with both of us sleeping for most of the flight. I woke at one point to find my 'new' wife's head on my shoulder as she gently snored. We were soon off the plane, and at that time of day, it didn't take long to get out of the near-empty airport. As we approached the taxi rank, a well-dressed man ushered us towards a modern, immaculate cab. It wasn't long after dawn, and the Indian driver looked exhausted. He had probably been working all night. As the sun was rising over the dunes, I looked around and noticed the driver nodding off. Shaking his arm, I yelled. "Hey, mate, wake up." With a startled look, he over-corrected momentarily and then continued. "You want me to drive?" I whispered to Ramone. "Everywhere I go, I've got people trying to kill me, and a sleepy, overworked taxi driver nearly finished the job for them."

We made it safely to the Hotel and were met by a team of beautifully uniformed staff opening doors and collecting our luggage despite it being so early.

"Welcome to the Shangri-La Hotel, Sir."

I was very impressed by the level of service the Hotel offered, but I was so exhausted all I could do was mumble. "Thank you very much."

For appearance's sake, we held hands as we walked into the Hotel's incredible foyer, where we offered hot mint tea from a tall man dressed in a red uniform covered in gold buttons and braid. He had a type of vest over this grand uniform covered in hooks holding small golden cups. He would take a shiny cup from his vest and lean forward, and a golden spout that was part of the vest would issue beautiful hot mint tea. Usually, checking into hotels is such a pain in the butt. However, the girls behind the expensive green and gold marble counter made it enjoyable and entertaining.

We were escorted to the lifts and then into our room. We had booked a modest apartment to suit who we were supposed to be. However, the room was huge and decorated with a Middle Eastern theme. Everything spoke of wealth and high quality but in a totally classy way. It was hard not to smile and forget why we were there. We spoke in hushed tones about the mission. Even though there was no reason to believe our room was bugged, we were cautious. In some places, it makes sense to go outside, and the outside verandah had a beautiful view of the mosque. However, there were identical verandahs on either side where someone could purposely listen or even accidentally hear while having an innocent smoke. With sincere excitement, I said, “Laura, how good is this?”

Smiling widely, Laura put on a husky voice, “Amazing how good that bed looks, very comfortable.”

I thought: *She can’t help herself. One way or another, she is enjoying making me feel uncomfortable.* In an attempt to get back to the mission, I asked.

“You OK to have a look around tomorrow? Remember we booked that rental so we can check out Dubai?”

Smiling, she replied. “That sounds great.”

She picked up the local paper sitting on the telephone desk. “I know you can’t read the Arab words, but have a look at that cruise ship. Maybe we can jump on a cruise before we go home. What do you think, Rob?”

Without knowing it, Ramone had caused a small glimmer of thought to fly across my mind.

“Funny you mention that, Laura. I just realised something: nearly every place we’ve been having ‘fun’ on this trip, there had been a cruise ship in town. Ramone’s face showed this thought meant nothing to her, and she started to unpack. I filed the beginnings of an idea away for another time. We silently figured out the sleeping arrangements, deciding the bed must look like two people had slept in it when housekeeping came in to restore our room. I stood on our verandah overlooking the Khor Al Baghal waterway. The lights reflecting off its calm waters gently illuminated the famous and magnificent Sheikh Zayed Mosque.

Ramone and I were starving, so we went downstairs and caught a Gondola that traverses an internal canal through the Hotel to a shopping and food precinct.

The would-be Gondola was crewed by two Filipino born-again Christians singing some modern Christian rock. It sounded good; they said it came from Australia. I had to respect their courage and personal faith, singing and talking about Christianity in a Muslim country that would have had their heads removed in some regions. We got off and walked to an array of high-end restaurants. The happy bride and I agreed on Chinese.

We enjoyed a wonderful dinner, including two bottles of New Zealand Sauvignon Blanc. By the time we were in the lift heading for our room, I had probably had enough wine to make me relax. I began to wonder if I had been hasty regarding the sleeping arrangements. Ramone was a looker, she was funny, and Ramone was tough, all the things I seem attracted to in a woman. Yeah, the wine was definitely kicking in. I gained some self-control and sat out on the verandah, giving her time to get changed in the bathroom and get into bed. And unlike a movie, I was on the lounge, and she was in the bed, and that is where I stayed until morning.

We dressed and went downstairs to the best breakfast banquet I have ever seen or tasted. The food was terrific, the service fantastic, and the decor exciting. Most of the other tables were occupied by Middle Eastern women attempting to eat their breakfast, still wearing their burkas to maintain their modesty. The Hotel was obviously seen as a safe place for them to come and enjoy themselves while their husbands went elsewhere. The tour car arrived, and we headed off to Dubai. With one major highway and little traffic, the trip flew by. Miles and miles of sand in vast ridges, some of which had huge water tanks near the road. The guide explained these were for watering trees planted along the highway to try to stop the sand from travelling across the lanes and cutting the highway in several places. Water was dearer than gold in the desert, but not oil. It must have cost a fortune.

We had a good look around Dubai, to think that only a few years ago, in the new areas, there was nothing but sand and now some of the most incredible architecture in the world. We visited developments such as entire suburbs reclaimed from the sea and several stunning hotels for the rich and famous. We shopped, or more precisely, window shopped, at the famous Gold Souk Markets and many other sites in this modern city founded on ancient ruins. Driving around the harbours confirmed the enormity of any agency attempting to catch or stop smuggling. The number of ships and the tonnage moving through this port was why Dubai was so popular with the smugglers. Our driver dropped us off at the Dubai Mall, with instructions to meet at the front in two hours. One thousand two hundred high-end retail outlets and over 200 food outlets occupy some 6 million square feet of space. It includes a massive aquarium with a multi-story glass front to entice shoppers and their children to stay a little longer.

This Mall is a small city within Dubai with 80 million visitors a year enjoying activities such as under-roof Snow Skiing, an Ice Hockey Field, Movies and Shopping. Eating wasn't a priority to Ramone, who gobbled down some K.F.C. leaving she called to me over her shoulder. "I'll see you in one hour at the front entrance."

Sarcastically, I thought, *Amazing trade-craft Ramone, she was putting a considerable effort into her cover as a married woman and tourist.* Not to be outdone, I complied.

"Yes, dear." Looking married and trained at that, I trudged off. It took me about twenty minutes to check out some electronics stores, and I was all shopped out.

Walking past the multi-storey aquarium, I headed towards the front of this mega-shopping centre. I found a small bench near the front door out in the middle, surrounded on two sides by banks of shops. As I sat down, I said hello to an older couple already occupying the bench. From their accent, I realised they were from New Zealand. I didn't say any more to them, although I got the impression they would have liked a chat. However, I was enjoying the solitude, using the time to think through what we had seen and heard. I was thinking about where our mission could possibly go from here. Our tour was a bit of a waste of time, but it allowed us, while maintaining our cover, to get orientated with this major port. It was also good having a local guide answer questions as they arise. My thoughts were intruded upon by the sound of two clear shots. Now, I know shots when I hear them, but where we were, I immediately rationalised them as probably builders nailing into the concrete putting in a new shop front. Shooting crimes were extremely uncommon in Arab countries, especially here in the wealthiest place on earth. Street crime just didn't happen.

Rationalisation of the sounds where there shouldn't be shots aside, I couldn't help myself. My training kicked in, and I found myself sitting feet flat on the floor, eyes scanning in segments, alert for anything that would present a threat. Married or not, in the back of my mind, I was also hoping Ramone was alright. This place was so big something could happen in one shop, and a million shoppers just around the corner wouldn't have known. Suddenly, about fifty yards away, a small boy dressed in jeans and a bright soccer tee shirt screamed as he ran straight towards me. I thought. He's *a good-looking kid with huge dark eyes, dark hair, well dressed, but he looked terrified.* Then, I saw the origin of his fear. Chasing the boy was a tall, thin man in an expensive Western suit. In turn, a shorter man his large gut hanging over his jeans, a black shirt, wearing a Ferrari cap came struggling after him.

A simple labelling system of people is basic training for snipers to keep track of multiple targets. So the tall one became Tall Guy. If the boy didn't look terrified and if I hadn't just heard two shots, this could be a hapless bodyguard trying to catch a disobedient, spoilt brat. But my gut said it wasn't. A two-second assessment of the situation and I knew what to do. I had my plan of attack; now I just had to wait for the three runners to enter the kill zone. I let the kid run past me. He was so scared he didn't even see me standing there just to the side of his path.

As Tall Guy passed me, I noticed he had a small black automatic handgun subtlety held close to his right leg, confirming my initial assessment. Then Mr Ferrari arrived, when he was nearly parallel to my position, I slammed the back of my extended knife-edged hand into his throat, coat hanging him. His momentum lifted him off the ground. For an instant, as he hung suspended on my arm, the millisecond his feet hit the floor, I jammed my knee into his solar plexus. His Ferrari cap fell off, exposing his completely bald head. There was a whoosh as the air expelled from his lungs. With his throat crushed, Mr Ferrari fell to the highly polished floor and would never move again. I reached down and took the Sig Sauer P226 Tribal Two Tone from his shoulder holster. As I ran, I pulled the action back to ensure the weapon was loaded and cocked, now it was.

Over my shoulder, I heard the New Zealand woman scream. But I had already left them behind chasing after the terrified boy Tall Guy was pursuing. The boy was now only just a little ahead of his long-legged pursuer. He made the classic quarries mistake and turned to see how much lead he had. The boy stumbled, falling heavily to the floor. Smiling, Tall Guy ran the five or so yards and scooped the little boy up with one arm. Panting heavily, he completely stopped, like he hit the pause button to catch his breath. I had lost sight of Tall Guy and the boy as they had run around a corner at the end of the bank of shops. Anxious for the child's safety, I ran flat out and turned the corner at a brightly lit Calvin Klein shop. Not knowing the race was over, I nearly ran right into them. There before me was a situation as bad as bad scenarios can get. Tall Guy was holding a gun to the head of one small squirming child.

In one action, I raised Ferrari's Sig Sauer and flicked off the safety catch. Tall Guy looked as scared and surprised as the kid. He had his gun pushed hard into the poor boy's cheek and was screaming something. The weapon moved up and down the kid's face as the gunman tried to catch his breath. Now, talking in a hostage situation is OK, and sometimes it even works. But not this time. He couldn't speak English, and I lacked Arabic. Negotiating wasn't going to fly. He was caught out in the open without his partner to help. He was scared. Reading his eyes, what I saw concerned me greatly. I had no idea who the boy or the Tall Guy was. It didn't matter; everything in me screamed. I had to stop him from kidnapping or killing the boy. I had a clear shot and figured now was as good as time as any. Any hesitation on my part was only risking this guy would panic and pull the trigger.

Knowing he didn't understand, I whispered. "Let him go, mate, let him go." Halfway through the word 'go', I squeezed the trigger, and the Sig Sauer bucked a little, and a clean red hole appeared on Tall Guy's forehead. He immediately collapsed, dropping the boy and his gun simultaneously. I ran forward half, just catching the child. "You're OK, little mate; you're OK, I've got you."

At least, that was the plan. I was kneeling in front of the boy, consoling him, when something hard hit my head from behind. As I slid to the floor, my last thought was there must have been more of them than these two. I didn't know it, but two Linebacker size men in expensive suits had arrived. After slamming me, one bent to the boy and effortlessly picked him up. While the other man unceremoniously dragged me by the collar to the shopping centre's entrance. After throwing me into the back of a shining black Hummer, the men climbed in, slamming the doors shut; the desert 4WD took off with a screech of rubber.

CHAPTER 6

Ramone had heard the gunshots too and, considering she was unarmed, had bravely run toward them. When she approached where we had arranged to meet after her shopping spree, she saw the first man I had downed his Ferrari cap still lying near his lifeless head. The American Agent ran past him and headed around Calvin Klein's corner to where I had caught up with the boy and his pursuer. Ramone was concerned as she could see the pool of blood surrounding the tall man's head and breathed a sigh of relief that it wasn't me. When she couldn't find any trace of me, Ramone was somewhat relieved but anxious to know what had happened. Most of all, she wanted to know where the hell I was. Her training kicked in, and she backtracked to see what she could turn up.

Still sitting on the bench when the action started, the New Zealand couple hadn't moved and were holding hands and looking very pale.

"Hi, do you speak English?" The couple nodded in unison. They had both slid down the bench, getting as far away from Ferrari's corpse as possible.

Ramone used the sincere anxiousness she was feeling to ask. "What's happened here? I was meeting my husband here. He is nowhere to be found. Did you see an Aussie hanging around this bench?"

Shakily, the woman looked up and answered. "Yes, dear, we talked to an Australian, a lovely man. But suddenly, he jumped up and knocked that man out. He's not dead, is he? He is, isn't he dear? He hasn't moved in all this time." Pointing to Ferrari's body some five yards away from where they sat.

Ignoring the New Zealander's questions, and with an even more worried look on her face, Ramone asked. "What happened then?"

This time, the man answered. "He knocked him down just like Sue said, then he took that man's gun and raced after a very tall man who was chasing a wee lad." Pointing towards the direction, he continued. “They ran around the corner to where that Calvin Klein Shop is luv. After a little while, there was another shot, but I’m not sure what happened after that. We were both too scared to go and look. Should we wait here for the Police?”

Ramone, feeling even more worried, started to walk away. “Thank you for your help, keep safe.”

With a strong New Zealand accent, the man raised his voice, causing her to stop as he said. “Luv, I can’t be sure it had anything to do with it, but two locals dressed in business suits came through that entrance. They were both big fellas, if you know what I mean.” He was pointing towards huge automatic glass doors over her right shoulder. Ramone had stopped in her tracks so she could hear him, struggling with his broad accent. “Anyway, soon after the commotion, I saw them leave carrying the boy and dragging a man. My old eyes aren’t as good as they used to be. I’m not sure, but it could have been your bloke.

"Thank you so much; I’ll find him.” She called over her shoulder in a hurry as the C.I.A. Agent walked toward the entrance. Even though only a few minutes had elapsed since the shooting, she knew deep down she was wasting her time. They were long gone by now, but as she walked, she mentally regrouped. Where was Steve Wallace, and who had grabbed him? How was all this in any way related to their mission? Ramone sat on a short garden wall outside this fantastic shopping mall surrounded by thousands of happy, noisy shoppers and tourists oblivious to what had happened. By the time she had walked back inside Mall Security had covered the two bodies. The local Police and Ambulances were starting to arrive, bells and whistles screeching to a halt directly in front of where she was sitting. The shoppers continued to pour through the glass doors with their booty, some jumping into cars and taxis, melting into the constant river of traffic. She worked through every scenario and every possibility. She was unarmed, unofficial and undercover in a foreign country. She was alone without the resources she would usually employ to locate a missing agent back in the States.

For the first time in her work life as an agent, Ramone was at a total loss as to what to do. Then, seeing a Mall Security Officer commandeering one of the entrance doors for the use of the Police and Ambulance gave her an idea. Ramone remembered that these days, all stores deploy CCTV units everywhere. Fifteen minutes later, she had flirted her way into the small Security office. The two Guards, who usually majored in shoplifters most days, if that, were drooling over their keyboard. While they weren't going to challenge Sherlock Holmes any time soon, they knew the one important thing at that precise moment. Sliding past one of them, Ramone sat down again, making sure this time her dress rode up her thighs even higher than when she requested to see the CCTV videos.

"You guys must be brave working in such a dangerous place." She was sure she heard them both sigh. She uncrossed and crossed her shapely legs yet again. "Who are those big men? They look official to me. Come on, fellas, a couple of sharp law officers like you must know who they are?"

Both Guards seemed to involuntarily push their chairs back in either shock or fear of her question. Ramone was just as surprised at their reaction but pushed on. She reached over to pick up a pen and post it notepad as though she needed to write down something. She knew from their reactions the answer she sought must be valuable in some way. Ramone allowed her bare arm to gently rest on the tattooed hand of the older one with the drooping moustache. He melted, even though his friend shook his head, attempting to discourage him from answering. He chanced another look at her legs. "My Dear, they are Crown Prince Abdul Al Sattar's men. That little boy is Prince Zayed."

He must have thought he had just earned his way into Ramone's bed because the disappointment on his face was deadset pitiful when she quickly stood, thanked them and left without another look or word. Ramone's timing was impeccable. As the lift doors opened, she was engulfed in a mix of onions and stale body odour.

She had to stand aside to allow three overweight Police Detective types to exit the lift. Ramone was positive that they were here to see the same CCTV video.

Once again, I awoke with a splitting headache; I was getting sick of being slugged all the time. I found myself in a small room furnished only by the cot I was on and a single chair. On one wall was a large mirror, and a bucket in one corner and a little barred window just below the ceiling.

It must have been a two-way mirror because I had only blinked my eyes three or four times, and with a soft click, the door opened. A man in a full desert Arab costume entered the room. He had the bearing of someone with authority, backed up by ability. Although he was Middle Eastern his accent made it clear he had been educated or had lived in the UK. at some stage.

"Ah, good show, you are awake, praise Allah. You are required in the main reception area. Do you need to access the bathroom first to wash? If you are thirsty, there will be drinks where you are going."

I said I was OK and stood up, trying to hide that my body was telling me I should be falling down.

He continued politely. "Please put your hands out in front." I was impressed that he had asked for 'in front', as this is now acknowledged as the more effective way to cuff a prisoner compared to behind your back. He placed high-quality handcuffs on my wrists, tight enough to work but thankfully not painfully so. As we walked along pristine white hallways and through gold-decorated doorways. I noted there were armed staff at every turn and wondered where I was. Holding my bound wrist out in front as I followed him I asked. "Where are we, and why am I here like this?" My guide would not answer my questions regarding my predicament, location or why I was here at all. After five twists and turns down this hallway, we came to a large open area. It was the size of a good hotel's foyer with an expensive blend of Middle Eastern and Western furniture. The walls were adorned with huge portraits of stern-looking grey-bearded men, most armed with gold and jewel-encrusted Scimitars and Jambiyas (curved swords and daggers). They had hawk-like eyes and noses and appeared to be related to each other, but I wasn't sure.

My eyes focused on the two highly polished display racks of Scimitars located beside the paintings, although I pretended to be looking at the portraits. A deep voice caused me to turn. "Don't make any plans to attempt to use one of my ancestor's Scimitars to aid your escape. My man here will not hesitate to shoot you where you stand." With a quiet rustle of his glistening Thobe on the carpet, the speaker flowed into the room and sat down. He sat behind a gold and green-trimmed marble table big enough to seat six people. The ornate chair he occupied could easily be described as a throne. Taken aback by the alert observation of my captor, I found myself facing a man of my height and weight with the same flint black eyes and hawk nose as the men in the portraits. Covering his head and much of his dark-skinned face was a white Ghutra held in place by a woven golden Egal. Over his radiant thobe, he was wearing a golden Bisht vest of shiny material with a decorated fringe. Everything suggested wealth and power.

He spoke again. "I have kept you alive to allow me to see the face of my son's kidnapper. To see what a foolish man looks like. Tell me, how did you expect to get away with that? What was it for ransom money, or did an enemy hire you? I can assure you whatever your motivation was to kidnap my son, you have made the biggest mistake of your very short life."

He continued quietly but leaving no doubt about his authority and controlled anger. "Do not become relaxed about your current environment; I assure you it is only a temporary respite. Your friends killed two of my most trusted and long-serving men. For this, you will pay dearly."

Smiling like a lion about to devour a gazelle, he continued. "Shortly, my men will take you to a far less comfortable setting where they will ask you these same questions. Now, I want those answers, but for what you have done, deep down, I hope you take a long time to answer."

I thought; *I may as well have stayed with the Bedouins to save time.*

He kept going in his deep, accented voice. "If you are foolish, you will not answer their questions or lie. If you choose to be uncooperative, my men will take days to ask the same questions, and you will eventually answer them. I have an excellent medical staff who will keep you alive as long as possible". Which is it to be?"

Somehow, I had to clear up this mistake. "Sir, I don't know who you are, and I didn't try to kidnap your son. I am a tourist from Australia here on my honeymoon. I saw two men chasing a small boy and stopped them. I..........".

His gesture was almost imperceptible; however, his stooge didn't miss it. Moving forward in a blur, he backhanded me, knocking me off the chair. I fell sideways, turning my shoulder to protect my head as my hands were cuffed. His voice was now as hard as the flint.

"Your two accomplices are dead, so this all falls on you. I have been told you are not even loyal to your friends, killing one to attempt to make out you were not involved, or perhaps keep all the money, hey?"

I was over this big time. I didn't expect a medal for helping the kid, but I didn't think I would be arrested and interrogated. "I don't know what the fuck is going on, but you have it all wron....".

Once again, out of the corner of my eye, a blur. The big man hit me again, this time a little more sideways. Thankfully, one of his sidekicks caught me as I fell off the chair.

Spitting some blood on the marble floor, I tried again. “I couldn’t even fucking confess if I wanted to. Every time I open my mouth, King Kong smacks me. Let me out of this chair, you big prick, and we’ll see who’s who in the zoo.” My comment brought smiles to everyone in the room except the big guy who had been hitting me. As I readied myself for another hit, there was an urgent knock on the door. A small man in an expensive Western business suit, white shirt and red tie entered the room from a side door. The one asking the questions looked happy to see the man arrive. “Faishal, come in, what have you discovered?”

“My apologies, Your Majesty, it took some time to collect and collate the CCTV videos you required. I had to wait for the Police to acquire them from Security. The Detectives were happy to hand them over to me, so I waited downstairs for them.”

I had heard this Faishal use the title Your Majesty and was trying to figure out what the hell was going on. Sounding impatient, the man sitting at the table demanded. “Alright, Faishal, load the machine. We will see what happened; it would seem this fool will not admit to anything, at least not without encouragement.”

With that, Faishal withdrew something from his coat pocket, switched on the player and inserted what must have been a DVD. Every eye, including mine, turned towards the wall-mounted 50-inch screen. Someone yelled to turn off the lights. Except my life depended on this footage; I nearly expected popcorn to be served. I was totally frustrated and confused by everything that was occurring.

Even having the lights off annoyed me because it would have been the perfect time to make a break for freedom. Things might have been different if the handcuffs weren’t securing my wrists and King Kong hadn't been standing next to me.

The vision came up. I recognised the little boy and two men I hadn’t seen before, probably bodyguards. One was walking with the boy in front of the enormous aquarium window, another similar-looking bodyguard walking a few paces behind. The little boy appeared excited and rushed ahead of his guards. I couldn't see why, but the bodyguard closest to the boy seemed to stiffen. Of course, there was no sound, but the bodyguard's reaction told it all. Both bodyguards reached under their coats; the frontman fell to the ground. You could see his left leg give a little kick and then nothing. The man at the back threw himself down and unholstered his handgun, but his head jerked to the left, shot from the right by an unseen assailant. The little boy appeared to scream and then took off amongst the tourists and local shoppers running towards the front entrances.

The man Faishal had called Your Majesty let out a quiet but heart sound of anguish. On the big screen, my new best friend, King Kong, now appeared; he must have been further back again. He ran forward and was seen to ignore what I assumed to be his men and went after the principal, the boy. Of course, this was what a well-trained bodyguard should do. A silence you could feel filled the room, with all of us holding our collective breath due to the gravity of the DVD. Very little time had elapsed, but the gap expanded between King Kong and the two assailants racing after the child. He was quick with his hands, but being so big, he wasn't built for sprinting.

There was a moment of no vision, possibly as one CCTV camera zone finished, and another started. The boy, followed by two men at various distances, was seen to run towards the entrance. The huge bodyguard was not currently visible.

In front of the parade in the distance were three white people, two men and a woman, sitting on a small bench that backed onto a little waterfall and garden. There were several shopping bags at the feet of the man and the woman, who, by the colour of their hair, were elderly. Of course, the other man we were watching was me, who was now handcuffed and bleeding from the nose. Now, on the screen, you saw me stand as though I had not seen the little boy chased by the two men. However, it was apparent this was a ploy, as everyone in the room could see that I had allowed the boy and the first man to pass. Suddenly, I launched my attack on the second assailant. Something fell from this man's head as he hit the deck.

There was a sound you hear in a movie theatre when something surprising happens, just short of a scream, a sort of quick intake of air. I was then seen to kneel beside the man I had just killed. None of us could see what I was doing until I stood up, and a gun was silhouetted for a short moment as I jammed it in my pocket. I shoved something else in the other side pocket. Of course, I knew this to be a spare mag. A second or two later, I was seen running off after the boy and Tall Guy, as I had named him. Running, I drew the gun from his pocket and, holding it in my right hand, I reached over with my other hand and did something to the weapon, quickly looking down at it without missing a beat. To no one, in particular, King Kong quietly said. "He was checking to ensure there was round in the chamber."

The terrifying race continued between the two banks of shops, heading towards the front of the vast shopping centre. Suddenly, the little boy turned the corner past the Calvin Klein Store. Once again, the vision went static white and those watching let out a frustrated sigh like those watching a dramatic movie when they put on an advertisement.

As the new camera cut in, the little boy looked around, his eyes as big as saucers, terrified of the tall man just three steps behind him. As he turned, we saw his feet tangle, and then he stumbled and fell. The tall man pounced upon him in one step, grabbing his skinny little arm so tightly that a grimace of pain flashed on the boy's face, immediately replaced by fear. The man held his gun pressed into the child's temple, a welt already rising from the barrel pushing against the young face. The barrel then slipped to the boy's cheek;

it was clear the assailant was puffing vigorously and now appeared confused. Arriving at this scene, I slid to a halt about five meters away from the brutal scene. Although there was no audio, everyone could see that the gunman, with a vicious snarl, was saying something to me.

There was the very slightest twitch in the gunman's eyes. I had no way of knowing, but I was sure everyone in the room knew there wasn't any doubt he was about to fire. He probably hoped he would escape while everyone hovered over the lifeless boy. There was a slight puff of greyish smoke from my gun, and it sounded like everyone in the room took another big breath in unison. Simultaneously, a third eye appeared between his two flinty eyes, and hair, blood, and brain matter flew from the back of his head. He then collapsed stone dead, still clutching his gun in his right hand and the boy in his left relinquishing both as he fell to the shopping centre floor.

I was seen to jump forward, pocketing my gun as I went, catching the boy before he hit the ground. You could see that I allowed my momentum to take the boy past the assailant's dead body, shielding the boy from seeing the corpse. I then knelt and hugged the terrified kid and could be seen to say something.

The massive form of King Kong appeared from around Calvin Klein's corner. His hand arched as he was seen to hit me from behind in the back of the neck with something. It was probably a sap, a small but dense, hard leather-bound club. His employment of the sap explained why I had such an incredible headache. The DVD stopped, and the screen became snow. In the soft light from the scratchy screen, I noticed the man sitting alone at the table was wiping his eyes caught by the lights coming back on.

He suddenly leapt to his feet and commanded. "Uncuff this man immediately!" Looking at me, "Sir, I am so very sorry for how we have treated you. I owe you a debt I can never repay, and I have treated you as an enemy. I believe it would be impossible, but can you please forgive me?"

Free from my bonds, I was busy rubbing my wrists, attempting to regain some feeling from being cuffed for so long. I was happy all this had been cleared up. But that didn't mean I was pleased. "Who the hell are you people, and what is going on?"

The man asking all the questions nodded his head, and Faishal responded. "Sir, you are in the presence of the Crown Prince Abdul Al Sattar, the heir to the throne of the U.A.E. The boy we now know you saved is Prince Zayed, first-born son to His Majesty. We are in your debt, Sir.

However, please do not speak to His Highness in such a tone." The aide was in shock, having never heard anyone speak in that manner to his Prince.

Faishal attempted to explain what had occurred. "Until we saw the CCTV video, we thought you were one of the kidnappers who, perhaps to either shut him up or attempt to look innocent, had eliminated his colleague."

Raising his hand to silence Faishal, the Crown Prince took over. "Thank you, Faishal. I can understand your upset, Sir. I cannot express my horror at mistaking you for a criminal. I am so, so sorry; you are a hero to my family and our Nation. Just as much I cannot express my thanks for what you did. For a child, you didn't know you endangered your own life. You didn't even know who that child was. You said you were on your honeymoon, so may I assume your wife would be worried about your whereabouts and well-being?"

He turned to the man he called Faishal, who I later learned was the Prince's Personal Assistant. "Find this man's wife and bring her here." They had emptied my pockets, so they knew my name and where we were staying. I stuttered. "We were on a tour from Abu Dhabi. My wife wouldn't return to Abu Dhabi without me. She may be waiting at the Mall where I disappeared."

The Assistant, understanding his master's wishes without further command, nodded in agreement and left the group. The Prince came around the work table and offered his hand to me. His body language showed me he was still very embarrassed about the treatment they had dished out to me. I didn't know much about how Princes acted. But I figured they probably lived their entire lives with no one brave enough to say they had made a mistake or were wrong. For this guy to be in this predicament, it had to be unexplored territory. I was sore from the beatings and annoyed as all hell. But I could understand how, as a father, I would react if someone attempted to hurt my son. I decided I would cut this guy some slack. He must have felt fuelled by hatred towards me for killing his friends. King Kong was just doing his job, thinking I had a hand in killing his friends and making him look inept.

I spoke quietly out of respect. "Sir, I am unsure what to call you." He chose not to interrupt. "I can understand how you must have felt. And to be fair, King Kong. I corrected myself. Um, I mean, your man here showed incredible bravery. He didn't hesitate for a moment. He did a great job following those kidnappers and getting your boy back. I could feel the stress leak from the room. The Prince, appreciating my grace, seemed to relax, and I saw the huge bodyguard's shoulders seem to lift a little out of the slump of failure and embarrassment. The Prince clapped his hands and ordered food and drinks. He turned to me and introduced himself. "To answer your question, my official title is Crown Prince Abdul Al Sattar, the heir to the throne of the U.A.E. I realise most Westerners struggle with royalty and titles; however, to maintain the status quo, these things must be. Please call me Prince." I wasn't sure if a 'commoner' like myself was allowed to touch His Highness, but out of habit, I thrust my hand towards him. "Pleased to meet you, Prince. I am Rob Johnson." The Prince shook my hand firmly and laughed.

Within a few minutes, several servants appeared with trays of drinks and platters of exotic food. I was surprised and more than a little happy to see the familiar bottle of Jack Daniels amongst the offerings. With a movement of his head, the Prince led me into a lounge area. I was thankful that it was furnished with Western-style lounges. I was far too sore to sit on the floor, royal cushions or not. I noted the Prince was matching his scotch for my Jack Daniels. Princes must be allowed to drink, probably as long as no one outside the household sees them. I must have been trustworthy and intelligent enough not to raise the subject.

King Kong was hovering but did not join us in the lounge area. The Prince explained how the Royal Family functioned and how he was a Prince and the United Emirates Minister for Defence.

As the Prince was about to proceed, there was a scream and a kicking sound as a side door to the reception area flew open. King Kong's hand flashed under his immaculate coat, reaching for his gun. My loving 'wife' came rushing through the doorway, shaking off one of the Prince's staff who was attempting to restrain her. Faishal became her next victim as she pushed against the wall. Bursting into the room and running towards me, worried King Kong as the Prince sat next to me on the white lounge. The big man moved incredibly fast over a short distance. He was about to grab Ramone when the Prince barked.

"Awqafa, awqafa," a command to stop."

Ramone, was oblivious to King Kong's near attack, or maybe she didn't care. She threw her arms around my neck, hugging and kissing me passionately. Ramone was playing the part of a scared honeymooner and deserved an Oscar for her efforts. For the first time since we had been together, the Prince sat back with an amused smile on his handsome face.

My worried wife continued her show. "Robby, are you OK, honey? I've been so worried and then being pushed around by these clowns. What the hell is going on?"

Before I could speak, she turned on the Prince and launched into him. "What the hell are you smiling at? You let us go right now. We are Australian citizens, and if we are not returned to our Hotel right now, you can expect a whole fuckload of trouble, whoever you are."

At least here, Ramone might get away with making out she was Australian, having done a reasonable job of softening her American accent. I also figured it was a certainty the Prince had never in his life been sworn at and never threatened, especially by a woman. In the last two hours, a man had sworn at him, and now this woman was swearing and screaming threats at him. His guards were probably amazed he did not order their imprisonment or punishment. This might have been the case if we had been his subjects or if the circumstances differed. The Prince smiled with royal grace as I attempted to calm my new wife, looking embarrassed and unsure of what to do.

Taking on my most husbandly assertive tone, "Honey, HONEY, may I introduce the Crown Prince. I am sorry you were worried, but we have worked out all the confusion and misunderstanding just now. It's all good."

'Laura', my loving wife, wasn't even close to being able to slow down that easily. She was about to launch a fresh attack and then propped. She wasn't stupid; suddenly, she heard the Prince part, and her face cleared. Her demeanour moved from fear to anger to embarrassment, understanding, and having new questions. Only a woman could move through those stages before your eyes.

Incorrectly, the Prince addressed my wife, sensing that he was safe to proceed. "Mrs. Johnson, please forgive me. I am so sorry about this terrible misunderstanding, but let me try to explain. Please sit down, and I hope everything will become clear. We were very wrong in thinking your husband was involved in the attempted kidnapping of my son. Would you like a drink or perhaps something to eat?"

She had only settled a little when, without notice, she went back to furious, brimming with adrenaline. Ramone interrupted the Prince. "No, I don't want a fucking drink."

Turning to me but attacking the Prince, she demanded. "How could you be that stupid? He's on our honeymoon, a tourist."

I attempted to calm her down by holding her and stroking her hair. Well, I never claimed to be an expert on women. It earned me a definite reprimand from my beloved. "Don't touch me. How could you get involved and then disappear like that?"

This lack of respect had to be getting close to too much for the Prince and me, to be honest. I just wanted all of us to relax and then get out of there. He was contrite, but taking this abuse and demands from a Western woman had to be pushing his limits. It was the Prince's turn to interrupt; ignoring Laura, he addressed me.

"My new friend Robert, my terrible behaviour has caused your honeymoon to cease prematurely, another debt I now owe you. Madame, until just before your arrival, we didn't know anything about your husband's past, but we could see he's a highly trained and skilled fighter, and his bravery is outstanding."

These compliments appeared to have the desired effect on my wife; she calmed down. Sensing the minor success, the Prince continued.

"Now, please, as I have asked your husband to please try to forgive me for these mistakes."

Witnessing this scene, I was embarrassed and concerned about Ramone's outbursts. However, if I was candid with myself, I was a little overcome by a strange feeling as my pretend wife defended me so vigorously. I just wanted to move on and go back to the peace of the Shangri La Hotel.

"Perhaps with your permission, we should be on our way, Your Highness."

"You may well be correct; it has been a trying day for all. Of course, of course, you are probably both exhausted after all the excitement."

Nodding, I said, "Thank you, Your Highness. We are both exhausted. Would it be possible for someone to take us to some transport?" Ramone chimed in, much calmer now. "Our tour driver waited as long as he could but returned to Abu Dhabi."

The Prince laughed. "Of course, we will assist you to return to your Hotel, but we would never allow an honoured guest to find their own way at this hour. If it is OK with you, my Pilot will fly you to Abu Dhabi. Which Hotel are you staying at?"

"The Shangri La, your Highness," I answered. The Prince smiled. "Wonderful, they have a heliport; we will arrange everything. Now, not only have I treated you terribly, but you have risked your life for my family, and it is our custom to reward your service to the Crown. Do you have any desires I may fulfil?"

Taken by surprise, I responded. "Your Highness, thank you so much. In Australia, it is not our custom to help someone and then receive a reward. Other than maybe a person buys them a drink or a meal, and you've done that. Sir, I mean Prince, we are very honoured just to have met you, Your Highness. I am so thrilled I was there at the right time and I was able to help your son. That, your Highness, is my reward with all due respect."

The Prince appeared surprised and pleased with my response.

"Robert, I liked it better before you knew who I was. Now it is no longer as easy, but of course, I am used to this barrier created at birth and in place for centuries. I hear your words, and they are very congruent with the quality of character you have so well demonstrated. What would your reaction be if I transferred One Million American Dollars into an account of your choosing?"

The Prince apparently felt obligated and was not used to people not seeking some reward or favour.

"Your Highness, I am honoured by your desire to reward me. Your generosity is overwhelming, but please fly us back to the Hotel and enjoy your life with your family. Your son is a courageous boy, and if it is meant to be one day, he will be a strong King you can be proud of."

The Prince smiled proudly. "Well said, you continue to amaze me, my friend. So many people curry favour from me, asking me for things constantly. I am sorry you will not accept my gift, but it only increases my respect and admiration for you. I will give you my card. Now, if you ever need anything in the future, show it or phone the number, and you will receive whatever help you require. It won't matter whether you want a table at a restaurant or are in trouble; this will open any door that bars your way."

With a sweep of his hand, the Prince stood and escorted the couple into a small lift that was immediately outside the room they had just exited. Twenty minutes later, after saying our farewells, we were seated in the most luxurious Helicopter I had ever seen. I had spent hours in Helos, but usually, they were noisy, shaky things. It was canvass and netting seats surrounded by fellow soldiers sitting forward because of the webbing and packs on their backs, everyone armed to the teeth. Now, we were seated on kid leather lounges, sipping our third flute of Dom Perignon. My cover wife had now moved from murderous rage to stunned shock in the presence of royalty and such wealth. I raised my Champagne to hers, and we both smiled. Who would have ever dreamt our little tour to Dubai would end like this? Especially, when the reality was that we were on a mission. Little did we know what was in store on our return to the Hotel. Now, the Shangri La Hotel in Abu Dhabi was, in our books, the best in the world, or at least so far in our experience. Probably seen as Budget, our room was a palace to us; the staff was terrific and the food out of this world.

We hadn't eaten much at the Prince's Palace, not because the banquet before us wasn't mouth-watering. It was a mixture of fatigue and restraint to avoid appearing impolite or like beggars let in off the street. We were both hungry but even more exhausted. We were looking forward to the view from our room towards the majestic Sheikh Zayed Mosque. And the beautiful room we had, with its gigantic bed and fluffy pillows, and for me, even the couch was a comfortable luxury. I felt the Helo bank a little. There was a polite knock, and the female attendant wearing a modern-style burqa that revealed only her dark, shiny eyes took our empty glasses with a slight bow and disappeared into another area of the Helo. I was amazed at how much room there was, seating for twelve and still a galley of some sort aft the seating.

We could hear the Helo lose some revs as the Pilot bled off some speed and looked out the window to see our Hotel looming up. The landing was soft without any bump or noise. The attendant came back and said.

"Thank you so much for allowing me to serve you. Please be careful as you climb down the steps to the hotel deck; hotel staff will assist you from there".

With that, she pushed a green button on the right of the door, which then slid to the left, causing a warm rush of air to meet our rosy faces.

"Welcome back, Mr. and Mrs. Johnson. I am El Abdul-Hakim, General Manager of the glorious Shangri La Hotel.

Once we get inside, could you please stop for just a moment?" We looked at each other, a question mark on our faces, but with the crazy day we had been through, we figured just about anything was possible.

Once inside, the Manager turned towards us. I noticed this man's suit was incredibly well made and probably cost three months of my Army pay. Bowing slightly, he continued. "Mr. and Mrs. Johnson, we have been informed that you are friends of His Majesty the Crown Prince. Please forgive us for not knowing this when you first arrived. All our rooms are exceptional, of course. However, I have taken the liberty of having your possessions carefully packed and moved to the very best room in our Hotel. It is the Presidential Suite.

Your own Butler will serve anything you desire. Please enjoy yourselves, and of course, everything is free of charge to you. Now, please follow me up to the Penthouse Suite, and then I will leave you to relax after your day of travel. We held hands, partly for our cover, more in trembling with fatigue and excitement. A happy couple smiled back from the bronzed mirrors of the private lift. The Manager rang the doorbell, and a Butler opened the dark wooden door, smiled and stood aside. Indeed, I thought this had to be some concussion-caused dream, but it wasn't. The whole day had been like a day off from our mission.

Ramone whispered. "This is like some friggin movie; it's just unbelievable."

Matching her, I whispered, "Yeah Ramone, we must refocus on why we are here. But for now, let's enjoy what we have tonight. Are you OK with that?"

She smiled. "Oh, hell yeah, I feel like I'm skipping school or something, but as long as we are back on track tomorrow, that's cool with me." She smiled again.

The General Manager bowed deeply. "I will leave you now; please ask your Butler for anything. If you want to speak to me, please do not hesitate, as you say, 24/7." With a slight bow, he left us to our luxury suite.

CHAPTER 7

Our Butler finished serving a sumptuous breakfast, and we enjoyed it even more, knowing this fantasy was about to come to an end. The reality of not only returning to our ordinary lives but back to the dangers of our mission was about to recommence hit both of us. All we knew for sure was we were moving on today. We needed to start chasing our leads. However, we weren't convinced about where this would take us regarding the outcome. We could keep travelling the world and identifying smugglers and their systems, contacts, and routes, providing high-value Intel. However, that wasn't our whole mission. Sure, that was important, but our real goal had a loudly implied urgency. Every day, this thriving industry of stealing artefacts and smuggling them to Western markets continued to mean more money to fund terrorist activities. Our mission was to discover the head of this monster and cut it off. I prayed that this beast was not a Hydra only to survive and some new leader and start up again somewhere else.

Being spoilt at the Shangri La Hotel took us too far from our work, both physically and mentally. So we checked out of the hotel with the General Manager waving and saluting as we hopped into a waiting limousine. Ramone and I had decided to go to the airport and establish a temporary base there; this made sense because we could leave from there once we had a target. I hoped our base would be in a bar but kept the thought to myself. My theory was honeymooners sitting in a bar would look kosher if anyone was watching us. I didn't think we were under any surveillance, but you had to be consistently vigilant. We planned to hole up and work through the Intel I had collected in Cairo, especially the USBs and the fat man's phone. The death of the Papyrus Factory Manager cum antiquities smuggler was so recent I was hoping his contacts were still current, as it would take time for rumours of his demise to spread along his smuggling channels. The Limo dropped us off, and we made our way to the nearest coffee shop, Ramone's choice, not mine.

Located within the airport, we sat where we could watch the Lounge's entrance and be sure no one was looking over our shoulders reading our Intel material. As it was all in Arabic, I couldn't help at all, so Ramone systematically worked her way through it all. I could at least think about what she was looking at as she read aloud. There was a ton of interesting information on the USBs, lots of cargo manifests, destinations, and freight forwarding agents. This Intel would probably be precious in the clean-up phase of this operation. It would result in hundreds of operatives being arrested and their cells closed down. Then we got to Ali Ben Adham's cell, the fat man's phone. Ramone worked through the contacts, calls, apps, emails, and internet searches.

Something was happening in the back of my consciousness. It is like some phone ringing miles away in a dream, the type you can hear but never answer. Draining the last of my coffee, I asked.

"Ramone, sorry, but can you work through the calls again? This time, we are not looking for the name so much as the call itself."

I had the beginnings of a theory, but I needed enough proof for even me to buy in on it. Slowly, Ramone ploughed her way through, and there it was, a ship-to-shore number or, more precisely, a shore-to-ship call and several of them. I tried to hide my growing excitement. "OK, this may be nothing, but can you run a check on that number and tell me what ship it belongs to?"

Ramone could sense the change in me. "Yeah, sure, but what are you thinking?"

Smiling, I replied. "All this data analysis and Intel work isn't my usual role. Until I'm sure I'd rather sit on it. Ramone, for now, please just check it. If it is who I think it will be, I will tell you the rest of my theory, promise."

As she did her magic, I pondered the entire mission. Depending on what Ramone might dig up with that number, things may be about to change. Now, I knew from my briefing papers that the U.S. Feds had a first-class team. Based in New York, they had seized several shipments of stolen Egyptian treasures bound for the world-famous antique shops and auction houses in that great city. I hadn't let on that I understood this was what Ali Ben Adham at the Papyrus Factory was crying about, that it was his shipment they had grabbed. But sadly, I knew the seizure would be like a big drug bust you see on the T.V. news. Score 1 or 2 goals to New York's finest and probably 21 to the smugglers of the drugs or, in this case, antiquities that got through. In my briefing papers, I had read there was a Top-Secret warehouse somewhere in New York. Here, recently seized artefacts were stored along with millions of dollars worth of other confiscated treasures from past millenniums. These artefacts were not exclusively Egyptian; they included giant Buddhas from Burma, statues and stone carvings from Inca ruins and even Roman spears and shields from France.

I was starting to feel more and more that I was chasing the wind by following down these leads and contacts. Sure, I had gathered some valuable Intel, but what long-term impact would it make on this illegal antiquity trade? I well and truly understand the importance of historical artefacts to a nation's culture and history. But for this boy from the bush, today was more important. The fact this industry was funding ISIS operations all over the world was all that mattered. Ramone got on her secure Sat phone and contacted Langley. After identifying herself using an encrypted password for that day, she was connected to the section able to access all communication databases worldwide. She gave them the info and requested the details on that ship-to-shore number.

Turning to me, she said, "They're gonna get back to me ASAP."

Unsure how long this might take, I suggested. "We should keep looking through those APPs and searches again? Same deal, we are looking for anything related to a ship or ships."

As she did, I wrote down the ones with the most potential. I was way out of my knowledge zone, so I asked.

"Is there any way to tell when these APPs were added and the searches carried out?"

Smiling, she responded. "Yeah, sure, mystery man, when will you tell me what's going on?" Her phone chimed. She picked it up after two rings and listened.

"Thanks, Pete, I owe you one. Thanks for your help; same to you, buddy." Now she had some Intel of her own. She returned to her question about me sharing my thoughts. "OK, lover, I'll show you mine if you show me yours."

"Ramone, you have to drag sex into everything." I said, smiling at her childish but funny joke.

She giggled. "OK, enough, here it is; that ship number was a cruise boat, the Southern Star."

I couldn't help but jump up and hug her.

I exclaimed. "That's got to be; it has to be."

Ramone looked puzzled. "It's gotta be what?"

Sliding forward in my chair, I said. "OK, let's put all this info into a time sequence. If we do, it might start to make more sense."

Firstly, U.S. Feds seized several shipments of artefacts from cargo ships, especially in New York, in the last six months or so.

Secondly, that big shipment we were both briefed about must have hurt fat boy Ali Ben Adham's enterprise, all his gang, and the whole system, I'm guessing it was that gear he was still crying about it when we had our little chat two days ago."

Reaching for my coffee to steady my excitement, I asked Ramone. "What day did he search for cruise ships?"

Ramone looked up from her notes. "18th June this year."

"**Bingo**, allowing for the international date line, yep, the very same day as that big seizure Ali Ben Adham searches for cruise companies. And I tell you what, wifey, I don't think he was planning a holiday. He was thinking about a new conduit to move his products. One that would not attract scrutiny from the US authorities."

Ramone had it now; excitement filled her voice. "Then he loads the Southern Cruiseline APP on his phone; every ship, departure date, port, and destination."

Ramone's eyes widened. "I see what you mean; he might have been thinking about using the cruise ships to transport his contraband, figuring the Feds would never think of doing more than a cursory search of such vessels."

Standing up, I lent over the café table. "Yeah, but it is interesting that the first of those shore-to-ship calls started within a few days. He contacted someone on board the Southern Star several times. I think it's already happening. I don't know how he got set up so fast, but I think he has already mobilised the new supply chain. Perhaps he had a friend or a criminal contact who knew someone on that cruise. Ramone, did your friend at Langley tell you who the call went to onboard the Southern Star?"

She shook her head. "No, I asked straight away, but the call went to the cruise ship's switchboard, and that's all he could tell. They would have transferred the call to a stateroom from there."

Thinking about all this, I realised that the pieces definitely fit together. Because in all the places I had captured new Intel and damaged the infrastructure of the smuggling organisations, there were always tourists and cruise ships present. I had learned a long time ago not to believe in coincidences. This evidence, as thin as it was in some ways when combined with the phone contacts and APPs, helped me decide our new direction.

It wasn't that common for me to get so excited, but I couldn't help myself.

"Hey Ramone, it's a bit of a long shot, but I bet there are a small group of Retirees, cruisers with money connections who may even have a nice little collection of

Antiques back home. Who knows, the ones involved may have already been paying customers of this smuggling gang or the antique dealers involved. They would be easily recruited and may even be paid in product adding to their private museums. It all sounds great, but I can't see any way for us to proceed without getting on that ship, the Southern Star."

She was quick and couldn't help but smile. "Are you serious? Firstly, Langley would never pay for us to go on a cruise. Secondly, I don't know much about cruises. But surely, they're booked weeks or months ahead of sailing. So even if a miracle occurred and they approved us going, there wouldn't be a room for us."

I thought about the good men who had given their lives in several different theatres of operations. I aimed to stop the next bullet or bomb paid for by this smuggling business. I hadn't been chasing all this down for some bureaucratic budgeting to stop me cold. But I knew she was right. It was going to be tough.

"Ramone, of course, you're right, but somehow we must. If we had months to set this up, we could probably have signed on as crew, but now......" My voice betrayed my frustration. Ramone, can you please check when that ships due in Dubai?

"A mile ahead of you, partner, I just checked. The Southern Star is in Dubai right now. We've got less than forty-eight hours before it sails off into the sunset. With or without us."

What was impossible just got harder with such a small window. Frustration and anger boiled over, and I spat. "It's got to happen; we have to get on that boat or ship or whatever the fuck it's called."

Ramone had presented our assessment of the Intel and our plan to her Control. She did a terrific job, but I could quickly identify the two stages of the call. They seemed over the moon about the Intel, with her responding to their praise and a few laughs. Then, the call hit a brick wall regarding the cruise.

Not being rattled, in her most professional tone, she revisited our theory and sold it again and again. I wasn't surprised at the resistance. I could imagine being stuck in Langley and being asked to approve an international cruise for a male and female agent. You had to be kidding, right? It must have sounded suspect at best, ridiculous at least. As a trained sniper waiting for the best shot, the precise moment to release that deadly projectile is my stock in trade. However, this was different; it was only a theory. As we waited, I was getting angrier by the minute. My certainty was firm, but my optimism regarding our plan ever being approved was diminishing rapidly.

Ramone sounded more desperate. "Well, Sir, would the idea gain approval if the Agency didn't have to pay for it?"

Of course, I couldn't hear the reply to such a silly question: how would we pay for a cruise or get someone else to do so?

Ramone terminated the secure call; she had to feel just as frustrated and angry as me. I realised she wasn't my enemy and she had tried her best. "Listen, Ramone; I'm sorry about before. I know it's not your fault. You know your organisation; can you think of anything we can do?"

Initially, she shook her head in the negative. Then suddenly, Ramone spun on her heel and clapped her hands in glee. She started smiling, which annoyed the hell out of me.

I demanded. "What's so fucking funny?"

Ignoring my angry tone and still smiling annoyingly, she asked. "Who owes you big time and is one of the most powerful men in this country?"

I was smiling now. "Of course, Crown Prince Abdul Al Sattar, the heir to the throne of the UAE. If anyone can get us on that cruise, he could. I used the card he had given me and phoned him immediately. We had succeeded in maintaining our cover story while we were with the Prince. Part of me hated misleading him, but I acted the role of a new bridegroom doing something special for his bride.

"Prince Sattar, I know I said I didn't want any reward for what I did, but I have had an idea. I realise that it is terribly short notice. Would it be possible to get us on the Southern Star before she sails two days from now? It would mean so much to Laura. Your Highness, in Australia, we have a saying; 'Happy wife, happy life.' Your Majesty, if it is possible, it would be much appreciated".

The Prince responded. "I am a little surprised, but I must confess I felt unhappy that I could not reward your bravery properly. So, this opportunity brings me some amount of joy. I am unsure how cruises work, so I will pass you on to my travel secretary, who will assist you. If it all works out, please enjoy yourselves, and I will cover every expense. And Rob, all going well; I am delighted to be able to give you this small gift."

I was incredibly grateful. "Thank you, Your Highness, for your generosity; please be assured that if you can't secure our passage, I am certain no one could have." Transferring my call to his secretary, she took some details and promised to get back to me in the next hour. Forty-five minutes later, my phone chirped. "Mr Johnson, this is Sharon Ross, Prince Sattar's administrative secretary; good news, Sir."

As arranged, an anonymous but immaculate white mini-bus arrived precisely two hours later. We were waiting outside the airport as we had been instructed. The driver loaded our bags as we got into the back of the van, settling into its luxurious interior. The transfer took nearly an hour, but we enjoyed the air-conditioning, drinks, and snacks as we flew along the smooth roads towards Port Rashid Terminal Dubai. Once we got to the dock, you could tell we were being treated as VIPs. This allowed us to breeze through all the security and administrative processes that took hours for most passengers.

Even so, I was very impressed with the level of security to board, with two visual checks of our I.D., boarding cards and x-rating of everything we were carrying. It raised doubts regarding my theory that the antiquities were transported on this cruise liner, considering these security processes. The Steward showed us to our stateroom, which was a large balcony suite. We freshened up and then went and grabbed some dinner. Neither of us had been on a cruise before and found the choices of what and where to eat initially pleasantly overbearing.

I was surprised by how quickly Ramone relaxed and got into tourist mode. It was impressive to see her adapt to her cover so fast. Yeah, right. That was until she opened her mouth, looking like a starry-eyed schoolgirl.

"This will be amazing, Rob (at least she was using my covert name)." "I still can't believe this is happening."

There was an irony in what she was saying because it was as true for us agents on a mission as it would have been for us as supposed honeymooners.

Smiling, I said. "The last thing we should do is add to Langley's fear about this 'holiday', so please stay focused. We have to identify whoever is smuggling artefacts on this ship. I'm still not 100% convinced that's the case, but it was a pretty strong chain, so here we are. But we must switch on and work hard on the mission, OK?"

Ramone knew I had reprimanded her; to her credit, she whispered back without any sign of anger. "Yeah, sure, I'm sorry. I am just a bit overwhelmed by all these incredible things happening to us."

She was tough, smart and had been in the CIA for eleven years or so. I could understand and made a note to cut her some slack. After all, we were now on the Southern Star, one of the best cruise ships in the world. I thought to myself: *it's interesting; I was trained not to allow hardship of any kind, whether it was cold torrential rain, freezing snowfalls, man eating mosquito or just sharp rocks under my elbows to distract me from my mission. Here, we were in the absolute lap of luxury, and I faced the same level of distraction.* My focus was what was required, but what was our next step? We were onboard, but how would we find our smuggler amongst over 2,200 cruise passengers and 1,000 plus crew?

Leaving the port was a spectacle of engineering, beauty and immense power as the massive ship moved away from the pier with three sounds of its fog horn. We stood on our balcony and enjoyed the view, sharing the thought with every other passenger. This was the beginning of an incredible adventure.

Of course, for us, the adventure could turn deadly. I could already feel the adrenaline start to pump through my system. Once the cruise ship cleared Dubai Maritime City, a vast man-made peninsular near Port Rashid Ramone, and I headed for one of the numerous bars to do some planning. Fewer people were on the starboard deck, so we took our drinks out there. The sea breeze would carry away our words before any prying or innocent ears could catch our conversation.

With this luxurious environment with a surprise around every corner I knew I struggled to concentrate on why we were here, and I figured Ramone was, too. "How ya doin with all this, Ramone?"

She responded. "It's still like a friggin dream, but I know we have to stay on mission. I'll be fine once we start to work."

Speaking as much to myself as Ramone I was trying to keep both of us on track. "Yeah, I know how you feel, and I agree I'll be the same. But just being here is a great start. Let's talk this through;

it's like looking for a needle in several hay stacks. We have around three thousand suspects. Obviously, we can't work with that figure; we need to circulate and get people talking. It may be the simplest innocent comment someone makes over dinner that tips us off." Little did I know how prophetic my words would prove to be.

We both jumped, spilling our drinks as a giant seagull-looking bird landed on the railing in front of us. We were still close enough to land for this to be common. Laughing at our edginess, we sat back down on our colourful deckchairs and took a long pull of our respective drinks.

Thinking out loud, I whispered. "Ramone, the way I see it, we could be up against a gang, but I don't think our fat friend in Cairo had time to establish some big crew on board. I bet it's more likely one or two staff who were already here and had some previous relationship with him. We should have thought of that. Any crew from Egypt might be a good bet."

Ramone responded. "Yeah, I agree; we need to check that out first. When you look at the crew, the majority are from the Philippines. Not a country usually connected to anything Middle East or associated with antiques. Probably staff accommodation is shared and small, no good for smuggling anything big, right? Plus, would these Arab or Egyptian guys trust them not being either Arab or American,? The Arab connection on one end and the American on the destination end."

Pleased with her assessment, I agreed. "Yeah, that probably makes sense. OK, maybe more senior crew, Officers, Hotel Managers, people with a bigger cabin and more authority and freedom?"

I was glad to see Ramone was living up to her promise; she was focused and even excited by our discussion. It was good for both of us to be working again.

I took the lead. "OK, we are both new to cruises, and I am positive I don't know much about life on board for either passengers or crew. We need to talk to fellow passengers about cruising. And crew when they bring us a drink or food about the onboard culture. Who does what, why and when? We are first-timers who would naturally be curious. So real low key and try to vary who we ask the questions."

Ramone caught on. "Yeah, true, we don't have to act about being new, we are, but there is no way of knowing who we will meet. You're right about that."

"The little bit of the logistics we saw as we boarded the dock was buzzing; an Officer supervised loading pallets of food and booze. It seemed locked tight. We also noted that the crew on board went through the same security as the passengers. I wondered: *was there a gap in the system that the smuggler or smugglers had discovered? Or was there a crew member being paid to look the other way?*

Ramone joined in as I took another sip of my drink. "Yeah, well, it's not hard to hide a few keys of Cocaine or something in amongst the tomatoes, or in our case, a box of little figures or ancient jewellery.

I interrupted. "But the smugglers still have to load and hide the big items, get the coffins, and mummies and statues on here somehow. If our best guess is correct."

She responded. "OK, are we getting anywhere? Or are we just getting discouraged?" We went on like this for over an hour; a waiter brought us new drinks twice as we mulled over all these issues. Ramone and I realised that physically searching the entire ship would be virtually impossible due to roving security, cameras, and locked doors. We were done in and hungry. Neither of us felt like changing for dinner, even though the dress requirements were only smart casual. So, we headed for the buffet that was out of this world. As per the plan, we made casual conversation with the crew members when they brought us water or took our plates. We sat beside a couple from the USA. Ramone did most of the talking, explaining that we were on our honeymoon and hadn't cruised before. They were super friendly and more than willing to give us advice.

Wiping butter from his ample chin, our new friend continued. "Well, this is our twenty-fourth cruise; we mainly go Norwegian, but Princess is great, too. Look for the most ports because sea days equals shopping on board days."

"Jim, you stop boring these young folks; they don't want to hear you talk all night."

Jim's wife Margaret was a lovely, friendly woman of about sixty-five, well-kept with short blond hair. I was surprised she could raise her food to her mouth due to the large amount of gold on her hands and wrists.

"We love cruises, unpack once, everything within a short walk, incredible food, and I love the shopping."

She said with a big smile, grabbing an emerald necklace hanging on a gold chain around her neck; she held it towards us. "I got this today; I just love it."

Ramone saved me. "Why, it's beautiful, Margaret."

Jim whispered to me. "See what I mean? The more time on the ship, the more it'll cost ya."

Putting my glass down, I replied. "Jim, I had no idea people did as many cruises as you two."

"Oh buddy, there are some who cruise two-fifty, three hundred plus days a year. Hell, some live on board full time three sixty-five days a year."

We bid our dinner companions goodnight. They were off to the dancing show, and with a wink, I said we were heading back to our cabin. Hand in hand, we walked back in silence. Neither of us believed that our cover was highly vulnerable or that any form of surveillance was in place, but we were still careful.

We had left the balcony door open, and the wind was howling into our room. It took a considerable amount of force to open the cabin door inward. I walked around the bed and slid the glass door to the balcony shut. Ramone poured us a drink and sat on the bed while I sat on the Lounge. OK, give or take the shopping talk, that was interesting. I am starting to realise how little I understood about cruises. Now, if some people cruise nearly all year round and some even live on board, that could make them strong contenders for what we are looking for. What do you reckon, Ramone?"

Taking a sip of her drink, I said. "I nearly fell off my chair when Jim said that. I'm thinking the same thing as you. It lines up with some of the issues we identified. Like, uh, if I was on board that much, I would know all the crew, and they would know who I was. Just think I could walk around unchallenged and, with a few exceptions, probably access places you and I couldn't even find."

Nodding, I interrupted. "Yeah, and you would get to know the crew well. If you were going to recruit some help, form a little 'gang', you would know who to talk to, who was safe. Who was up for a bribe or some extra off-the-books work? It all makes sense now. All we have to do is work out how to identify these 'professional' cruise passengers."

CHAPTER 8

As I was thinking about this, Ramone picked up the Star-News, a glossy little paper informing each passenger of the ship's features and the next day's itinerary. Opening the two-page newsletter, a small gold envelope fell onto the bed. Ramone tore the envelope open, and she smiled.

"We have been invited to attend drinks and hors-d'oeuvres with the Captain and frequent cruisers at 1400 Hours tomorrow." Emphasising Frequent Cruisers. "Surely luck favours the well-prepared, hey?"

I couldn't believe my ears; we had probably been invited as first-timers to inspire us to become addicted cruise passengers. Of course, the other alternative may have been because someone knew The Crown Prince was paying our bill. Either way, this was an excellent opportunity to get a look at the target group we had only recently identified. Yawning, I stretched. "I don't know about you, my lovely wife, but I'm beat. Let's hit the sack, for me, the lounge, depending on your preference, and revisit all this in the morning."

Ramone laughed. "I bag the bed, big fella. Goodnight, sweet Prince." More laughter. We slept incredibly well thanks to the magnificent ship's design; even though there was a stiff breeze and rolling sea, we slept peacefully with just a gentle rocking. We awoke early, ordered cabin-service coffee and pastries and enjoyed them on our balcony. Later, I went to the gym and, after a good hour of punishment, decided a massage would be just what I needed. Entering the Spa, a pretty receptionist in a pseudo-nurse's uniform that was strategically unbuttoned enough to entice but still look classy and professional welcomed me.

Fortunately, I was able to get a massage immediately, so I entered a pleasantly scented room with the mood lighting turned right down. I was instantly calm and relaxed.

As instructed by our budding receptionist, I undressed, wrapping a small white fluffy towel around my nether region. I lay on the massage table, my face protruding through the hole especially built for this purpose, giving me a fantastic view of the floor. I heard the door open, and like most men, I fantasised about a buxom, scantily-clad maiden coming to rub baby oil all over me.

"Good morning, Sir, my name is Sal. Do you like a hard or soft massage?"

With my fantasy rapidly exiting my mind, the question worried me greatly. The masseur's voice was baritone, and my dreams shattered. "I hope you are talking about a massage, Sal?

"Very funny, Sir."

I chose the hard massage and braced myself. After my fantasy disappointment, I decided to make the best of it and enjoy myself while asking a few questions. "So Sal, where you from?"

Squirting some oil on his hands, he responded. "Staten Island, New York, Sir."

"Please call me Rob; Aussies aren't big on Sirs and Misters. So, you been doing massages long?"

Sal answered. "About four years ago, I qualified, worked for a while in N.Y., then scored this gig about two years ago."

Figuring most people like it when others show interest in them, I asked. "Is it good? I suppose the novelty of being on a ship wears off pretty quickly."

He worked on my hams. "Yeah, but I do get to see places I probably wouldn't have. Although the money is not great, I have no expenses, and at least I know I will get paid every week. I have a bit of a plan; two more years, and I'll decide where I want to be and have saved a few bucks for fun."

The conversation ceased as I relaxed, and he exerted himself, kneading my stiff muscles. He gave me one of the best massages I had ever experienced. As I left, I thought, what a nice young guy, just the right type for a job like this. Making my way to the pool deck, I found Ramone beside the spa pool under the shade of the walking deck above. She was with five other passengers with tropical-looking cocktails on the table before them. Her face lit up on seeing me approach, and she stood up, embracing me and kissing me passionately. I returned her kiss, and after more than a while, I released her and sat in the vacant chair. Ramone made the introductions, and a waiter eagerly asked me if I wanted a drink. I was never an umbrella and cherry sort of guy.

So, I ordered the usual and put my sunnies back on so I could observe without being too obvious.

The conversation was all travel and cruises, not adding anything new to our Intel. Between the massage and now some alcohol, I switched off for a little while. I gently took Ramone's hand in mine and said. "Baby, we have that function this afternoon. How about we have lunch and some sack time before we go?" This comment brought the expected guffaws and remarks regarding honeymooners from the circle of tourists. As it turned out, we had no time for a nap by the time we enjoyed an American-style BBQ lunch. We found the theatre where the cocktail party was to be held and made our way to two seats off to one side. A waiter produced a tray with beer, champagne, or juice; we decided on champers to create the right impression.

The Cruise Director, a bubbly, attractive New Zealander, was master of ceremonies and, after a bit of a warm-up, introduced the Captain. He was a man in his mid-fifties with a well-groomed head of white hair and who, resplendent in his crisp white uniform, looked like he had just come straight from Pearl Harbour. He shared a few funny stories from his forty-something years at sea. The loyalty program was explained to everyone; it equated with a point per night on a Southern Star cruise.

As you gathered points, you moved through different levels, Bronze through Gold and Silver, right up to Platinum for those having achieved 76 nights or more. Benefits came with the various achieved levels; well, yeah, that was all very interesting. I was still hoping for some personal identification of the long-term cruisers. Thankfully, I wasn't disappointed. After a lot of compliments and back-slapping lubricated by some enjoyable cocktails and finger food, it all came together.

The Captain, assisted by the Cruise Director, announced an Honour acknowledgement in his soft Norwegian accent he announced. "Ladies and gentlemen, please stand when my lovely Director calls your name."

With all the pizzazz of a game show hostess, the pretty blonde Cruise Director studied her iPad and began to call the honour roll, followed by the number of cruise days. "Mr. and Mrs. Watts 8,496 days."

And so, it went on. The Watts were clear leaders, but over twenty couples stood smiling and waving, all with thousands of cruise days to their credit. I had to get a copy of that list so we could slowly work our way through it. These had to be our Targets: conservative image, constant cruisers, and an invisible part of the furniture to the crew. I had asked Ramone to try to take photos with her phone as best she could without looking too obvious. Now, all we had to do was 'borrow' the MC's IPad. Then, we needed to meet all these couples, potentially the smugglers we were tracking. The cocktail party wound down, and we approached the Cruise Director. We gushed our thanks to her for the exclusive social invitation. I felt a bit bad stealing her device, but it was necessary. As Ramone hugged her and kissed both cheeks, I casually lifted her iPad, and we left the theatre. We returned to our room to devise a strategy using the names on the iPad, which I was grateful wasn't locked. We needed to vet the members of this elite group. It was a little hard to believe these elderly cruisers, some of whom cruised three hundred and fifty or more days every year, were our smugglers.

By now, it was happy hour at all the bars on board, so at great personal sacrifice, I volunteered to have a drink while looking for the frequent cruisers. If you were a 'professional cruiser', you would know all the lurks and perks on board. Happy hour at every bar was a winner. They would come out of their cabins and suites like hibernating grizzlies to get a gut full of half-price booze of their choice, returning home to be ready for dinner. At least that was my theory; now I had to find the right bar, no loud sports bar or crowds of 'unwashed travellers' on their first cruise for this group. I figured the Spinnaker Lounge was a winner with its extensive wine cellar and subdued ambience. I was starting to sound like a friggin travel writer, but, I was out of my depth, and I knew it. I had enjoyed a few drinks there the day before, so I headed down two decks and entered through the swinging glass doors.

Serving drinks was a dark-eyed Filipino Bar Attendant who had spent some time in Australia and liked talking. I had never thought I was God's gift to women, and I had never had to flirt or use my charm for work. Whatever it took, I was willing to give it a go. My missions in my Army days and now with the National Security Centre usually started with me in muddy camouflage gear or ended up that way. The only female company I experienced was usually being bitten by every known insect on the planet. This spy stuff was a whole new world. Looking at her left breast to read her name tag was the start I needed, and she didn't miss it either.

"Hi....... *Maria*, I am so glad you are working this afternoon. How have you been?" A dazzling smile said she was fine, and I had to agree.

"I am doing great, Sir, thank you for asking. Can I get you the usual?" The Spanish sort of American accent of the Philippines was as alluring as she was.

"Sure, a double on the rocks, thanks." Happy hour meant you paid for one drink and got two, which was a valid reason to talk to Maria. I had to order and drink fast, a job I adapted to quickly.

"Maria, I know all the male passengers probably try this, but when do you get off? I would love to buy you a drink and talk about Australia some more?" I couldn't believe her smile could get any whiter or broader or her eyes any darker, but in concert, they did.

She responded. "Oh, I would love to, but the crew is not allowed to frat...., I don't know the word, but we just can't date passengers; I am truly sorry."

"I think the word you were looking for was fraternising with passengers. You sure there is nowhere we can have a quiet drink, no strings, no expectations?". I could see her resolve begin to weaken, and I felt guilty, as the last thing I wanted was to hurt this girl or get her fired. But a bartender is a goldmine of info.

She smiled again as she wiped the bar in front of me. "Yeah, I s'pose there is one way. We couldn't have a drink, but we could get to know each other on the walking track, and who doesn't talk to the person alongside them there?"

I smiled as well and asked. "Well, it's not exactly what I was thinking, but it's a great start. What time can you make it?"

In a soft Filipino accent, she whispered. "The boss is starting to watch us; we have been talking for a long time. I will meet you on the track near the spa pool at 1730 Hours; gotta go."

When Maria left me at the bar, I'd had four double J.D.s lined up because the happy hour was over. I had tried to monopolise Maria as much as I could get away without her getting into trouble. I felt good from the drinks I'd already had but was still switched on to what was needed. Looking at my glass swirling the ice around, I wondered what pretty Maria could tell me. I downed my drinks and returned to my cabin. Ramone took one look at me and raised her eyebrow. "I can see you have been working very hard. My poor dear. You look all worn out." Sarcasm was dripping from her every word.

I frowned. "Well, now I feel like we *are* married. Yes, it was a hardship, but I did my best. I have a date; I mean an appointment with one of the crew at 1730 hours to find out some more."

"What have you found out so far?" Ramone enquired.

I felt a little defensive under her questioning. "Ahhhh, not much yet, but the door is open; I am sure I will find out some good Intel when I speak to her."

Ramone didn't miss much. "**Her**, so you have had what looks like more than a few drinks. Then you are meeting a female crew member who so far you haven't asked a single question. That sounds so worthwhile". The sarcasm was back.

"Ramone, you must have got a Masters in Sarcasm at University to be this good."

Smiling now, I said. "You're jealous, aren't you? If I was meeting a fat male waiter, it might be profitable. But, because I am meeting a beautiful Filipino girl, it all changes to no value."

"Oh, honestly, men, your only direction is where your dick is pointing. A beautiful girl, seriously?"

"Enough, enough, my good wife. I have to get into my running gear."

Smiling now, "Another couple of double Jacks, and you won't even be able to walk you turkey."

"You're such a sweet talker, honey-bun. You may be right, but we will just be walking, not drinking. OK?"

I grabbed my clothes and slipped into the funny little bathroom, happy to escape the flood of sarcasm; whoo!

I got to the walking/running track just in time and saw Maria was there already. She was smart enough not to look like she was waiting for someone and was standing at a small outdoor table, doing up her shoes.

I wondered whether I was enjoying myself or continuing to play the part of an interested male passenger. But bending over to do her laces, I couldn't help but notice the view from the rear was enough to raise my heart rate without further exercise. Yeah, I know, I was fooling myself. Maybe the J.D.s were having some effect. I walked past nonchalantly, and within five steps, Maria had caught up with me and was keeping pace. We walked briskly, finding this was an excellent way to maintain privacy as most other older walkers were strolling along. By the time we had done ten laps of the ship, we were both shiny with sweat, and our conversation was a little puffed.

After enough of general talking about the Philippines and Australia, I gently steered us to the main topic. Maria was extremely helpful as she knew all the high flyers very well, this being her eighth cruise with them. I discovered she was very easy to talk to and willing to describe each couple as we worked through the near-resident passengers. I kept showing a relaxed interest in them and my sincere amazement they had cruised so often. We finished our walk, and I felt like a teenage boy, unsure whether to shake hands, kiss or just say goodbye and walk away. Unlike that adolescent boy, I had gotten all I wanted from this lovely person. I felt a bit fake using her this way. As great-looking as Maria was, it wouldn't go any further. I couldn't trade Chris back in Australia for a shipboard romance. Plus, I was still on a mission. It turned out I was kidding myself anyway. If she was interested that way, she didn't show it. "I have really enjoyed our walk and talk. See you at Happy Hour, hey?" With that, she was gone. Maria had talked about two couples that seemed to match my expectations as smugglers. As I strolled back to my cabin, I digested the information, hoping I was identifying the target. I mustn't fall into the trap of shooting an arrow into the wall and then painting the bullseye around it.

CHAPTER 9

Ramone had calmed a little and could see I had returned with some Intel. We cross-referenced the couple's names in the Cruise Director's iPad to find out where the two couple's cabins were. We discussed how to proceed from here; starting with surveilling them, including searching their rooms. But first, we would also follow each pair and orchestrate our eventual meeting with them. We knew most elite passengers were on a particular floor, so we hung around the lifts until we confirmed our targets. Although security on the Star was impressive, it wasn't that difficult to wait for a cleaner to open the cabin. They would jam the door open so they could restock the room. This would enable us to sneak in when the cleaner went to their trolley for something, close the door and put the Do Not Disturb sign out. The crew member would hopefully assume the passenger had returned to the cabin for some reason and would move on. Once we finished, we would leave the door open and the sign removed, allowing the cleaner to return and freshen up the cabin. This ploy was taught in every Intelligence Service School because it was simple and worked. It removed the chance of opening the door and finding the occupants still in their cabins.

Ramone and I executed this strategy on both couple's cabins and found absolutely nothing to raise our suspicions or confirm their involvement. We noted that each couple had left their dining card information on the bedside table. This information lets us know their table number and the seating time each dined. Getting someone moved so we could eat with the individual couples would be nearly impossible due to their established routine of near-constant cruising. Although we had not played our VIP card since coming on board, I hoped that would enable us to pull some strings. It worked for one couple, the Fosters; we would join them this evening. However, the Somersets would be challenging; it was entirely out of the question as they always dined alone.

In preparation, Ramone and I dressed more formally and discussed our approach when we met this first couple. The Fosters liked to visit all the different restaurants on board, but tonight was Italian night, so we headed for La Cucina. When we arrived at the entrance to the Restaurant, a beautifully suited Maître-de welcomed us. If he was shocked at our presence and joining the Fosters and another couple, he didn't show it. Our target dinner companions, on the other hand, showed ample confusion on their faces as we walked to their table. Ramone and I had decided we would play dumb regarding why we had ended up sitting with this group.

Smiling warmly, I greeted the two couples. "Good evening, everyone; we are so pleased to join you. We don't understand how it has happened, but please allow us to join you."

John Foster wasn't very tall but had an air of authority and confidence he had probably earned the hard way. Although he appeared in his sixties, his body talked of an athletic past, and his handshake was dry and firm. Narelle was perhaps a little younger than her husband, with hair beautifully styled but kept in her natural grey colour.

Like her recently retired stockbroker husband, she also spoke with confidence comfortable in herself. From her muscle tone, she exercised regularly and was trim and tanned, wearing just enough jewellery. They explained they had always cruised several times a year but were now looking forward to being able to do the longer forty and sixty-day cruises.

The other couple from Canada were of no interest to us from a mission point of view and enjoyed just listening to the Fosters. Their silence for most of the evening was beneficial. By the time dessert arrived, I was ninety per cent sure the couple was not our smugglers. We may have been on a luxury cruise liner in a fantastic restaurant instead of a dirty street or some smelly interrogation room. But it was like most investigative work; elimination always took most of your time. Dinner finished, and we all left for our respective cabins. As Ramone and I walked along the thickly carpeted hallway, I couldn't help but think I would like some place for a quiet drink and think. Ramone opted to return to the cabin, so I headed off to the bar near the pools. It wasn't air-conditioned, but this time of night, it should be peaceful.

To my surprise, Maria was on duty. "Hey Maria, you work all day and all night?" Smiling, she replied. "The usual guy pulled a 'sicky'. Hopefully, he will feel better tomorrow night because it makes it a long day. Anyway, don't worry about it, the usual?"

"I responded. "Great, thanks. Say, I hope I didn't bore you with all my questions. I still can't believe people cruise so much."

She looked around to ensure no one would hear her drop her usual formality. "Not at all, Rob. I really enjoyed our time together. I was telling my friend from the Spa all about our talk. Speak of the devil." She waved to someone behind me. But, when I turned around from the bar, whoever it was had moved out of sight.

With a giggle, she continued. "Anyway, here's your drink, Sir. Can I please have your cabin card to charge it for you?"

Noticing a couple had sat at the bar explained the formality. I handed over the card, "Thank you, I hope you have a great night."

She rang the drink up on the register and handed me the slip; I had given her an extremely generous tip as a thank you. I had two more and worked through the information we had gathered so far. I was starting to get tired and decided to call it a night. Throwing down the last of my drink. "Awesome Maria, hopefully, I'll see you tomorrow at Happy Hour, goodnight." As I walked away, I had a sinking feeling in my gut that I would have both understood and acted upon if I had been in a sandbox somewhere or even in the Australian bush. But I couldn't understand it here in a floating paradise.

The next morning, Ramone followed the other couple, the Somersets, from breakfast and all through the day. She wondered if it was all a waste of time when they headed towards the second smaller theatre. Ramone didn't think there was a show on but kept tracking them at a safe distance until they rounded the corner. An A frame announced Star Bingo, and the time meant it was about to start. She now knew how to meet them. Ramone kept going, figuring many passengers would innocently wander around and get lost. If the Somersets saw her following them, claiming to be lost would allow Ramone to recover quickly. Asking Mrs Somerset where she was going would appear innocent and initiate contact. There was a small desk at the entrance to the theatre where two of the dancers from the nightly show were selling Bingo cards.

Ramone joined the queue alongside the Somersets and could tell from the interaction with the dancers they were Bingo regulars. She decided she would go it alone, quickly figuring there would be no talking once the calling of the numbers started.

"Hi, this is my first go at Bingo; lookin' forward to it, though."

"Ah, another American, don't you worry honey, it's easy as fallin' off a log." Mrs Somerset said, smiling broadly. Ramone had planned to strike up a conversation with the target couple and then sit next to them so that she could talk to them before and after the Bingo games. All good so far. She knew nothing about Bingo but was ready to wing it. Ramone sat beside the overweight American woman who was sipping on a large Mint Tulip and was organising her Bingo cards and dopper pens. The conversation flowed smoothly with the usual questions; 'Where are you from?' and 'Which college did you go to?' whenever USA citizens meet in foreign places. Ramone had so many covers for America she just slipped into the one she deemed most attractive to the Somersets, and it seemed to work. They were from

Alabama, which, of course, Ramone picked from their accents when she had first eavesdropped on them outside.

Jed and Doris Somerset had made their money selling farm machinery first and then the stock market. Doris was wearing more gold and diamonds than a small jeweller may stock, but she was warm and friendly. And although Doris was worth a fortune, the older cruiser was instantly likeable and down-to-earth. Ramone quickly established a good rapport and, with a skill developed during years of undercover operations, extracted as much information as she could mine before Doris held up a gold-covered pudgy hand.

"Sweetheart, we gotta stop now; Bingo is starting; you concentrate and good luck."

And that was it for the next thirty-seven minutes. She knew she had to play to maintain her cover and be there to talk some more at the end. Ramone did it well, winning $150 and Doris $75, Jed nothing, so he just grouched and carried on. The CIA Agent was trying to remember if he had said a single word other than moans and groans.

When it finished, smiling Doris turned to Ramone. "Well, sweetheart, you sure caught on quick."

Jed seemed to awaken from his silence. "That caller drives me crazy; he could talk the horns off a goat, as we say back home."

Doris, hoping the caller hadn't heard her grumpy husband admonished him. "Oh, Jed, that young fella is OK. He's a good dancer, too; you don't like him because he's a homo."

Jed admitted. "That's not true, oh yeah, it probably is true. I s'pose I should be grateful he ain't no rag head, hey Dor?".

Doris was looking around, hoping no one could hear them. "Please, Jed; there are so many foreigners on the crew you'll get us into trouble."

The older man was unrelenting. "I don't give a rat's ass, and you gotta know that."

The embarrassed wife attempted to end the scene with a nervous laugh. "OK, OK, sweetie, let's all have a drink before he gets us thrown off the ship, hey honey?"

Ramone liked these two real people; what you saw was exactly what you got. She kept it going. "That would be great, Doris, but let me buy the drinks with my winnings. What would you like, Jed? I figure Doris is up for a Mint Tulip, and I will join her?"

Doris must have felt the need for something stronger. "Dear, I know it sounds a little unladylike, but I would rather have an Alabama Slammer if that's OK with you?"

Ramone smiled at the older woman's honesty. "OK, sounds like two of them, Jed???" Shaking his head, the older man answered. "I ain't at no Tupperware Party with you two, you know. I'll have a double Southern Comfort straight up, please."

Laughing, Ramone stood up and walked to the bar, thinking, no *way, these can't be our smugglers.*

I couldn't find Ramone anywhere, so I figured another Happy Hour would do me no harm. I went to the Spinnaker Lounge again, hoping to meet some more potential Targets; maybe Maria would be there too. As I entered the Lounge, there was a small group of passengers singing someone Happy Birthday, and a lot of the bar was joining in. Approaching the bar, I was disappointed to see another Bar Attendant serving. When she came over to serve me, I couldn't help but notice she had been crying and even now appeared close to breaking down again.

With a smile, I said. "Hello there, where's Maria today? I hope she isn't sick or anything, is she?"

With that, the girl behind the bar nearly collapsed to her knees, caught herself and sobbing loudly and rushed through the service door.

The other Bar Attendant, a muscular Filipino named Angelo, whom I had met several times, came over and shook his head, looking at the closed door. I noticed he, too, looked despondent.

I asked. "What's going on, mate? Is everything OK?"

The Barman replied, but you could tell he was putting on a brave face. "I'm fine, everything is fine, thank you, Sir." Then he couldn't keep it in any longer and nearly sobbed himself. We have just heard that our friend passed away today; it is a big shock, Sir."

My stomach sank, and I immediately thought, where is Maria? "Angelo, I know you have been told to keep it quiet, but are you talking about Maria?"

A tear slipped from his right eye. "Si, I mean, yes, I know you two talked, so I will tell you the truth, Sir. I can't believe it; they are saying she killed herself."

I felt like someone had punched me in the solar plexus. I had trouble breathing and struggled to talk for a few moments. "Angelo, what do you mean?"

He softly continued. "They found Maria in her cabin; she had cut her wrists." He started to lose it again.

"Angelo, I don't want to intrude, but I agree. She seemed happy and well content with her life and loved her work on board; I cannot see her hurting herself, no way." Slowly shaking his head, he went to serve another passenger.

I walked back to my cabin, but really, I didn't remember the trip. I opened the door to find Ramone watching a Jason Bourne movie on the ship's channel. She looked up smiling, looking very happy with herself.

"Hi, I had a great day. I won $150 Bucks and spent the afternoon with couple number two, the Somersets. The money is all mine, by the way, and the Somersets, well, they are just lovely people. No good re our mission, we are back to square one, I am sorry to say."

I looked at her like I was seeing her through smoke or a cloud. "I think we are on the right track; sadly, it's cost a lovely innocent girl her life."

I explained everything about Maria, and we slowly worked through my contact with her. We attempted to identify anyone who may have overheard our conversations and came up with nothing.

Ramone asked. "OK, let's look at another group. Who knew you met or talked to Maria?"

Shaking my head, I said. "No one, really; our conversations at the bar would have looked natural enough. I would have looked like a tourist cracking onto her, but nothing serious or threatening. Well, it seems Angelo knew because he mentioned it. He only told me the truth about her death because he had seen Maria and me talking. He must be OK. Otherwise, he wouldn't have been so upset or doubted the cover-up story of her death." I said.

Ramone interrupted. "There must be someone else who knew, think."

Suddenly, I remembered the last time Maria served me a drink. "Hang on; I just remembered Maria said she had told a friend who works at the Spa about our talks and how I was interested in the frequent cruisers."

As Ramone got off the bed and grabbed a bottle of water from the mini-fridge, she stated. "Yeah, but didn't you say that was her friend."

"Yeah, the thing is whoever it was saw us together again last night."

You could tell Ramone was well-trained in evidence collection and chain logic. "So, you saw the person. Easy, we can grab her and find out the truth."

Shaking my head. "No, as Maria waved to them, I turned around to see who she was waving to, but I couldn't see anyone by the time I looked."

Nothing was conclusive, but we had made some progress. “OK, not perfect, but at least we knew she works in the Spa.

CHAPTER 10

National Security Centre
Canberra
Australia

Colonel Goodrich had been on the back foot as soon as the meeting with Brigadier Dodds had started. He could understand the Brig's concerns about Major Steve Wallace "swanning all over the globe", as the Brig put it. But Goodrich knew Steve Wallace too well to think he was enjoying a holiday. Deep down, Goodrich knew the Brig had nothing but trust and respect for Steve Wallace, gained from Steve's performance on past missions. Something else had put a burr under the Brigadier's saddle. Wallace would be on task even though the setting was highly different to the usual Asian jungle, far-flung city, or even the Australian outback. The Brig grated on and on.

"Pete, having him seconded to the C.I.A. annoys me. We all know he's one of our best men. I don't like the loss of contact or control. The C.I.A. was damn quick to ask for an Aussie agent when they needed one. But they are way slower sharing the Intel he is collecting."

Goodrich now understood the Senior Officer's concerns. "Yes, I know, Sir, it's far from ideal, but I have complete faith in Wallace. Even if it is slim, the possibility of closing down the money trail or the Hawala agents funding these terrorists makes this Op an extremely high-value target."

The Brig agreed. "I know, I am just bloody frustrated by the set-up."

Smiling, the Brig softened. "Pete, I was never very good at sharing my toys. I know you are right about Steve Wallace's abilities under fire. Well, the truth is I'm worried about him. He may well be out of his depth. His skill set and experience are not undercover investigations, especially an extended operation like this one has spun out too."

C.I.A. Headquarters

Langley Virginia U.S.A.

Assistant Director Dave Myers oversaw the operation and was less than happy with the direction it had taken. The Intel Ramone his assigned operative had sent through was certainly of high value. Even though Meyers had a team of analysts working through it all, sitting at his desk, he stared at his cold coffee and wondered where this op would end up. The Intel was rich in new Targets. There was a gold mine of new names and contacts and some old 'friends' that had been on the Agency's watch list for some time.

However, Myers' boss, the Director of Counter Terrorism, was unimpressed with the thought of his Agent being shacked up on a cruise with some strange Aussie. But, being a realist, he figured you couldn't have it both ways. As much or as little as he trusted anyone, he had faith in Myers.

The seizure of Egyptian artefacts by the Feds in New York had been the spark of an idea for this operation. More importantly, the constant rumours that a lot of this smuggling was going on not just as a criminal enterprise but to fund ISIS and other terrorist groups left no other option. An operation to shut it down had to be executed ASAP. It all made sense. It was a straightforward business: find the artefacts in the desert, dig them up, then export them and sell them as unencumbered antiquities at legitimate auction houses. By doing this, they turned the stolen history into money, which equals guns, bullets, and even missiles. He knew Ops Planning couldn't see any way to identify all the key players without infiltrating the smuggler's gangs. Hence, the current operation. But none of that meant that he had to like it.

These twenty-first-century smugglers quickly occupied well-established infrastructure and transport systems established to service anything illegal. The guys in planning thought that arresting the Australian gunrunner provided a gateway into the system. The incarcerated smuggler's criminal credentials weren't expected to facilitate a total infiltration into the upper echelon, still, they might get them a meeting or two. Credit where credit is due; this Wallace guy had done some top-class work to this point. And Assistant Director Myers was glad he had decided to assign Ramone to buddy up with him. By doing that, he had taken back control of the Op, at least now if anything went wrong, they would have each other's back. It didn't hurt to have an Agency Operative reporting directly to him. The Aussies were good guys, but he hated getting his reports via the Australian N.S.C. With Ramone there he would be well informed.

He didn't doubt that the Australian Security Centre would eventually pass through the report. He just didn't like getting it second-hand. Myers was happy with the way the op was going, even though the two agents seemed to stumble from one fight to the next; they were still making significant progress. He had led enough warriors in his day to recognise a top-quality soldier and operative. Anyone who could find his way through this maze and collect high-value Intel and, in the meantime, survive several attempts on his life was well above average. Fair enough, Wallace needed rescuing from those Bedouins. But Myers couldn't help but wonder if he would have made it out by himself if left alone. The USMC Action Report demonstrated he was one very resourceful guy, this Aussie Steve Wallace.

Southern Star Cruiseship

"Look, chill; I don't know what you are worried about. I took care of the Filipino bitch. What a waste, pity her mouth was as big as her tits."

Offended by such crude speech, the older man of the two spoke as though he just chewed on a peppercorn. "Now, now it was regrettable that had to be done. But please, don't be so uncouth, my young friend."

With a vane flick of his blonde hair, the young man smiled. He always found some way to yank the old man's chain. *He was so old-fashioned he was nearly as friggin old as the stuff he was smuggling.*

This thought brought another smile to the young man's tanned face. In turn, the old man hated this brash young American, but he had learned to bury this hatred to keep the young man on side. He was his eyes and ears and, at times, muscle operating on board without restrictions.

The older man continued, not realising the young man's thoughts were silently ridiculing him or choosing to ignore it. "I don't see what you have to smile about; we don't know what she told the Australian before you silenced her. Just as importantly, we don't know why he is so inquisitive about a certain group of passengers of which I am a member."

Remembering the bonus income the old man represented to him, he switched to serious. "Good news is our Mr. Robert Johnson is just as you said, he's Australian. That means he can't be C.I.A. or F.B.I. or anyone else. Now his hot wife is American, but let's get real, they are on their honeymoon, same again."

Harrison half filled his crystal tumbler with twenty-year-old scotch, offering the younger man a drink didn't cross his mind.

Sal noticed this, but made himself feel better by thinking; *Lucky, I don't like scotch, you selfish old prick.* Sweeping back his hair with both hands more to make him feel better than any cosmetic effect, he continued to allay the old man's fears.

"Firstly, how would anyone know we are here and busy with your boxes downstairs. Secondly, can you see any of the same alphabet agencies or Police Forces sending an Aussie and an American undercover on a cruise like this? I don't think so. My take on him is the guy just asks a lot of questions. Maybe he was short on conversation topics or just liked to know everything about his surroundings. Of course, the other reason he's talking to a Filipino bar girl is that even though he is on his honeymoon, he may have just been trying to get into Maria's pants."

Noting the old man's look of horror at this comment, the younger man put his hands up in mock surrender and continued. "Sorry, but who knows. The other good news is he is booked in with me at ten o'clock. So I'll be able to gently get him talking and see what he is all about."

The old man was far from convinced, but there weren't a lot of options available.

"OK, well, that's a break; see how you go and let me know as soon as you can get over here. If Johnson turns out to be something other than a happy honeymooner asking too many questions, we will need to get rid of him, too."

The young man's tanned forehead creased as he thought. *I don't know much about the old man's past, but I can tell he must have been a heavy hitter in his day. He as cold and ruthless, as he is friggin annoying. But hey, the extra money is good.*

The young man swept both hands over his blonde locks to clear his head a little. Sal always made sure to call him boss at least once during every meeting to stroke the ancient ego.

"Boss, when you say 'we,' you really mean 'me.' I hope there's some bonus money coming my way. I didn't really expect all this wet work."

Not expecting a reply, none was forthcoming. After checking the hallway was clear, the younger man closed the heavy cabin door and walked into the hall towards the lifts.

I found Ramone sitting in the coffee shop; in front of her was a huge iced coffee piled high with whipped cream and chocolate shavings. "Hey, you're doing it tough, Mrs. Johnson." Looking around to make sure we were alone, I went into a whisper. "You better be careful when you get back from this mission that you don't want to have to go on a diet."

Glaring at me, "Get fucked Mr. Johnson, you actually sound like my husband."

I laughed. "Well, that's a lovely way to talk to your dearly beloved. I am starting to feel like the honeymoon's over already."

Ramone nodded. "OK, truce, if you knew me and saw me with this monstrosity in front of me, you would stay well clear as this is a definite sign I must be in a foul mood."

"OK, sweetness, I didn't mean to make the mistake of waking the grumpy grizzly; what's upset you?"

Ramone couldn't help but smile, spooning a heap of cream into her mouth before talking. "I checked in on my secure sat-phone. Oh, that asshole, my boss just carried on about progress and cost. He has no fucking idea how tough this assignment is. Because we happen to be living in luxury, all of them back at Langley probably think I am screwing you silly all on an Agency paid holiday."

I started laughing. "Well, your keepers might be right about the first part. And the second perception, I just don't know. Unless that's why I am so tired in the mornings, are you helping yourself while I am asleep on the couch?"

Between the cream fix and our joking, Ramone was starting to calm down. "Very funny; I know you're trying to make me happy. Thanks, but I have other plans. If it weren't so early, I'd be on my third Margaritas by now instead of this."

Looking at my watch, "Listen honey-bun, I gotta go get a massage; you're dead right; this is one very tough gig. I'll leave you to eat or drink that milkshake. How about I meet you at the poolside B.B.Q. buffet for lunch in an hour?" As I stood, I was pleased to see Ramone smile goodbye and attack her iced coffee. Once again, speaking with a mouth full of ice cream. "I'm going to slip back and wash my hair; I'll catch you near the pool, hey?"

The young man punched in the cabin number on his desk phone and waited for the old man to answer.

"Hey, boss, the Australian just left; he sure is careful. We talked about a heap of things on board, but he eventually got around to the same questions he'd been asking Maria. I still don't know for sure, but there is something that's not right. Leave it with me, and I'll keep looking. Even his body makes me wonder; he's fit and hard, and I would have loved to ask him how he came by some of those scars."

The old man sighed. "OK, just keep your head down until we know what to do."

The old man hung up without further comment.

In a crew uniform of crisp white Bermuda shorts and a Blue Polo shirt with his shiny name tag, he had the run of the ship. Occasionally, he was called upon to visit some passengers preferring the privacy of their cabin rather than the Spa. He was virtually autonomous, give or take a weekly report to H.Q. The young man made his way to Deck 8; coming out of the lift, he turned toward the Starboard side. The ship's hallways were longer than a football field, one on each side of the enormous floating hotel. Knowing the cabin he was looking for was in the middle, he walked without reading the cabin numbers until he arrived in the three-hundred section.

Seconds later, he was standing in front of 8362, the honeymoon abode for Mr. and Mrs. Johnson. Before entering the cabin, he surreptitiously looked up and down the incredibly long hallway one last time. He was relieved to see there was no one nearby. He swiped himself in using the special staff Entry Card that he would never usually have in his possession. He smiled as he remembered stealing the card from a friendly little cleaner named... Well, he couldn't recollect her name, she was hot and happy, he knew that.

The door opened with a metallic click, and he entered the cabin. He was sure the couple would be at lunch as Mr Johnson had told him his plans to meet his wife at the B.B.Q. buffet. Still, he moved quickly, searching carefully, first the obvious, then the less; he found the Sat-phone taped under the coffee table.

OK, well, that was interesting. Did they hide it so it wasn't stolen? If this was a hotel, he could believe that. But no way on a cruise; it just didn't add up. They, or at least one of them, was trained, maybe just a cop, perhaps something more.

The phone was locked, so he would have to leave without taking it with him and having time to break into it. If he took it, they would know someone had turned over their cabin.

He was missing something; it was there; he had seen it subconsciously but couldn't identify what it was. Hang on! The room, the way the personal items are arranged, the clothes in the wardrobe. It had the feel of two people, maybe friends sharing a room, not two honeymooners living in bliss. The room hadn't been serviced; although the bed was messed up, closer inspection showed that one side hadn't been slept in. It looked strange as well; it was like one of them slept on one side, and the other occupant didn't even leave an impression. He couldn't tell, but he wondered if he got here earlier enough in the morning whether Mr or Mrs Johnson got the couch. His gut feeling was ninety per cent convinced the couple must be fakes. He thought I bet if I just observed them as they move around the ship or perhaps ate a meal together, I would be sure. As he was about to leave, the bathroom door suddenly flew open. Mrs Johnson was totally naked, holding her towel in one hand and a hairbrush in the other was framed by the doorway. He hadn't heard any shower noise from there because the door had a sealed steel configuration with a low bulkhead, so the cabin couldn't be flooded.

The young man recovered quickly. "I am so sorry, Madame. I just came into the cabin to check something; when there was no answer to my knock, I came on in."

Ramone quickly moved the fluffy white towel to cover her nakedness. She didn't miss that this guy was taking a good look at her and that he was trying hard but failing to hide a dirty smirk.

More annoyed than embarrassed. "Ah, OK, well, as you can see," reading the masseur's name tag. "Next time, knock louder. You really should go."

The young masseur was thinking furiously through the options. He faked embarrassment, stuttering. "For sure, Mmm, Mam, once again, I am so sorry." With that, he went to leave.

Safely wrapped in her towel, Ramone was too smart to be conned that easily. "What did you want anyway?"

She looked around the room for signs the room had been searched to confirm why this man was in her room. From where Ramone stood, she noticed the phone had been moved. While it was still taped to the coffee table, the phone was placed ninety degrees differently from how she had left it.

Sal was young but very street smart and had trained in and survived the drug scene of the worst New York could offer. He saw Ramone's eyes catch the phone. He wasn't sure what had happened but knew he was sprung.

Slowly moving closer to her, he answered her question. "Mam, I needed to tell Mr. Johnson someth............"

Mid-word, and without any hesitation, he landed a right hook on her jaw, she recovered quicker and more than he ever expected. As he went to follow up with a left jab to Ramone's naked stomach, she blocked it with a Chudan Ude Uke using her left forearm to sweep his hand to his right. The towel had long fallen to the floor, but she was far too busy to worry about modesty. As his arm swung wide, it opened his chest and midsection. Ramone delivered a perfectly timed Mae Geri Keage, kicking Sal solidly in the chest. The instant pain told him that the karate bitch had cracked at least two ribs. He had never met a woman who could fight like this. It was clear confirmation of her being more than just a blushing bride. He spat. "You bitch, now I'm going to fuck you, but not before I hurt you."

But now he was sure of it. He was also starting to wonder if he would get out of this cabin, let alone report this information to the old man. Ramone knew her front snap kick had done this guy some serious harm, but she was too well-trained to rush in. She feigned another kick but overplayed it. He lurched forward, closing in and was able to hit her foot so hard she spun away from him off balance in the confined spaces. Every breath was excruciating to Sal; he knew he had to end this quickly if he was to survive. He rushed her and shoulder-barrelled her into the wall. He was lucky cabin walls were more rigid than domestic dwellings. She was unconscious before she hit the floor, falling beside the bed crammed up against the bathroom door she had just come through less than two minutes before.

"Fuck, Fuck, Fuck." The young man swore out loud, holding his ribs and trying to breathe as shallowly as possible. Concerned only about being caught, he felt nothing for this Karate bitch except a slight swelling in his shorts. She sure was a looker, and being naked and wet caused him to stop and enjoy the view for a moment. Touching his crotch sub-consciously, he forced himself to focus on the work at hand. Sal was a cool operator but not foolhardy. He thought h*er husband could arrive at any moment, wondering why she hadn't met him for lunch.* I've just got to do it and get out no options; it's a no-brainer. He grabbed a pillow from the bed and, covering her face, smothered the unconscious woman until he was sure she was dead.

He looked around the room. He was amazed the room wasn't wrecked for the intensity of the fight. In fact, not a thing was out of place. He knew his big problem was moving a body anywhere in broad daylight without being seen by every ship's CCTV and avoiding over two thousand passengers. Overboard was the only answer, but a body falling eight floors might be seen by a cleaning crew member or a passenger enjoying their balcony.

But seriously, what choice did he have. He picked the naked woman up and let her fall a short distance onto the huge bed. Her lifeless legs spread, and a gasp escaped his tightened lips. If Sal knew for sure that he had the time, he may even, well, he didn't. He had never nailed a deaden before, but she was a knock-out and still warm. Gravity caused her large breasts to fall either way, but they were still very nice. Quickly looking at the cabin door, he cupped one of her breasts and smiled. Even in death, his reptilian conscience had found a way to abuse her. He was no pervert. At least, that's what he claimed. It had been what attracted him to his current profession, and those complaints in New York were bullshit. You put oil on a body, and you can't help it if your hands slip under a towel occasionally or along a leg.

Getting this job was the best thing to happen to him, and he knew it. He had escaped the bail hearing in New York, and here he got to massage women all day long. Even some of the old ones were still OK looks, wise. And so far, no one had complained if he touched a little bit here or there, probably the highlight of the cruise, hey? He pulled his handkerchief from his pocket and was careful not to leave any fingerprints as he unlocked the balcony's sliding door. As he slid it open, the sea air rushed in. The curtains billowed around him, clutching at him, nearly smothering him due to the force of the wind. He went back to the lifeless body, bending over the naked woman. He grimaced as his broken ribs complained when he threw her over his shoulder. With one hand happily cradling her soft, warm butt, he swept the flapping curtains aside with his other hand and stepped onto the balcony. Holding her back from the edge, he placed her on the steel balcony chair; he had a quick look in all directions, not forgetting to check the upper decks.

It seemed clear. It was impossible to be one hundred per cent certain, but still, he looked around one more time. Satisfied, he picked up the beautiful naked body in both arms, leered at Ramone once last time and with none of the respect one would show."

The Ship Spa.

I had shown up at the Spa to ask Sal for his help, Ramone had disappeared and after searching the ship I was really worried. I was desperate and figured he was worth a try.

"Rob, I didn't see your name in my diary." Sal stated sounding like a question.

"Sal, I can't find my wife, I was wondering if you'd seen her." I pleaded.

"Most husbands would be happy Rob.' Sal said with a smile.

I showed my displeasure at this joke, and asked. "What happened to you Sal, you look a bit knocked around?"

He attempted a weak laugh that didn't fly. "Haha. Oh, Rob, I tried to hide it from my clients. I got into a bit of a scuffle with that dickhead Filipino assistant chef over nothing. But you know how it is, man, on board, it can get a bit close, hey?"

I tried to sound sympathetic, to encourage him, and I decided to imitate him. "Oh man, sorry to hear that, you OK?"

"Yeah, I'm good. I should have ducked when I dived. I am a lover, not a fighter, but the stupid prick just pushed too hard."

"OK, mate, as long as you're OK. Can you send out a bit of a call for me?"

He smiled. "Yeah, will do. I hope you find her, Rob. I am sorry I was a bit uncaring before. I didn't understand how worried you must be."

Something in me wanted desperately to end the conversation, so I acted as if I was grateful and left the Spa. "Cool, Sal, I'll leave you to it. Please do your best, and thanks."

CHAPTER 11

It was dinner time, and although I wasn't at all hungry, I had to rush to make the serving time and continue to collect more Intel, but more importantly maybe hear something about Ramone. As I walked the long hallway, I thought, *I'm late*; when *I get back to my cabin, I'll have to quickly dress for dinner.* As soon as that singular thought crossed my mind, I was guilt-stricken when I realised it should have been 'our' cabin, not just mine. *Was I already sure Ramone was gone? It wasn't like her to disappear like this.* I joined a table for six *and made my* excuses for Ramone's absence. "My lovely wife isn't feeling well; please excuse her." Over dinner, our conversation was varied and then, like when you are fishing, a bite or, in this case, some new information takes you by surprise. In between courses, a Lawyer from Tucson, Arizona, bragged about how many cruises he and his silent wife had been on. "You know, Rob, there are a few suites on board with all the bells and whistles, but did you realise there are four 'OWNED' suites on a ship this size?" I felt like I had just been hit by a black marlin when I was rigged for smaller fry. "No, Sir, I did not; how's that work, Walt?"

Enjoying being the bearer of this revelation, he continued. "Nearly every cruise line sells some suites." The word 'sells' slapped my face like a wet fish. The Lawyer continued. "For the life of me, I can't really figure the R.O.I. man (Return on Investment) for the cruiseline. But they weigh every fuckin lettuce leaf, so selling a few suites must be good for them." Walt's wife hadn't spoken during the dinner thus far but decided to speak. "Walt, please watch your language at the table". Walt glares at his fair wife. "Anyway, the suites are '*absofuckly' (*making the inverted commas gesture*)* amazing, and they get all sorts of gifts and freebies." I can't remember the main course. I was too busy reeling with the importance of what the half-drunk Lawyer from Tuscan had just informed me. As I returned to the empty cabin, Ramone's well-being was at the forefront of my thoughts. However, I had learnt that sometimes solutions came to me when I distracted myself thinking with something else. This new information about people owning a suite was full of possibilities; it made perfect sense. A permanent resident on the cruise ship would be the ideal smuggler. They would have unbridled access to nearly every part of the ship. After a while, they would become virtually invisible, always wandering around, never perceived as a threat.

The crew would treat them with a casual respectfulness founded on long-term relationships, everyone knowing everybody. OK, I still had no idea what had happened to Ramone, and now I may have stumbled on the strongest lead we'd had so far. I grabbed the Sat phone from under the table and tried to fire it up. I wasn't sure, but, I figured Major Goodrich and the Brigs would want to know if it was me missing. Ramone had told me her pin, so the phone lit up, and I hit number one, hoping that would take me through to Langley.

It took all my convincing skills to get to talk to Ramone's Control Special Agent Munroe. When I finally got through to him, I spoke for a full four minutes, and he still wasn't convinced who I was. I was worried about Ramone and frustrated by this guy's attitude. He seemed more stuck on the fact that I was on her phone than with what I was saying. Worry and impatience overflowed in my voice. "Look, *friend*, I am working for or with you, C.I.A. arse-holes. I understand how careful you have to be, but I'm desperate. Now, I linked up with Agent Ramone at your embassy in Amman. Agent Smith handled it all; come on, man, talk to him, please."

Munro had an annoying, arrogant sort of speech pattern, like a Lawyer who assumes everyone else possesses half their I.Q. Obviously, he knew who I was but wasn't giving anything away.

"We don't have an Agent Smith in Amman, but OK, I'll look into it and get back to you." The phone went dead.

If I didn't have to value the phone so much, I would have smashed it against the cabin wall. I knew how these spooks worked. Firstly, off the cuff, there was no way Munroe would know whether there was an Agent Smith in Amman. Secondly, back in the Amman Embassy, I seriously doubted whether the Agent's name was really Smith in any case. For all I knew, the guy we met in Amman may have been Munroe, for that matter. I wanted to resume my search for Ramone, but I also needed to wait on that phone call back to see what Langley wanted to do once they confirmed my credentials. I sat in my cabin, swinging between worrying about Ramone and thinking the mission through. It's just like searching the bush or the desert; you start again, knowing you must have missed something. All the discussions with Maria, other Bar Attendants, crew and passengers tumbled around inside my head like pebbles on a beach.

Eventually, I began to rehash my most recent conversation with Sal the Masseur. What, if anything, had I learned from him? Then my thoughts started opening up like the sun slowly rising over the horizon until the light flows like molten gold over the landscape. The truth began to dawn on me. What had I totally missed? What had he said? Then I remembered an old interrogation law. Often, it wasn't what was said but how, or what wasn't said. Deep in my gut, I started to feel that something was wrong about him. "Fucking Sal", I swore to myself. I thought he was just a nice young guy from New York working his way around the world.

I had three questions for young Sal, and I was going to get some answers one way or another.

1. Why hadn't he mentioned the owner's cabins.

2. When he could see I was so worried about my wife missing, why didn't he suggest I inform Security and have the entire ship's crew join in the search, make public announcements and so on.

3. How did he really get those bruises on his face. I thought about the answers I expected to get to these questions, and it made me feel physically sick. I hoped I was wrong on all three counts, but there was only one way to find out. The last question worried me if my gut feeling was on target. Someone trained and experienced like

Ramone could put a few bruises on Sal, especially if she was fighting for her life. I jumped up off the bed and was about to head out of the cabin when the Sat phone chimed.

"OK, I believe you." Munroe sounded a little friendlier, but I could hear something new in his voice, something that worried me. The Agent continued.

"Look, there's no easy way to say this: Ramone had a G.P.S. Transponder implanted into her shoulder. My heart sank knowing what must be coming next.

"Now, in real-time, I'm looking at the Southern Star's location from our Satellite live and at Ramone's location simultaneously." I heard his voice had a slight tremor in it. Now, I knew what I had heard but hoped I was wrong? Over the years, it had always sounded the same when an Officer phoned to inform a mate's wife or parents their loved one had been killed in action. Munroe coughed, hesitated and then spoke.

"Ramone is close on a hundred-plus miles behind your ship. There is no land and no vessels in her proximity. I am sorry, but it looks like she is in the water and has been for hours. Her body is hundreds of miles from anything. I am truly sorry. She's gone."

I thought: *If I was only in Australian waters, I could go back and search for her deploying a Border Protection or a Navy vessel.* But it was impossible on a cruise ship in the middle of nowhere. Ramone was gone forever. Rage built in me until I thought I would explode, and then it was replaced by a strange coldness. I didn't know if Ramone was alive when she went into the cold, lonely ocean. But one thing was sure: if Sal had anything to do with it, he would pay for Ramone's death. Munroe broke into my silence. I realised I hadn't said anything since he had delivered the sad news. He must have realised I was in shock and grief at the news and was kind enough to give me a moment. Having said that, Special Agent Munroe's moment of compassion was fleeting.

"Now I've spoken to the Director, and the mission is still active. You and Ramone have done some great work. So, the boss doesn't want to waste any of it, especially after losing Ramone. He wants you to keep going and get the job done. Give me a call every three days for a SITREP (Situation Report), make it at 17.30 Hours your time. The Director is having kittens over this Op; he's calling me hourly."

Feeling numb, I couldn't concentrate. I had seen plenty of death, but for many reasons, now knowing Ramone's fate had really knocked me. I couldn't stop returning to the thought: *Was she dead before she hit the water? Did she suffer?* I signed off the call quickly, unsure I could keep it together any longer. "OK, Munroe, I'll keep you up to date". I pushed the end button and fell back onto the bed. I must have slept for about three hours, a sleep tormented by visions of Ramone being thrown overboard. In my nightmare, I could feel her total isolation from everything, her fear of dying so alone.

The water was ice cold, and huge black shapes appeared, never actually becoming sharks but circling in ever-diminishing circles. Brushing her with their sandpaper skin. She screams and screams, but I can't hear her, but somehow, I know she is crying out. I woke saturated by my own sweat. I sat up, starting to call her name, only to choke on my impotence. I couldn't help her. I hadn't helped her. I had let her down. Getting off the bed, I entered the compact cabin bathroom. I saw another man's face in the mirror, an older man and wondered why this had hit me so damn hard. I staggered into the shower cubicle and tried to burn away my exhaustion with steaming hot water, followed by icy cold.

By the time I was dressed, I had the semblance of a plan. I was going to grab Sal and get some answers. This time, he would tell me everything, he wouldn't enjoy the experience, but I would. Sounding as happy as a passenger should be on a wonderful cruise, I phoned the Spa and booked another massage. I couldn't help but wonder what would go through Sal's mind when he saw my booking on his computer screen. Sal would have to keep his act up. Being on a ship crew, you can't just hide in your cabin forever. He would be confessing his guilt if he tried to hide. I was hoping he would be stewing, worrying about what I knew. He would be hoping I still knew nothing. I figured normal volume conversation, or a T.V., was inaudible between cabins. However, I knew from being able to hear far too graphically the couple next door having noisy sex and arguing that the cabin walls were too thin to mask the noise from any form of hard torture. My interrogation of Sal had to be quiet. Any bashing, screams, or sobbing may bring Security to my door, resulting in my imprisonment in one of the ship's security cells.

Of course, I knew the ship would have no reason to have any contemporary truth serums or chemical interrogation drugs. With access to any modern drugs unavailable, I had to reach way back into my Interrogation Technique Training and articles I had read. I remembered that back in 2009, the Czechoslovak State Secret Police had reportedly used Hyoscine, also called Scopolamine, to successfully obtain confessions. This Scopolamine was also used to treat several medical conditions. Fortunately for me, one of them was Motion Sickness, more commonly called sea sickness, a constant problem for some cruise passengers. Beggars can't be choosers. I wandered down to the sick bay and innocently looked around, reading notices about onboard hygiene and Doctor's hours. Noting that the Infirmary contained the surgery and another door marked Pharmaceuticals, I returned to my cabin. I waited to ensure there would be less traffic around the surgery. 0300 hours saw me picking the lock on the Pharmaceutical storage unit and I began searching for the Scopolamine. There it was. I grabbed four bottles and re-locked the cabinet and door on my way out.

I had attempted to get sleep by drinking more than a few J.D.s, but their effect only lasted a few hours. I was grateful for 24-hour dining, so I headed up to the buffet. After a quick breakfast over my third black coffee, I thought about my plan. I was to happily wander into my massage appointment, with my main goal being to read Sal's demeanour. This was more to help guide my interrogation approach rather than to confirm my concerns about him. By now, I had no doubt because of the adage I had been drilled into me during training; 'where there is any doubt, there is **no** doubt'. Booking my appointment so I would be the last appointment for the day meant the Receptionist would finish before I would be finished. This suited my plan. I headed down the hallway and headed outdoors for some sun and fresh air before getting to work on Sal. I walked towards the ship's stern, walking past the pool full of happy overweight passengers and then ran up the stairs across the walking track I had walked with Maria just a few days ago. This stirred up the embers of anger and revenge, but I quickly pushed them back out of sight. For now.

On entering the Spa, the Receptionist looked up with another perfect smile.

"Welcome, Mr Johnson; lovely to see you again. Sal will be out shortly."

"Thanks, Kelea," I said as I sat on the snow-white lounge.

Sal came out within a minute or so and walked straight up to me, his hand extended, ready to shake mine. His tan seemed a little faded today, and his smile was just a little more plastic than usual. I took his hand and noted it was wet and clammy. All these little signs were not our familiar, confident Sal. I was happy to know he was already shaky. His fear would facilitate the drug I would fill him with, combined with the rough treatment I was going to mete out to him. I had to keep it quiet, but he would still suffer for Ramone's sake. We went into his office and through to the treatment room with its massage table and burning candles. I enjoyed seeing him grimace as he closed the door.

"So, Sal how's it goin?" There wasn't a gram of me that felt sorry for him. But he was clearly suffering; he could hardly keep it together. My being there had rattled him as I had hoped.

"Yeah, I'm great, Rob". I noticed as he spoke he turned away to hide his pain or worries.

Without warning, I started verbally hammering him, taking on a threatening tone where volume wasn't possible. "Now, Sal. I'm a bit surprised that a caring guy like you, who knew how worried I am about my wife, hasn't phoned me to see whether she turned up. And even now, you haven't asked whether I found her." Menacingly, I continued. "Now, Sal, you and I are going to walk out of here and go to my cabin for a talk." In a shaky voice, he tried to be brave. "What, no! No way am I going anywhere, and I have no idea what all this bullshit about your wife means. You're fuckin crazy, man."

My anger was growing, as I said. "Sal, you have got to work on your customer service. We are way past the play-acting. I don't know what happened, but I know you know. You're smiling, you little prick, I'll...." I was starting to think I would just take him apart right here, right now. I gotta grip on myself, grabbed his hand, and swung it up his back. I knew I couldn't escort him through the ship's entire length like that. But I wanted him to know I was willing to hurt him and was in charge. Confidently, I warned him. "Now we are going to go to my cabin. Like I said, you try to speak to anyone or make a sign, and I will end you where you stand. You hearin me, Sal?" He was catching on fast but still had to try. "Yeah, OK, but what's this all about?"

As an answer, I slapped him hard across his smug face, being careful not to draw blood. His face reddened as he registered the shock, and I had him. But we had to move now. I pushed him towards the door. The journey back to the cabin was stressful for both of us. Sal because he didn't know what was in store for him, but I figured he was starting to have some idea. For me, because controlling an unwilling prisoner without handcuffs or touch was a subtle challenge, especially moving amongst hundreds of crew and passengers.

When we got five doors from my cabin, Sal must have figured I would relax that close, and he would have a chance. Swinging around suddenly, he attempted to slam me into the hallway wall. I was ready for it. Stepping back, I allowed him to follow through and pushed his face into the nearest wall. He staggered and turned around to face me. His good looks were shattered like his nose. Sal's crisp white uniform was now covered in his freely flowing blood. Thankfully, a quick glance revealed an empty hallway in both directions. I bundled him the last few steps as I opened my door. I kicked him hard up the ass, pushing him into the room. I followed him in, kicking his tangled body again, which was now jammed up against the foot of my bed.

One of the first things you learn about fighting and interrogating is if you gain momentum, you don't let up. I wanted to hurt him bad, but my original thoughts regarding noise kept me in check. I stuck some tape over his mouth and pressed it home. I then secured his hands behind his back with some cable ties. I pulled them in over-tight and was happy to hear a grunt of pain. Wrenching him up off the floor, I slammed into a chair, placing more cable ties on each ankle. I secured him to the chair legs. When I was in the Infirmary, I had also acquired a small funnel, which was now sitting next to the Scopolamine bottles. Not knowing the equipment's true purpose didn't diminish his fear. When his eyes fell on what was waiting for him. His eyes widened as he had guessed correctly that they were ready for him. I was smiling like I was enjoying it because I was.

"Now I'm in a hurry and need to know a few things. If I could put a blow torch to your balls and get away with it without upsetting the whole ship, that would be my preference."

He became excited and mumbled something unintelligible through the tape. I slapped his chest, knowing his broken ribs would magnify the pain, and he settled. I had decided to try without the drugs in case he was easily scared. I continued sarcastically. "I know, mate, I know: it's all a big mistake. I've got you all wrong. Let you loose, and we go and have a drink together, hey? A fleeting look of relief flashed across his reddened face. At least until I hit him in the ribs again. "Yeah, right. No way, you slippery son of a bitch. OK, these are the rules. Not one fucking word from you unless it is an answer to my question. Once I remove the tape, if you scream, I will likely forget my plan to do this quietly and inflict some serious pain. Now we good? Nod if you understand and are willing."

He nodded, so I started my questioning. "Do you know where my wife is?"

Tape off. "Fuck you, how would I know anything about her?" Tape on, plus I gave him another vicious poke in the injured ribs. "Now that was the wrong answer, and you obviously need an attitude adjustment too, my old mate Sal. Are you going to come clean or not?" At this, he nodded vigorously. Tape off. This Ad Hoc torture was already boring me to death. Sal's eyes looked up and right, signifying he was creating what he was about to say. Speaking through his teeth, Sal answered. "You're not going to like this, Rob, but your blushing bride liked a bit on the side, on the front and even on her back. I heard half the crew had ridden a winner home with her. Now, your good wife going missing could be anything, but there are so many possible suspects. I wish you luck. Now let me out here, and I mean right fucking now."

Tape on.

It took all my control not to just finish him right then. Credit where credit's due; he was keeping his head, and he knew how to push my buttons, especially with him believing Ramone and I had been married. My voice didn't betray the depth of my anger.

"Look, Sal, you know, and I know that's bullshit. Now, are you ready to talk or not?"

Tape off.

Wagging his head sideways, he tried again. "I don't know anything. I don't even know why I am here."

Tape on.

Poke in the ribs.

Knowing some of the truth helped me be sure he was lying. I was really getting sick of the games. I was used to interrogating prisoners without any constraints. It was time for some truth serum. Sal's eyes widened as I opened the first bottle. I would have loved it to be inject able. However, I was forced to administer the drug orally because the Scopolamine was only in tablet form. To accelerate absorption, I had made several batches of white powder by grinding up six tablets at a time. I figured if the interrogation took a while, it didn't matter. Even if someone missed Sal, they wouldn't necessarily look for him with me. Seeing I was his last client, I might get a call, but I could dismiss that quickly enough.

I mixed the first powdered tablets in some water. Then I removed the tape from his mouth, forced the funnel between his teeth, held his nose and poured the mixture down his gullet. He gagged and spluttered but kept it all down. I decided not to waste the time waiting for the meds to kick in, so I asked. "What do you know about smuggling ancient artefacts aboard this ship?"

His eyes told me he knew something. I removed the tape, but he had recovered his composure.

"I don't know what you're talking about. Are you fucking crazy one minute your wife's missing and now some loony tune stuff about antiques or some crap?"

Tape on.

Slapping him across the face, I said menacingly. "OK, Sal, I can wait, but you do know you're eventually going to tell me everything. It's only a matter of time."

Due to the massive dose, it only took a few minutes for the Scopolamine to start to have an effect. His eyes glassed over, and as I once again tore the tape from his now-red mouth, his words were slurred. Scopolamine works by slowing or blocking certain nerve transmissions, so it was no surprise he sounded as though he was drunk. I had decided to work backwards by concentrating on the mission first and then finding out about Ramone.

Starting again, I demanded. "OK, now tell me what you know about smuggling ancient treasures?"

He stumbled and mumbled and needed constant prodding to get back on track. Displaying no powers of concentration, some questions took several attempts before a logical reply was forthcoming. However, after nearly an hour, I knew how the items got on board and where they were stored. I stopped and poured another Scopolamine mix down the funnel. He gagged again but kept it in. I was the last person on earth to be concerned about him overdosing on the stuff, but not just yet. However, I was still wanting more answers. I realised the entire process was a bit rustic and lacking sophistication, but it was slowly producing results.

The new dose kicked in fast as it piggybacked on the first mixture.

I started again. "Sal, I know your knee deep in this shit, but who is in charge?"

Tape off.

He slurred. "I really don't know, I, I, I, I, I, I, I, can't tell you that."

Tape on.

I hadn't any compassion for this scum. "Listen, you can stutter all you like, but you must know who you are working for. Who are you most scared of? If the stuff is stored in the private lockups, then that means it must be one of the permanent owners on board that's involved.

I kept going. "Now, no bullshit, Sal, tell me what I need to know while you're feeling good. Because if I get sick of waiting noise or no noise, I will use something different to help you talk, and I promise you won't feel good after I've finished."

Probably due to a blend of fear and the drugs, Sal visibly decided to cooperate. Nearly crying like a tap, he opened up.

Tape off.

"OK, OK, everything was his idea. I was just following orders, hey? Now, he owns a suite and has the run of the ship. He knows everybody and has a secure storage area down on Deck Two."

The drug was working well, but it didn't totally hold the person like pain or torture.

Tape on.

I kept him going. "Now, Sal, what else do you get when you own a suite?"

I could see Sal's eyes were starting to droop. As loud as I dared, I shouted.

"Stick with me, Sal."

He lifted his head and opened his eyes, but as they say, 'the lights were on, but no one was home'. I slapped him hard across his face; he jerked upwards, bringing the chair with him. The tape was still on, but I covered his mouth with my hand just in case. My unmeasured doses may have been too much. He was out of it. To distract from the next big question, I asked.

"OK, Sal, you were talking about the benefits of being an owner. What else? Come on, not much longer now, and you can sleep all you want."

Tape off.

Slurring his words like a drunk. "Free unlimited Internet, man, not just free but forever mobile as we sail all over the fuckin world, man. Can't be traced because, at any one moment, there might be, who knows, five hundred, a thousand users online going through the ship's hub."

Tape on.

I sat on the bed for a moment and thought it through. Sal was right; all the C.I.A.'s tracking and hacking resources wouldn't ever pick this up. We had stumbled on to it from the land end, and only because the fat man had kept the info on USBs and his phone, luckily for us, that was for sure.

"Sal, Sal (I spoke as loudly as I dared), Sal, you with me, buddy? Now, just two more questions and you can rest, OK? Now, who is your boss? What's his cabin number? "Sal, what number suite buddy tell me now?"

Tape off.

Slumping in his chair, drool fell from his mouth onto his tee-shirt. "OK, OK, there are only four of them; you want 1203. Mr Ian Harrison, he's an arrogant fag; he's from London, I think."

Tape on.

I could see Sal was close to passing out. "Sal, you're nearly there. Just a few more questions, mate." I was sick of calling him mate or buddy, but I knew I had to get him to relax and just talk.

"Do you know what happened to my wife? Where is she, buddy?" I knew where Ramone's remains were, but it was a good test of whether his answer was honest by asking it this way.

Tape off.

"I don't know, man. I need to sleep; I am wasted." His words became more affected as the overdose of truth serum overpowered his nervous system. I had to hurry before he lost it.

Tape on.

"Come on, Sal, what happened? Suddenly, it flowed a bit like molasses, slowly and slurred. His answers were not totally coherent.

He began to inform me of all he had done instead of the specific items I wanted to focus on.

Tape off.

"It was an accident; he told me to get rid of Maria; she had a big mouth. She had told me how nice you were, and then I saw you talking to her at the Pool Bar. It's your fault I had to do it." He stopped talking for a moment.

My mind pictured the vibrant young girl who was so happy with her job and life. Sal started up again. "I made it look like suicide, and everybody bought it because it's common for the odd crew to top themselves. They get lonely, somebody dumps them back home anyway; it worked to cover up Maria. Little Maria with the big tits is in the little morgue. He giggled. "she's down there near the stuff we are smuggling (another giggle)."

Tape on.

Every fibre of me wanted to crush his windpipe there and then, but I still needed to know about Ramone. If the story about Maria's sad ending enraged me this much, there were certainly no guarantees I wouldn't rip him limb from limb if he had anything to do with Ramone disappearing. Thankfully, he seemed to have had a second wind and woken up. Now, he was talking, and I wanted him to keep going.

"Buddy, what accident? You said it was an accident. Didn't you mean to kill Maria?"

"Oh, not Maria, man, that hot wife of yours."

As he continued, my skin began to crawl, and his smirk turned into an unmistakable leer. I didn't want to hear any more, but I had to know the truth, I asked with subdued urgency.

"What do you mean, Sal, what happened?"

All of a sudden, I couldn't shut him up. It was like a dam bursting.

"Harrison told me to search your cabin, so no big deal. I went in and looked around, nothin scary, no guns or electronics or anything. I found that big-ass Sat phone stashed to the underside of the table. I was just leavin' when she comes out of the shower. Whoa, that lady is or *was* smokin' hot."

The drugs meant any normal inhibitions and caution were non-existent. He had apparently forgotten who I was. But knowing that didn't make it any easier for me to hear this filth. His head was drooping again. "Sal, what happened next?"

Sal's head flew up as his eyes tried to focus.

"Anyway, she, like, drops the towel (at that, he actually licked his lips) and we fight."

I so wanted to hurt this sleaze.

"She was a mean mother; she nearly kicked my ass. I was glad to finish it still standing. Fuck me, it was like a fuckin porn movie with a female Bruce Lee. Man, she broke my fuckin ribs."

I let him keep talking; he was drugged enough to enjoy the foggy memories and was like a river of molten lava flowing slowly downhill. My questioning and prompting were no longer needed, as momentum was driving his recounting of Ramone's last moments.

He continued. "Anyway, I figured I had to dump the bitch's body somehow, and it's a fuckin big ocean man. What can I say? She was hot, man, what a waste anyway. I threw her over the balcony. I saw the splash, and then she was fish food. Hey, have a nice swim bitch. She got what she deserved. She fuckin hurt me, but she paid the check in the end." He went quiet and I wondered if he had passed out.

"I didn't tell Harrison man, he would have freaked. couldn't tell him, Nah."

I'd heard enough; I willed myself not to go there. I didn't want to imagine what this deviate might or might not have done to a naked Ramone. I was a lot calmer than I had expected to be, all considering. Maybe colder is a better description. I have killed many men, sometimes from a distance, others so close I could hear them stop breathing and smell their sweat. Training and experience had confirmed if you allowed emotions such as anger to come into the processes, you lost focus. You lost awareness and made mistakes. The killing machine the Military had created and honed to razor's edge in me had kicked in like an emergency generator when the power went off. I sat there in front of this waste of space and thought it through. He deserved Maria's treatment, but I couldn't fake his suicide because they may eventually carry out an autopsy or a toxicology screen once the ship arrived at the next port.

Of course, any such analysis would reveal his Scopolamine saturated system and slapped face, in addition to the wounds inflicted by Ramone. Alarm bells would sound as this drug isn't popular either for recreation or suicide by nature. He had decided his own fate. He was going to be 'fish food' as well. I toyed with the idea of waiting for the drugs to wear off, so he got the complete trauma of flying past all the decks until he hit the cold waves below. Then, he would begin to fight the ocean, eventually succumbing to its power. Then, blissfully giving in, he would breathe in the salt water, feeling his lungs fill with the cold brine. He deserved all the fear and pain I could cause him. However, the risk was too high to wait. I was aware of the shipboard daily routine for this time of day. This meant that at any time, a cabin steward might come in wanting to turn down the bed and refill my ice bucket. It had to happen, and now.

I was still unsure if he had thrown Ramone overboard while she was still alive or unconscious. He wouldn't have cared about her either way. I wasn't even sure he had thrown Ramone from our balcony. My only concern was not getting caught. I couldn't have him screaming all the way down, causing a man overboard alarm to be raised and possibly a rescue as well. Visualising Sal flying towards the cold waves eight floors below us, I knew I needed to shut him up.

I replaced the worn tape over his mouth but made sure his nose was clear to breathe, hopefully, salt water very shortly.

I cut the cable ties around the chair legs and immediately replaced them by binding his ankles together. He was like a drunk, aware to some extent of what was happening but not really involved. I lifted him off the chair, double-checked his hands were still tightly secured, and threw him on the bed. Walking towards the balcony, I was mindful that by carrying out these actions, I was probably imitating his actions the day he murdered and disposed of Ramone's remains. Opening the sliding door, the same curtains billowed, embracing and smothering me. Momentarily, I was blindfolded by the flapping curtain. Wrestling the material away from me, I pinned it back with one of the balcony chairs and stepped onto the little platform. Casually, I poked my head over the balcony rail like any passenger would.

Long ago, I learned that just because I was engaged in some sinister plot or action, that action may mean nothing to others. I knew the same step was benign to the casual, uninvolved observer. This was my cabin; it was not unusual for the occupants to wonder what was above and below their balcony. So, I did just that: I looked everywhere. To my relief, I saw no one in any direction. Helping me with this, it was dinner time. A silver moon was dutifully climbing the sky, causing the dark waters to sparkle and deepen. I went back inside the cabin. Sal wasn't going anywhere soon, so I cleaned up the place. I decided any evidence of this afternoon's interrogation should follow Sal. I didn't want my cabin steward wondering why I had a trash can full of cable ties and empty bottles of Scopolamine. I collected everything and put it in a laundry bag. I then tied it to Sal's belt. Even though I am a trained assassin and can be as cold as ice, I was still surprised at how angry I was. What I was about to do was out there even for me, but this mongrel deserved more than death. Of course, this anger had a focus. Without thought or remorse, he killed a lovely young Maria and a great person and Agent in Ramone. When I picked him up, he seemed to be asleep. As I carried him to the cabin balcony, I couldn't help myself. I made sure I pressed his broken ribs as much as I could. I was pleased that the agony woke him. I was rewarded by hearing a muffled scream through the tape.

I whispered in his ear. "That lady you killed was terrific and didn't deserve to be treated like the garbage you are. Say hello to the sharks, Sal." Fear sobered him instantly, and his eyes widened as understanding struck him, and he began to struggle. I took another quick look around, picked him up and tossed him and the laundry bag over the railing and away from the ship. I didn't look or wait in case anyone had seen anything. I didn't want to be linked to the flying body. I stayed back from the railing and listened, relieved I heard nothing. I walked back inside, grabbed my bottle of J.D., and took a deep swig straight from the bottle, followed by another. I had a lot to report, but I was shaking from adrenalin and anger, so it was better to wait. After three slugs of the smoky whiskey, I started to calm down. I phoned Munroe straight away. I was in the mood if anyone got in the way this time. Thankfully, my call went through quickly, the Agent answering in a bored voice.

He let me finish my report without interrupting, and he was no longer bored when he spoke. He was probably as excited as Special Agent Munroe ever got.

"Boy, oh boy, you sure get results. I am glad you dealt with that prick. Poor old Ramone, hey?"

I enjoyed reporting. "Yeah, her killer said she fought like a tiger. I got the impression he thought he was bloody lucky to have beaten her. OK, Munroe, where do we go from here?" It was all happening very fast, but I had to ask.

The C.I.A. Agent tried to reassure me. "Well, now we know who, where, and a fair bit of how. You have two sea days, and then you visit Venice. I'll get back to you when we have a plan." He continued.

"In the meantime, I want you to look around the storage area and do some surveillance on this Harrison."

I was over this mission. It had gone on too long and was beginning to become a never-ending story. Losing Ramone was the final straw. You could hear it in my voice as I responded. "Then I can get off at Venice, fly home, and you guys can take care of the rest. How does that sound?"

I could hear the hesitation in his voice. "Yeah, sort of; stick with our plan, and I'll talk to you in forty-eight hours at the set time. I am glad you made this report. It's good for me to be updated just in case something happens to you.

He really had a way about him, our Agent in Charge. "Thank you, Munroe. I'm getting a little misty when I realise just how much you care for my safety and well-being." I said sarcastically.

My sarcasm wasn't missed. "Sure, sure, but seriously, be careful. You may have eliminated the cutouts below Management, but these grubs often have a backup grunt somewhere. Talk soon, buddy, and by the way, that was fuckin top-class work. I'll make sure your bosses hear how well you're doing."

I heard the sat line close and took another swig, draining the dregs of the bottle. Under the circumstances, I was amazed when I realised I was starving. I couldn't face the dinner table bullshit where everybody tried to outdo the people around the table. The buffet sounded too crowded for me tonight, so I reached for the cabin phone and punched in Room Service. I knew I would have to order two of everything because Ramone's absence could not be noticed until I was off the ship for good. I figured this would work as the Steward would knock, and I would collect the tray at the door without them entering the cabin. This would be normal for waiters; the other person may be in bed or in pyjamas. I ordered the food and sat down on the chair that a short time ago had accommodated Sal's interrogation.

CHAPTER 12

Trevanion Auction Rooms
East 74th Street
New York

He studied the beautiful wood and the craftsmanship of his Empire Style Pedestal French Directoire Desk. Not for the first time, he imagined the conversations, decisions, and perhaps intrigues this beautiful piece of furniture from the 1800s had witnessed. Its rich 'plum pudding mahogany' trimmed with moulded brass borders reflected the subtle lighting of his study. He hated the phone that was now sitting on the green leather desktop. The modern instrument didn't fit into the room's ambience, conflicting with all that was royal and impressive from a past era. He hid the phone in one of the desk's drawers when not in use. Jonathan Sherwood was a fifth-generation fine antique dealer; he was the Master of all that surrounded him, and he enjoyed this as if the Squire to the Manner born. Besides the phone and him, there was nothing in the book-lined study younger than a hundred and fifty years old. And here was this ugly plastic and copper wire phone assaulting the room's idyllic peace. Another reason he was annoyed was it meant he was forced to talk to this imbecile.

Even worse, what the fool had to say was not pleasing him.

Sherwood spat. "Harrison, seriously, could it be fucked up any better?"

Sherwood instantly thought; T*his business drags me into the gutter now. I sound like a truckie.*

Harrison wasn't used to being spoken to in such a manner. "Now, Mr Sherwood, speaking like that isn't going to improve things."

Sherwood pushed on. "Well, nothing could make it any fucking worse. You have bodies everywhere and are down on key staff by losing Sal. Do you know what happened yet?

"No, He has just vanished without a trace."

The New York businessman yelled. "And now you tell me you have this Johnson fellow sniffing around. By the way, do we know who he is? F.B.I., Treasury could even be C.I.A., I suppose? If he is, we need to proceed with extreme caution."

Harrison attempted to calm the New York dealer. "We don't think so, Mr Sherwood. After all, he's an Australian and on his honeymoon. We think he's just a curious fellow, motivation unknown. Sal searched his room, he didn't report anything strange from that."

Sherwood was still angry at losing that last shipment to those slimy Feds. He couldn't afford to lose this load as well. The only consolation was they hadn't discovered his involvement. He couldn't get close enough to any of them to offer a bribe, and the word was they were not interested. What could you do with men who turned their backs on easy money? He had per-sold the entire shipment that had been seized, and his buyers were less than happy. They had not only wanted their money back but once the media released the story, they became anxious they might become involved in the debacle. The genuine vendors, Sherwood, put them under one umbrella labelled ISIS for simplicity. They were even less happy because Sherwood had to refund the money, blocking their funding stream. To think it was nearby, probably still in New York at some secret warehouse, added salt to his wounds. Losing all that stock meant refunding monies. It hurt, but worse was the damage it had done to his reputation as a procurer of the virtually impossible. Sherwood often drifted off when he spoke to this clown. The antique dealer now drifted back again. Harrison was still rabbiting on. Sherwood couldn't stand the arrogant pig, but this new route seemed an innovative move even if arranged quickly.

That was until this assault wave of trouble seemed to sweep over his multi-tiered network. Someone had taken out the two key players at the Egyptian enterprise. He knew from experience, in true Egyptian style, that they would fight and scratch. Eventually, someone new would take over and reinstate the infrastructure that had been lost. It was a little like evolution. The strongest would survive and win the prize. In this case, the award was the contacts and profits the fat and now very dead Mr Ali Ben Adham had developed. Sherwood had survived no, more accurately, flourished on three distinct levels: the highly transparent and respected antique business his father and grandfathers had owned before him. He had also operated on another level, for the last twelve years, the covert and thoroughly murky world of smuggling and selling illegal antiquities. The third and most recent stratum was the commission income the Antique Dealer had gained from facilitating the sale of artefacts for the ISIS group and the resulting distribution of funds using their Hawala agents. He still couldn't believe such an ancient trust system could work so effectively.

Even though his legitimate clientele, the rich and famous, could be ruthless and arrogant at times, it was just business. He found them predictable and civilised. He really hated having to deal with these filthy terrorist criminals. They were uneducated, greedy and short-sighted bullies. Worst of all, they were zealots, and anyone in this category was usually irrational and, therefore, dangerous. They didn't possess any respect for history or the artefacts from millenniums past. He always felt he needed to wash his hands after dealing with these lowlifes, even after a phone call. Sherwood understood his position. He realised he was vulnerable because these peasants would assume he could be replaced in hours. In his mind, that was ridiculous, of course. However, he was realistic enough to know that wouldn't help him if he upset his new masters. His ISIS contacts above and on the lower levels, the smugglers lived and worked in places where a life was of so little value anything was possible. He smiled as he thought that the fat man in Cairo had died of 'natural causes', natural, that is, to a man in his line of work.

He had heard there was some drama in Petra and then some more at Wadi Rum. While he figured it couldn't be the same guy, he still wondered what was going on? Now, on the ship, this Johnson, if that was his real name, was sticking his nose in where it didn't belong. After losing the last shipment, the antique dealer was worried about being under surveillance by someone, so he had brought in a communications and technology security expert. The smelly, dishevelled geek was an ex-CIA techo who knew the importance of money. You could trust people like that, sort of. The guy had analysed Sherwood's organisation's needs and set up systems to ensure the safest way to communicate the required messages and the hardware and the software to carry them. He even trained Sherwood to use different encryption and phones. At least that let him talk freely to cretins like Harrison as he cruised around the world. But Sherwood was still cautious. What he didn't know was that there is always that weak link in every system. In this case, it had been the deceased Mr Ali Ben Adham in Cairo who, against all instructions, had contacted Harrison directly and kept a digital record of the contacts.

To Sherwood, it was all about the money, and the money was substantial. He knew that the accounts he deposited the funds into were fronts. Some of the money was rerouted within minutes to other secret accounts worldwide. He also understood the Hawala system benefited from it greatly. This system allowed him to 'keep' money that wasn't his and invest it on the basis that he guaranteed its buying power vouched for when required. Once and only once,

Sherwood had spoken face to façe with a 'representative'. It hadn't escaped him to note while the white Lawyer type wore an exquisite Saville Row suit. He looked like he could and would kill you in an instant if ordered to do so. Now, the business world was full of sharks, but Sherwood still felt a chill down his back when he thought of those eyes and the way the man smiled, all the while he made threats. The dead eyes had locked onto Sherwood's as he spoke. Sherwood's chest had tightened as he struggled not to squirm in his seat, trying to look confident. His forbears would be outraged to see he had thugs and murderer's numbers in his secret phone. More so to know he was willing to employ them to achieve his goals. Mr Saville Road continued to make the terms of the business deal perfectly clear. "Mr Sherwood, you will make a lot of money working with us. However, make no mistake, if you were to steal from us, you and all your family will die. If you talk to anyone, the same outcome and none of you will die quickly, Mr Sherwood. We are wonderful partners but terrifying enemies."

Sherwood knew then he should never have started working for them, let alone continue with all this smuggling and intrigue. But the money was outrageous, and knowing he would claim his commission on those 'special' sales and still receive a monthly retainer from ISIS was irresistible. They had no idea he was using their money to make himself even more cash. His off-shore accounts were bursting with his secret income. So except for having to deal with these low-class scum, he had never had it so good. It was a straightforward money distribution system. When the shipment arrived, he was to notify them by secure email, and they would reply with a number from one to twenty-eight instructing him which account or accounts to use.

Each time, only some of the money would physically be transferred. The rest would just be available through Hawala. It had been working successfully for the last twelve years, and being an optimist, this recent seizure was an obstacle that he would overcome. It would continue for at least another five years.

So many cruise ships came and went to and from New York. All he had to do was polish and refine this new system and then duplicate it on as many ships as he could recruit a willing owner. Many were old customers of Trevanion House, with huge mansions all over the U.S.A. Now they lived on board various cruise ships, some still liked surrounding themselves with smaller antiquities. They had downsized into their luxurious floating staterooms on board, circling the world. Sherwood would pick his mark, offer an illegal item as bait, and then recruit them to host a shipment of crates. Theoretically, that's all that was required, no actual involvement other than making their storage facilities available to Sherwood's men. On the other hand, Harrison made an art form of being too involved and over complicating what should have been just that simple.

On Board Southern Star

Deck 12

Room1203

Harrison sat in the vast lounge of his suite. He swirled the twenty-five-year-old Baron De Sigognac Cognac around the warmed crystal balloon, filling his hand while inhaling the rich fumes reminiscent of Arabica coffee. Deep in contemplation, he had been giving the whole sorry business a lot of thought. Sal had fallen off the planet. None of the crew had seen him. Even though there were still so many unanswered questions, there was definitely something strange about Johnson. After a warming mouthful of cognac, Harrison thought, This Johnson character was bobbing up too often, Sal hadn't really found anything for sure, but there's just something. Sal wasn't too concerned when Johnson made another appointment with Sal. Harrison had told Sal to check in after his appointment with the inquisitive Mr Johnson. Then nothing, not a trace. Sal hadn't turned up or phoned in a report. He had simply vanished. Harrison, being a long-term resident, could chat with the crew without any fear of them suspecting anything had made subtle enquiries but nothing; Sal had vanished.

The scuttlebutt on board was his hand had slipped on one too many well-oiled inner thighs of a married passenger once too often. The assumed story went along the lines that the woman had complained to her husband, and the offended party had apparently thrown young Sal overboard. This, while drastic, sounded highly feasible and was the only explanation for Sal's disappearance. This seemed to be of no surprise to anyone as Sal's lecherous reputation was well known. It sounded a little far-fetched. But you never knew who these oldies were. There was always the possibility the outraged husband was an ex-Marine or something. This component was added to the rumour and became fact by doing so. The theory was plausible, as the young masseuse's body had never been found.

Harrison, on the other hand, was more than a little concerned. It was not about losing Sal so much that it wasn't crucial from any operational viewpoint he could be replaced. It was more the fact the number of either missing people or bodies was becoming ridiculous. This had to result in increased Security and investigation. Of even more significant concern was someone was asking too many questions. He didn't believe in coincidences and certainly not the scuttlebutt running around the ship. Harrison was too careful for that. He knew it had to be connected somehow to this fellow Johnson. With a deep sigh, the elderly smuggler thought, *Ah, Venice tomorrow how I love Venice.* He took a small sip of his incredibly expensive brandy and enjoyed the smooth burn of the dark liquid. He then picked up his cell phone and punched a number.

PIER Stazione Marittima
Port of Venice
Italy

Despite myself and the horrible last few days, Venice was more beautiful than any reputation could have prepared the visitor for. If I hadn't been on a mission, I would have been overcome by the multi-faceted beauty of entering the ancient port by cruise ship. A fantastic concept for that time, a city built on a swamp, first occupied in 400 A.D., near the Venice Lagoon. And now, slowly but surely, the sea was taking back what had been stolen from her. Shops surrounding the famous square had boardings attempting to keep the tide at bay, and buildings were sinking back into the mud. We passed many islands and villages, some abandoned, others thriving. Picturesque churches and monasteries appeared to be sitting on the water as we viewed them from our ship's balconies.

As we approached the cruise ship terminal, water taxis were buzzing around. I could see the famous Gondolas staying in the side waterways, only occasionally crossing the Main Canal. We moored at Pier Stazione Marittima. From my balcony, I watched as each crewman began to carry out the required actions as with each port the ship visited, settling into a 'done it all before' routine. Evening fell, and an amazing lightning storm lit up the skies and the surrounding waters, reflecting off the huge glass windows of the cruise terminal buildings. Thunder cracked and echoed its way around the buildings and structures of Venice proper, casting a ghostly temporary light invading every cabin and public area. I decided I had two primary objectives: the first was to have a close look at this Mr Harrison. The second was to investigate his storage unit in the owner's private storage facilities. I had no idea what this lockup would look like. But I figured it would hardly be Fort Knox in the constraints of a cruise liner. As Sal had confessed, I hoped Mr Harrison's secure area would be full of stolen antiquities to confirm all my theories. The Southern Star does an outstanding job protecting its passengers and their possessions. I knew from the exiting and entry procedures that onboard Security is taken very seriously. This led me to believe accessing this secure storage area may be challenging. But of course, I had to try. I needed to visually confirm the evidence before the OP could proceed.

I figured Harrison had visited Venice on previous cruises, so I wasn't sure which shore excursion he had chosen or if he even going to get off the ship. I hung around the lift foyer near his cabin. He turned up just as I was close to giving up on him. Maintaining my cover, I chatted with people waiting for the lift. Some went to the Piazza San Marco, some to the Renaissance Clock tower with that encompassing view of St Marks and the entire city. Others in the group were going to take a Gondola ride and take in the Rialto Bridge, the Grand Canal and all the colourful canal-front homes. They would get off and visit the famous Murano Glass Factory and other unique stores, have lunch, and then get back on a Gondola. In the meantime, I wanted to follow Mr Harrison and start building a workable profile on him. With that in mind, I had I.D.'d him and noted that he had a blue disembarking pass. This meant he was going on a shore excursion. I rushed to the excursion desk and purchased a blue pass. Although he was ahead of me, I knew he had to wait for the ferry, so I went through Security and onto the wharf. I joined the queue for the Burano Island tour. Burano is a small fishing island famous for its Lace Works. It has diverse markets and beautiful bright-coloured shops and houses.

I was standing just three couples behind Harrison, waiting to be called onto the small boat that would take us to the island. I took in every physical detail I could glean from observing him. After a short time, our ferry arrived, and we boarded for the trip to Burano Island. It took us past several private yachts. One had its own heliport and lifeboats that were bigger than the ones on the cruise ship. One of the passengers sitting next to me turned to me and started talking to me in a striking Yorkshire accent. Gesturing towards the yacht, he explained.

"I read all about it in an article. Apparently, it's owned by a Russian Billionaire. Cost him $263 Million and was named Dilbar."

The Englishman recited that it was some 360 feet long and 50 feet high. We could see several immaculate crew scurrying around, cleaning windows and mopping decks. During the trip, I kept chatting away with my fellow travellers to blend in while casually observing Harrison. This was the closest I had been to him, and I was interested in seeing him up close. He was a bit older than I had expected, mildly tanned, and his silver hair was styled and set in place, not moving at all as the breeze blew through the ferry. He appeared to be a man of wealth, and he projected a calm confidence that comes with position and control. His eyes were shielded behind aviator-type sunnies, so I was careful not to stare. Eventually, we slowed as a small wooden jetty came into view. The ferry turned away from our island, the Pilot put the craft into reverse and came alongside the old but well-kept jetty. A young deckhand jumped off and secured lines fore and aft, deftly tying the ropes around the small bollards. Several locals were fishing from either side of the deck. They looked up without any genuine interest and watched the passengers disembark up a short mobile gangplank. We all filed down the short jetty and walked over to the shade of a large lemon tree.

The plump Italian Guide then raised a colourful umbrella and called us together. With a local accent and lots of practised jokes, she informed us we would have a guided tour for an hour and then two hours of free time for lunch and more shopping. With that, she turned and, looking back over her shoulder, called.

"Andiamo, Andiamo", let's go.

Like a small flock of multi-coloured sheep, we dutifully followed her as she took us to lace factories and shops that were so white you were glad to be wearing your sunnies. All the women oohed and aahed, and all the men looked forward to lunch and vino. I wasn't any different on that score. Still, by keeping away from Harrison, I continued to evaluate his fitness, alertness, and ability to focus. His once athletic body was straight and toned except for showing a slight paunch. Without being obvious, he moved like a cat, two or three steps, then a good look around before proceeding again. The formal tour ended, and people headed in various directions. I had realised the group splitting up would make it a lot harder to keep him in sight and me out of sight, but I had to try.

I was thinking: T*his is the prick who ordered Sal to search our room, which resulted in Ramone's murder. He might not have ordered her death or even know about it, but he's as guilty as Sal. I would love to grab him, take him into the bush or behind a shed somewhere and beat the last details of his smuggling ring out of him.* However, I was aware that doing that could jeopardise the whole Op. I wasn't about to waste Ramone's ultimate sacrifice and all our work when we were so close to the end of the trail. For now, my plan was fluid. I wouldn't do anything but observe him until my orders or circumstances changed. Set free by the guide, several of the cruise passengers set off in the same direction. They were like lion cubs adventuring out into the big world, individual but still looking for each other for support. I lagged behind them, using them as a mobile blind between Harrison and myself. This continued for the next fifty or so metres of stores and stalls. Eventually, one couple entered a store, and the others moved to the other side of the alley, leaving me alone and exposed. Harrison didn't seem to be checking behind him and seemed to be moving toward a destination he had in mind rather than shop.

I continued to follow him. This was the hardest tail I had done because we were moving up a closed alley of stores and stalls on both sides. It was challenging to follow Harrison without being obvious. Making matters worse, he suddenly looked around like he was expecting someone. For the seventh or eighth time, I was attempting to look fascinated at some lace or trinket to hide out in the open. I could not tell if Harrison was playing a game with me. I was sure if Sal had told Harrison about me asking questions otherwise. Otherwise, he wouldn't have searched our room on that fateful day. If he knew who I was, he would have noticed me on the excursion ferry. Whatever the case, I still had to follow him. Trying to look innocent, I picked up a lace tablecloth, or at least I think that's what it was. As though I was interested in its quality, I held it up to the light. Then, making a good show of it, I stepped to the right to improve the light. As I did so, a hole appeared in the cloth, dropping the lace item. I then saw a similar hole on the stall owner's forehead. Blood and brain matter was sprayed all over the lace displays behind him.

Being unsure of the origin of the shot, I dropped the tablecloth and rolled under the stall table. I now knew who Harrison had been looking for when he got to a specific part of the market. There was no doubt the shot was meant for me. I knew for sure that if I had stayed there a moment longer, the next shot would duplicate the sad result of the unlucky storekeeper. I crawled under the tent's rear wall and found each stall backed onto another booth facing the opposite direction. However, they had left a small service alley between the rows of tents. I ran down this corridor until I had probably passed Harrison's location. I noted numerous ropes and power chords were traversing the small alley. I stopped and pulled a rope attached to a tent post on the left side of the alley. I then slid to the right between two market tents and waited. I could hear footsteps running towards me coming along the service corridor. As the man reached my location, I wrenched the rope up to ankle height. The assailant crashed into the brick paving face-first. Attempting to protect his face, he shot both his hands out, exposing the hand holding the gun. I stamped on his wrist, and the handgun went flying.

Before he could recover, I was on top of him. I placed one hand on the back of his skull, stuck three fingers in his mouth and pinched a handful of cheek. I twisted it until I heard a sharp crack as the vertebrae in his neck separated. Now he fell on his face, dead. I picked up the handgun and searched his pockets for spare mags and I.D. Now, at least I was armed. I shoved the pistol in my waistband and the extra mag in my pocket. I crawled back towards the market side of the stalls. I got a glimpse of a small tattooed man in a dark blue shirt and white trousers working his way along the line of stalls. The blue shirt was doing an excellent job of hiding it, but I could see that his right hand was pressed into his trouser leg, and I was sure it held a sidearm. The last thing I wanted to do was have a shoot-out, causing more collateral damage by accidentally killing an innocent shopper or another stallholder. I could have nailed him where he stood, but the weapon I now had meant the bullet would pass through him, probably injuring someone behind him. So I held my fire. He continued to nervously work his way along the stalls. He was clearly a pro, switched on looking under the tables and between the different merchant's displays.

I allowed him to pass my position and stood up. I never took my eyes off him, ready to shoot if I had to. I suppose he could not conceive that his target would have ended up behind him. After all, prey runs before the hunter, doesn't it. This fact allowed me to get close to him. Mercy was not a factor; these guys were due. They were there to kill me; there was no doubt about that. I thought I had been following Harrison all day, and it was me that he was leading me to the slaughter. I had been so naive to think I was still under his radar. The blue shirt was still slowly walking along the line of stalls. Diligently, he bent to search under another table of lace items. As he stood up, I placed the barrel of the Beretta PX Storm in a 40 S&W Calibre I had taken from his friend behind his right ear. "Don't make another move." I could tell he understood what I wanted, even if he didn't understand what I had said. I pushed him between two stall tents into the service corridor. I had no desire or plan to talk to him.

So, as soon as we were out of sight. I squeezed the trigger as I touched his skull with the muzzle of the Beretta; the front of his head exploded over the tent. After looking around, I tucked the handgun into my belt and pulled my shirt over it. I squeezed between the tents, entering the main row of merchant stalls. Calming my breathing, I just stood for a moment thinking. I was starting to realise I was out of my depth. So far, I was managing each attack, but with no Intel and no backup, I was running lean. How many more assailants may still be on the island? I had lost Harrison, and I had lost my confidence in regards to following him, now knowing he was onto me.

I looked ahead and was surprised to see Harrison still poking along, looking at merchandise without a care in the world. He was probably confident that this team of hitmen had already ended me. I moved toward him and was on high alert, wondering if I had neutralised the current threat or if there was more to come? Up ahead, I could see Harrison enter a small Taverna. A short stone wall surrounded the hotel's front yard, where diners sat at tables that filled a wide alfresco area shaded by a vast grapevine. Resisting the temptation to rush up to the restaurant, I eventually arrived there. I walked down the three stone steps to the cool, shady eating area. I saw Harrison was ensconced at a corner table facing the street. A few more steps inside, I found myself in a small bar area decorated with fishing nets and wooden crayfish pots. Inside were a few more tables and chairs and a wooden bar with four or five stools along one side of the room. A doorway with a sign directing patrons to some restrooms caught my eye. I headed that way, hoping to find a back door in case I needed one.

As I entered the narrow hallway, I saw three doors fed off it: a Male and Female Bathroom and a red wooden door to places unknown. I hoped this red door would take me outside the building. Moving down the hallway to my left, an attractive Italian woman came out of the Female Bathroom. Smiling shyly, she stepped around me. As she squeezed past me in the narrow passageway, I saw something shiny in her right hand. Reacting instinctively, I tried to slide away from whatever the weapon was. In the tight constraints of the hallway, she made to strike low into my left kidney. Twisting my torso, my attempt to avoid the blade was only partially successful. As I swept my arm down between her and my body, the blade penetrated my left bicep. Excruciating pain shot through my system. However, I recovered instantaneously, using the momentum I allowed my body to continue rotating. I led with my right fist and connected with her forearm, causing her to drop the long-handled Stiletto dagger. I followed with a quick left that caught the side of her head. She staggered a little, but she surprised me with her toughness and answered my attack with three quick punches of her own.

The strikes were power-trained and well-aimed, blocking as best I could, her second hit caught me just above my left eye. Blood was flowing freely from the now open cut. I couldn't see out of that eye. I skipped away from the onslaught, knowing I was fighting a well-trained, disciplined assassin. I had to be able to see properly. I quickly wiped my eyes to restore vision. A change in tactics was called for, so I stepped into her. I grabbed her by the shoulders, drawing the assailant close to my body, limiting her ability to punch. I had to be quick before she could knee me in the groin, which was the obvious move on her part.

Holding her tightly, I swung her into the wall and, with all my strength, crushed her pretty face as it hit the old stone. I felt her collapse in my arms and let her fall to the cobblestone floor. Concerned she may come to and come after me again, I picked up the red-hilted Stiletto. These Italian knives were not made for cutting. I pushed the dagger into her throat where her collar bones met, and after wiping my prints off it, I left it there.

I had had enough. I tried the red door and found it to be unlocked. The old hinges complained a little as I opened it. Several stone steps led to a small private courtyard with a wrought iron table and two chairs. It looked like the staff used it for their breaks and to have a smoke. I carried the dead assassin's lifeless body into the private courtyard. I sat her on one of the wrought iron chairs, propped against the wall. I saw a near-new cigarette in the ashtray and placed it between her fingers. I had changed my mind. Using my handkerchief, I removed the dagger from her neck and tossed it over the garden wall. Hopefully, anyone looking into the courtyard would simply see a lady reclining in the shade, enjoying a smoke.

I went back into the Tavern and entered the bathroom. I had limited resources, but I had to patch up my bleeding bicep if I was going to get back on the cruise ship without Security bailing me up. I removed my shirt and singlet and tore the undergarment into a makeshift bandage. The filthy sink ran pink as I washed the blood from the wound on my arm. Luckily, it wasn't too deep, but stung like a thousand wasps. The cut above my eye was small and had stopped bleeding, so the wound was nearly invisible when I cleaned it. After drying the damage with a paper towel, I bandaged my arm and put my shirt back on. Looking in the bathroom mirror, I could still see some blood on my sleeve, but I *was* looking for it. Back out the red door and into the dappled sunlight of the courtyard. I headed past the lady, having her last ever smoke. With five quick steps, I was back on the main path between the brightly coloured shops and stalls. I was now in survival mode. Doing anything with Harrison would have to wait.

I had a few things to think about, so I headed back to the jetty, buying a cold Castello Di Udine Birra Moretti, a local beer from a street vendor on the way. I sat on a stone bench under a windswept tree and thanked God I was alive to do so. I thought about the implications of the last few hours. I thought I was tracking Harrison and had fluid plans: kidnap him to interrogate or observe him. If he needed some persuasion, I would have provided this with pleasure. However, the attacks on me told me several things. Firstly, Sal had obviously discussed me with his 'boss' Harrison. Secondly, Harrison was not reluctant to order extreme violence to solve any threat to himself or his enterprise. His ordering the three assassins to kill me while on the Burano excursion was proof of that. Thirdly, it was clear he had deadly contacts to order a hit so quickly and with such a deadly team as I had just eliminated. I was totally convinced the three were not locals, some fishermen and a waitress who killed people as a second job. No, they were too skilled, too slick and too well-armed. This meant they had been rushed to Burano Island from parts unknown in time to ambush me during this cruise excursion. This was no easy feat. I wondered *if our Mr Harrison was just a retired businessman or something much more sinister.*

I saw our Guide approaching the tree I was sheltering under and smiled at her, lifting the remnants of my Birra in a salute; she waved.

"May I join you, Signore?" she asked in her sultry Italian tone.

"Of course, please," I said, gesturing with my hand as I made room for her on the cool stone bench I was sitting on. I ensured she sat beside my good arm, hoping she would overlook the blood stain on the other.

"How did you enjoy my Burano? It is truly a beautiful island, no?" She enquired. Smiling, I replied. "It sure is Signora; the beauty of it all nearly killed me."

Not understanding my real meaning, she laughed happily at this comment. The guide continued.

"Oh, that makes me very happy to hear. I was born just down this path. I love this place."

Nodding, I agreed. "I can understand that. It is wonderful."

I could see the other passengers working their way back to where we were sitting near the jetty just behind us. The women were smiling and talking. While the men looked tired, laden with several shopping bags filled with lace items, I assumed.

I noted Harrison wasn't amongst them and was mindful that the return ferry was scheduled to pick us up in the next few minutes. As it had done thousands of times before, the small boat arrived, turned away from the island, and then reversed alongside the jetty. Once again, a crew member jumped out and secured the ropes. Because the tide had changed, he slid the small gangplank across the gap between the ferry and wharf and then stood aside. I watched all this, and as I embarked with the tour group, I walked straight into Harrison. Distracted by the ferry, I hadn't seen him approach the group at the last minute. And because I was surrounded by my fellow passengers, he had not seen me sitting amongst them. A look of shocked surprise flew across his face and disappeared just as quickly, but I had seen it. He hadn't expected me to make it back to this ferry or anywhere else. I hadn't really needed any confirmation of my thoughts about Harrison and the attempted hit on my life. Still, he had undoubtedly reacted with that surprised look. He recovered quickly and turned to walk across the gangplank. I let a few more tourists get between us and boarded the ferry. We arrived back at PIER Stazione Marittima and, like weary sheep, climbed the multi-story gangplank onto the cruise ship. After showing our bar-coded cabin card and the obligatory hand sanitising, we found ourselves at the Security checkpoint.

Once again, our cards were scanned, and then any shopping bags or backpacks were sent through an X-ray machine like those used in every airport. I complied with all these processes and was relieved to avoid any discussion about my injured arm. I walked through the metal detector arch and thought, *I'm home free.*

"Sir, is that blood on your sleeve?" The accented question came from a well-built, possibly Croatian Security Guard.

Smiling, I recovered. "Oh yeah, it sure is. I feel pretty stupid. I caught my arm on a nail at one of the stalls and tore a bit of a hole. I'll be fine after a shower and a couple of band-aids."

Fulfilling his duty of care. "Sir, it might be wiser to visit the Doc. I wouldn't want to get infected or something."

Wanting to end the discussion, I said.

"Thanks, you're probably right." I smiled and started walking towards the lift, praying that was the end of it.

Of course I ignored his advice, and returned to my cabin. Ramone had told me in case I ever needed it, she always travelled with a good first aid kit. I found it in her bag and patched myself up, grateful for a neat stiletto puncture rather than a gash requiring stitches. I washed the wound with J.D. and then threw down two quick swigs of Jack Daniels. I figured I had earned them. I didn't really care if I hadn't. My grumbling stomach reminded me that I had been too busy while visiting the Tavern to enjoy their famous marinara. It may have been lunchtime on that island excursion, but I was the only thing on the menu. Even though I was OK. I began to feel a little dizzy, perhaps shock or stress caused by fatigue. Sugar always helps with any residual shock. A quick visit to the buffet, including some dessert, would clear my head and make me feel a little better. As I walked through the restaurant entrance, "Washy, washy." The lovely Filipino crew member sang as she squirted hand sanitiser onto my open palms. After a good round of the buffet, including two Crème Broulees, I felt so good I made my way to the back deck bar. I had to think through some things, so I settled in with a J.D. to watch the impressive ship's wake.

CHAPTER 13

I awoke with a slight hangover. I ordered room service and, hit the shower and was fully dressed by the time my coffee and eggs for two arrived. That worked and now feeling a lot better, I left my cabin. Today, I had a plan to access the owner's storage units. I couldn't impersonate a crew member, but I had chosen clothing that a CCTV's casual glance could suggest I was crew. Working my way to the stern of the enormous floating hotel, I headed to the lower decks. After what happened on Burano Island, I figured my cover being virtually non-existent. I had no way of knowing how many baddies I was up against, so another attempt on my life was highly possible. This slowed me down a bit. From now on, I would be forced into circling the deck and doubling back several times to see if I was followed. Surprisingly, I seemed alone, yet I remained alert and recommenced my trip down to the lower decks that were out of bounds to passengers. I used staircases to avoid the CCTV surveillance in each Lift Foyer. Fire Evacuation Plans mounted on the landing wall of each stairwell enabled me to check my progress.

Finally, I was at my target destination. I unlatched the steel door and stepped over the Gunwale, entering a spacious cargo hold sectioned off into secured areas, each the size of a Sea Container. I had expected a dark, stale, diesel-smelling cargo hold, but this was a spotless, freshly painted, well-lit, and ventilated room. Using a vertical steel bracing post as cover, I surveyed the cargo hold for security cameras. Finding none, I moved to a wall. I surmised that the security depended on physical attributes rather than technology. They probably relied on the fact the deck was unknown to most people and off-limit to all the passengers except the four residents and, of course, the crew. All the items were stored behind heavy-duty wire and locks. I could see eight secured areas, four on either side of an alley wide enough to use a forklift. Four appeared to be for ship's cargo, probably holding high-value goods such as Duty-Free stock, maybe booze. I walked into the central alley. As I suspected, one was filled with cartons of beer, wine and spirits from around the world. Another had a clipboard hanging on the gate. This one appeared to hold shelves stocked with silver, such as cutlery, platters, jugs and so on.

I moved across the alley to the other four storage bays. Knowing only four owner cabins were on board, I walked along that side, reading the identifying placards attached to the strong steel gate at the front of each storage unit. This gate, or, more precisely, the front wall of each storage unit, had a chain and lock. When unlocked, it would slide across, enabling access into the secured area and the ability to place or remove items within the unit. One unit had some cartons at the rear of the cage. Two cages were utterly empty. There were no names on the placards, however, they were identified by their cabin numbers.

I found Harrison's Number 1203 between the two empty areas. Six large wooden crates fully occupied Harrison's secured site. A forklift must have stacked the crates as they were stacked up two high. I took the small lock-picking gun out of my pocket. I had found it and the other burglar tools I would need amongst Ramone's gear when I had grabbed the first aid kit. Starting to work it, I inserted the picks where the key would usually go and pressed the trigger. After about twenty seconds, the whirring and clicking sounds stopped with a loud click as the shiny padlock sprang open. I pushed the sliding steel gate sideways, just wide enough for me to squeeze into the crowded enclosure. Then, I closed the gate behind me as my excitement level began to rise.

I sidled past the front boxes that were as tall as me and was pleased to find a space behind the stacked crates at the back of the pen. This afforded me a place to work hidden from anyone wandering past the two rows of secured yards. I had brought a small electric drill, which I withdrew from my pocket and began to drill a hole into the nearest box. I gently blew on the hole as it formed, pushing the sawdust inside the crate to ensure I didn't leave any sign outside. The box was strong but not overly thick. The drill bit broke through and was free in the cavity within. I withdrew the little drill. Suddenly, I could hear two women talking in rapid Filipino, their voices getting louder as they got closer. Praying I was hidden from all directions, I froze. The women stopped outside my enclosure and were talking and laughing. Then I heard one of the steel gates screech as they slid it open, followed by the clinking sound of them handling bottles. After a few minutes, the gate creaked shut, and the sound of the women's voices receded to nothing.

Re-focusing, I inserted a small tube-like device like a small diameter hose. On one end of the tube was a tiny lens with a built-in light, and on the other end, an eyepiece. The instrument was like the spy hole in most hotel doors, except this peep-hole, when lit up, magnified and provided a clear image of its vision area. I then flicked a switch that illuminated the inside of the box. I put the eyepiece to my eye and moved the tube around to change the sight picture. I couldn't interpret what I was looking at in terms of a complete item, as I could only see some of it. However, I could see blue paint and the black and white of hieroglyphic figures. It must have been a large piece, maybe a statue or perhaps even a sarcophagus. Whatever it was, it provided all the evidence I needed to pin Harrison's skin to the wall. I was thankful that Ramone had packed all this covert search gear. I took some pictures through the straw and reversed my trip into the secure lock-up.

Pulling over the sliding wire gate I locked it up again. From there, I returned to my cabin, but only after taking several detours to see if I had picked any up followers. There were none, so headed to my level and entered my cabin. The existence of the antiquities confirmed our suspicions and proved all our theories regarding using cruise ships for smuggling to be correct. The next objective was to follow this smuggling pipeline further up to the money. I had played a part in this, but I was thrilled that all our work and, most importantly, Ramone's life had not been wasted on an incorrect theory. From this Intel, they would identify the destination and its dealers. Then, hopefully, the final objective: the experts would follow the money trail.

They would discover the bank accounts and hopefully arrest anyone associated with these accounts. And more importantly, the Hawala contacts, which were essentially the same as accounts but so much harder to trace and identify. The final phase was that these contacts and accounts should eventually lead the Agency to each terrorist organisation funded in this manner.

I was concerned I may have spooked Harrison by my presence on the ship, resulting in his minions dumping the evidence overboard. However, I now knew that the size of these items and the structure of the cruise ship itself made this impossible. I was relieved because that meant that even though Harrison was alerted and probably worried, he was clearly limited and unable to destroy the major evidence. Although I hadn't confirmed the specific details of the cargo he was smuggling, the size and number of the crates suggested big-ticket items. I could only imagine the value of this shipment, but those crates had to hold big ticket items. Some players would be counting the dollars, the others counting guns and bullets. This was especially so after the Feds in New York had already restricted their income stream by impounding their last shipment.

As I walked back to my cabin, I mentally regrouped. Sitting on the balcony i thought it all through; *From where I had started back in Canberra, Australia, to now, Intel-wise, the mission has been a great success. However, for a lot of the time, I was stumbling along, we were fortunate that the small leads led me to the goal. To me, it seemed the mission never had a defined target. We discovered a lot about smuggling artefacts. But finally, it was all starting to come together and make sense. Ramone and I had identified several diverse layers of this smuggling economy. We had discovered some of the people finding and digging up the artefacts. From the ancient tombs of Petra, on the highway where a crumpled business card taken from an assassin's wallet that led to Cairo. This was where we collected Intel that cracked the mission wide open.*

Then, the realisation that Dubai was one of the busiest legitimate ports in the world, but also had a dark side. Our fat smuggler from the papyrus company had used this famous port as a smuggling conduit for a range of contraband. Then he had come up with an idea not previously thought of. Of all places, a magnificent luxury cruise ship was unwittingly providing the facilities to transport these stolen antiquities. By recruiting a suite owner, he sidestepped the ship's security system and hid large items in the open recruiting a supposed benign Retiree living in luxury. However, the details were not yet apparent by the ship's route where the antiquities would be unloaded. It was, however, sure that the artefacts would be offered to buyers in New York or London and around the globe.

Intel-wise, I believed I was probably at the end of my mission brief. One way or another, every atom of me wanted to end Harrison. Not just because he had ordered and coordinated the attempt on my life, but more importantly, I was sure he was ultimately responsible for Ramone's and Maria's deaths. Not to mention the many future deaths associated with his being part of the funding machine of who knows how many terrorist outfits. He didn't deserve to live, but maybe keeping him vertical a little longer may serve a higher purpose in identifying his masters and or customers. It is better to find out who bought the items and who the money went to or through.

Most valuable would be the Hawala contacts, some of which may have helped finance 911. Those who flew under the money transfer radar, those faceless people all over the world who are trusted enough by the terrorist groups to guarantee payment. I couldn't see what more I could do as my cover was in tatters. Harrison knew who and, in a way, what I was. But, at the same time, I knew the same about him. He was a murderer and a stolen antiquities smuggler. And I knew where he stored the goods. The trouble was, what could I do about it? If the contraband were drugs, I would have already thrown it into the ocean.

But in reality, the pieces in the storage area must be protected by everyone. By the smugglers and dealers for the antiquities' dollar value. By the terrorists because of their value translated in terms of arms and ammo. However, there was a massive irony in play. There was also a need to protect them by the legitimate authorities for the altruistic, a more universal reason that these ancient items must be preserved for all mankind. That way, the people of the world now and future generations could view them in museums. Here, they would be stored and cared for by trained curators and not neglected in the den of some private collector. On board, we were all tied up by the unique circumstances. The illegal cargo wasn't going anywhere until we docked in New York. So, there was nothing to do regarding the antiquities stored below. However, there was always Harrison's attitude about me. The way I figured it, Harrison had no choice. He would continue trying to eliminate me. This had to be a good move for him or them; the smuggler would have to assume I had reported to someone, but it still made sense for him to remove any further threat. I was unsure if he still had the resources to organise a hit on me while on board now Sal had been removed from play. This was an unusual reality, a reversal of my normal operations. I was usually the one trying to kill a baddie somewhere, but here I was the target this time.

This mission continued to be way outside my normal routine operations. I was used to clear missions: go here, eliminate Tango 1 and come home. The only variable was, should I make it look like an accident, or did I send an unmistakable message by making it a blunt and apparent assassination? My more straightforward mission was to go here, pick up this package, and return home again. This mission had gone on and on undercover, different locations and no clear target. Nothing simple about this one. Even considering what had been achieved, I still couldn't see a definite end of mission, especially when I was answering to the N.S.C. (National Security Centre) back in Australia and the C.I.A. in the U.S.A. I hated the idea, but I figured I would let someone at a higher pay level than me decide from here. SITREP time, I phoned Agent Munroe on Ramone's Sat phone.

Munroe answered in a happier way than I had ever heard him speak.

"Hey, what's happening? Have you got that evidence we need?"

"Yeah, Munroe, I looked at Harrison's storage lock up. We know he's got artefacts crated up in there. I couldn't identify the item, but I saw hieroglyphics and blue paint seemed right for what we were looking for."

The joy in his voice was unmistakable. "Well, Merry Christmas. Were you able to get some shots?"

"Yeah, I gotta few. I'll send them to you ASAP. Your guys should be able to confirm what the piece is. I could only glimpse a small part from that small spy hole, but the item is larger than me."

Munroe just kept sounding happier every time I spoke. "Awesome, buddy."

I continued. "The reason I phoned is what do I do now? Harrison knows me, and it may be just a matter of time before it's my turn to become fish food. He might not know all the details, but one way or another, he must see it as a good plan to get rid of me. I was wondering what you thought about me getting some help. Or better still send home. If not, maybe someone to cover my back but also to keep surveillance on Harrison. Munroe quickly returned his usual non-committal tone.

"Listen, buddy. I'll think about it and let you know, OK, I better go, talk soon."

The line went dead, and I felt very, very alone.

The C.I.A. Agent took four hours to devise a plan and bounce it off his Boss, Assistant Director Myers. When he phoned back, it took me four seconds to think he was a friggin idiot.

Monroe put on his confident act. "OK, now, buddy, I want you to listen. Hear me out before you get excited, OK?"

With a sinking feeling, I agreed to listen. "Yeah, OK, I gotta tell you I am always worried when someone says that. OK, what have you come up with?"

Monroe continued. "Well, I know it's goin to sound fuckin strange, but we want to give you more support, but we don't want you to know who it is. Now, hang on, boy, let me explain, OK.

"I have been talking to your controls in O.Z., and they agree with me that we have no idea how many baddies are on board. We figured our Agent could stay under the radar more easily if you two weren't hanging out or being seen talking too much. This is what we...."

I lost it. "No way, are you fuckin out of your mind? Now I know why they call you Special."

He was on a roll, ignoring my sarcasm. He continued like I hadn't spoken.

"Anyway, this is what we are thinking: he can watch your back, the baddies will think you're on your own and show themselves. And this guy is a surveillance expert so we can ramp up the Intel collection. I know it's a stretch. You with me so far?"

I was bordering at lost for words.

"Whoever thought of this was off their friggin rocker. I won't know who is a white hat or black hat that could be dangerous for everyone."

Again, Special Agent Munroe continued as if I hadn't spoken. "No, I am for serious. The Brass back in O.Z. have approved it this way and a..... (I could hear a keyboard clicking as he found the name). Some Colonel.......Oh yeah, Goodrich or something is on board, too."

He kept selling the idea to me. "Good news, big fella, the guy we are sending is better than good at this shit. You'll thank me for this plan."

I grunted my surrender. "I seriously doubt that. I suppose I have no choice anyway."

Laughing, Munroe continued. "Roger that. He will board at the next port, Dubrovnik." A click, and he was gone.

As he terminated the call, you couldn't tell from how he spoke to Wallace, but Munroe was very worried about the Australian and the mission. For the second time that day, he punched in a series of numbers that put him in direct contact with Delta Force HQ Fort Bragg. Earlier, he had spoken to the Ops Officer there, discussing the possible mission.

The D.F. phone answered on the second ring. "This is Colonel Randolph."

Munroe had worked with the Colonel for nearly twenty years off and on. They had been in harm's way together a few times and shared as much trust as anyone could in their chosen field ever did.

"Ivan, did I wake you? You're so fuckin old you probably need a nanny nap every day about this time."

The Delta Force Officer was just as relaxed. "Amazing, you called right at this minute. I was just wondering how my tax dollar was being wasted. I guess I know now, what do you want? Is it a go?"

Munroe smiled. "Yeah, buddy, have your boy on that ship ASAP. All his crew papers and boarding details await him when he checks in at the airport."

The Delta Force veteran had heard it all before. "Now listen, Munroe, are you sure you want him to operate without your man's knowledge of his identity? It seems a bit strange to me, even dangerous in some scenarios?"

Munroe was firm. "You grunts are all the same, he said the same thing. Ivan, it's the way I want it played for now. His cover is blown. This way, your Operative stays clean by not being seen with him."

The Colonel conceded. "You're using him as bait aren't you? That makes some sense, I guess."

Munroe smiled. "To be honest, the whole plan is highly fluid. I don't want all the players in the know, at least for now. I need your guy to work an overwatch for Wallace/ Johnson, have his back, see if he's being followed, you know the drill. I was going to get him on board at Dubrovnik (Croatia), and in fact, that's what I told Wallace. But I've been thinking we get him on in Venice; otherwise, our Aussie is on his own too long. Who knows what they will try to pull after the attack on Burano Island? Ivan buddy, one other thing...."

The Delta Force Officer was understandably cynical. "Munroe, I can feel your hand unzipping my fly. What have you got up your sleeve next?"

"No, no, Ivan, nothing scary. I was just going to say I would get your man down here for a briefing, but rushing him into Venice, no chance. I'll email the file to you. Urgent. Any questions, get him to call me."

As always, the Colonel was first a soldier, and a soldier followed orders.

"Roger all that, until further notice, my Op will take care of Wallace but not make contact without being ordered to. He'll also get the smuggler's room bugged and trackers on the artefacts. Keep in touch, Munroe, talk soon. Out." and he was gone.

Munroe sat there looking at his computer screen but did not see a single character. He had some serious thinking to do. *Close the mission down and count the Intel and baddies they had collected on the way, or push it a little harder. And if he did keep it going, where to from here?*

CHAPTER 14

I was finishing a breakfast of crispy Canadian bacon and pancakes smothered in Maple syrup washed down with several cups of strong black coffee. I could feel the cruise liner's powerful mid-engine slowly push the ship away from the pier. Once clear, we sailed majestically from Venice past Burano Island and entered the open sea. In the next few days, we were destined first for Dubrovnik (Croatia) and then onto Athens, Santorini, with some passengers eventually disembarking in Barcelona.

The Captain's Nordic accent over the ship's Public system interrupted my thoughts.

"Good morning, ladies and gentlemen, to all our passengers who have stayed on with us. I hope you have enjoyed beautiful Venice. And, those of you who joined us last night, I trust you have now settled in comfortably."

The Captain continued. "Some of our team have left us for well-earned leave, and other highly trained crew have replaced them. Please let the new crew members know if there is anything you need. We now begin our Eastern Mediterranean and Holy Land Cruise. Of course, your daily newsletter will keep you informed. Maritime Law requires all passengers to attend our Life Boat Drill, which is scheduled for this afternoon. Your cabin Steward has placed the details on your bed with the time and your reporting station. Enjoy yourselves, everyone, and I will try to say hello as I move around the ship."

As I munched on my pancakes, I was thinking; *I'm on my own until Dubrovnik, so if I had brains, I should keep my head down and keep a loose surveillance of our pensioner cum smuggler Mr Harrison. Not knowing what resources he had, I figured having failed to kill me on the island, I had to expect he would try again. That's what I would do.*

I made a mental note that I would have to manage the Life Boat Drill regarding Ramone's absence, as thus far my deception had succeeded. So far no one had realised I was on my own.

Up on Deck Twelve in a galley adjacent to the buffet area, the newest crew member was sweating away. He arched his back and swept his long blonde fringe from his tanned forehead. He had just raised the two stainless steel bars opening the giant commercial dishwasher. Opening the heavy door resulted in another wave of hot, wet steam flooding over him, the ninth such load for the shift so far. Anyone observing would see a young, fit-looking fellow who was washing dishes. He could be, at best a labourer, lowly born, with a minimum education and limited prospects. They would have been very, very wrong. Ben Winfrey, nicknamed Oprah for obvious reasons, held a dual Post Graduate Degrees, spoke four languages, and had excelled in every aspect of his Military career.

This included six years in the United States Marine Corps and being accepted as an Operative in Delta Force. He was highly trained in long-range and short-range weapons, several styles of martial arts and surveillance operations, both mobile or static, human or technical. He was also highly skilled in deploying and piloting RPAS (Remotely Piloted Aerial Systems), which most people call Drones. This menial job, washing dishes, suited his primary mission as it had set periods around meal times. This allowed him the freedom he needed. In such a subservient role, he was virtually unnoticeable and, therefore, invisible. Winfrey had already located the suite owned by Tango One, Harrison, and the cabin occupied by Principal One, Mr Wallace/Johnson. He had also started to orientate himself, identifying locations around the ship where he could over-watch without being seen or appearing obvious to anyone. As Winfrey emptied the industrial dishwasher, the C.I.A. Agent returned to his mission briefing. Even that didn't follow in the usual way of doing things. Winfrey had tried to look like he was concentrating as

Colonel Randolph explained why he was talking to him instead of Special Agent Munroe. He had found it strange not to have a proper briefing from Munroe. His mind drifted away from the dish-washing, he imagined how it would have gone if the C.I.A. Special Agent had delivered the briefing.

"Now Lieutenant Winfrey (external Management never used nicknames as it might seem too personal), now you're going on a cruise, but don't think for a New York minute it'll be cruisy for you." Blah, Blah, Blah Winfrey was so glad he didn't have to put up with Munroe's shit. In his experience, C.I.A. people always felt obligated to speak down to anyone in the Military.

Winfrey was grateful that his own Colonel, instead of Agent Munroe, was doing the briefing and then let him read the file. The Colonel continued.

"Now Oprah, our Aussie friend, has done some great work identifying the Tango, a guy called Harrison. For all intents and purposes, he looks like a rich old guy living the dream on a cruise ship. Make no mistake, he's a grubby smuggler and has organised one if not two attempted hits on our friendly, plus he ordered the murders of at least one C.I.A. Agent and a civilian."

Colonel Randolph nodded to himself and continued.

"You have a three-stage mission. 1. As soon as you can, plant some listening devices in the Tango's cabin. We are banking on him being in contact with his handlers or buyers. Normal tracing doesn't work because every call goes through the ship's central comms system. This means the actual caller can't be traced. Once you've set those bugs, at least we can listen to that side of the communication. Maybe we can pick up some Intel, a name, a date, or something Via satellite. Knowing exactly when he's on that call, we might even be able to trace it to him as further evidence." The briefing continued. "2. We figure you'll have time before they unload the artefacts, but the second part is to install those tracking devices in the crates our

Aussie friend located. 3. Winfrey, until further notice, you must covertly protect that Aussie Agent named Steve Wallace. He is running under the name of Robert Johnson, a cruise passenger. He's already proven he can look after himself. But we both know that he may be outnumbered, distracted, or just unlucky next time. So, I want you stuck on him as much as possible; do whatever you need to do to keep him safe. OK?"

"Copy that, Sir, but what do you mean covertly?" Winfrey responded."

Looking tired, the Colonel answered. "The deal is we don't want Johnson or the enemy to know you are there."

Winfrey put on his poker face and nodded, but he was thinking that could be interesting in some situations. *How does Principal Wallace know who to shoot or hit when it hits the fan?*

The Colonel could see the D.F. Officer thinking. "Yeah, I know, that could get tricky; if he notices you, he will probably think you are there to hit him. Anyway, that's the deal we have to play."

Winfrey, a soldier, accepted his lot. "Copy that, Sir."

Colonel Randolph started winding up the briefing.

"OK, read the file, and you're wheels up in three hours. It will be pretty tight, but your cover is solid, and I know you are quick to adapt. Any questions?"

Randolph stood up and arched his shoulders unsuccessfully, trying to release some tension.

"No, Sir, maybe I might have some after I read the file."

The Colonel nodded. "I'll answer them if possible; if we can't, we will contact Agent Munroe."

Grabbing a coffee, Winfrey went to the workstation he had been allocated and began studying the Operational File.

Less than twenty-four hours later, the Southern Star was still moored in Venice. Two athletic-looking young men struggled up the ramp, carrying a bag in each hand. Although above average height and athletically built, the blonde man was dwarfed by the second man, who was well over six foot six and built like a professional wrestler.

Ascending the crew's gangplank, the giant exclaimed. "Man, look at the size of this fuckin boat."

The smaller one, taking in the fantastic scale of the gaily painted cruise ship, had to agree. "It's friggin amazing!"

One of the Security Officers overheard their comments. "Hey, Shrek, don't let them sailor boys hear you call it a boat."

With a smile the Filipino. "If you want to stay out of trouble, call it a ship, yes?"

Both new crew members showed their papers and were issued special crew swipe cards that were waiting for them. Security ex-rayed their bags without concern, and the two men headed for the lift.

Just in case the security check to get on board noticed them, the tech boys had secreted the state-of-the-art listening devices within his portable stereo. With a joke to the Filipino Security Officer, he stepped through the archway of the metal detector. The broad-shouldered Officer manning the detector smiled and said. "You only just made it, man; we're casting off ASAP."

Winfrey laughed. "Yeah, it was last minute, alright." He thanked the man as he picked up his bags. He knew he wasn't rostered on until dinner tonight, so he settled in. Enjoying a coffee poured from the crew galley bench, Winfrey walked over to the two-seater table and took out a copy of the ship's itinerary. He had never had to rush as much as he had to get on board in Venice. There was a sea day tomorrow and then Tuesday a day tour of Dubrovnik for the passengers. Then, another day at sea, Athens, Greece and the famous Santorini.

Even though he had only just started working on board, Winfrey planned to get the listening devices in Harrisons' room during dinner this evening. Working in catering, he had already been able to access the dining register and knew the wealthy smuggler's dinner reservation time. It had to be at dinner tonight as Harrison ate breakfast and lunch in his suite. The Delta Force Lieutenant hoped that by Santorini, Harrison would have talked to his Control, and back in Virginia, they would have enough Intel to close the onboard phase of the operation down. He was a born optimist, expecting everybody home safe, terrorists running out of ammunition within hours. Yeah, right. Deep down, he knew this was unrealistic, but this approach had always kept him going.

Winfrey was hard at it three hours later, establishing his cover job. Being trained as a dish bitch was a bit insulting, but all new staff got training. The young man demonstrating the dish washing routine was thorough, but Winfrey's mind was elsewhere. He was keen to get the listening devices in the target's cabin and wondered how to get away during dinner, the busiest period in the galley. It may have been mundane, but it would be a challenge. One way or another, he had to get to that owner's suite while Harrison was at dinner tonight. The galley Supervisor was an overweight, bald, sweating man who swore and cursed more often than he spoke ordinary words, all with a strong Eastern European accent. He had all but ignored Winfrey's arrival to the team, not even accepting the younger man's hand when it was offered. The Supervisor hadn't been seen since he had left him in front of the industrial twin-door dishwasher.

One hour into the dinner rush, the Supervisor walked by. Winfrey, slumping his broad shoulders and leaving his hair dishevelled, braced himself for a mouthful. "Boss, I know I'm brand new, but I feel terrible. I don't think it's like sea sick, but I'm really dizzy. Maybe all the rush to get on board, I dunno."

His Boss sarcastically spat out his words. "You are fuckin jokin; you just got here. Every time they do it to me. They replace a Filipino workhorse with some surfie that can't fuckin hack it, first shift. Ha!

You gotta get used to the heat and steam, my poor little boy. He spat sarcastically.

Winfrey whimpered. "I'm sorry, Boss. I'll be OK from now on, I promise."

Taking a step closer to the Delta Force Officer. "Yeah, alright, Princess, just you get all them fuckin dishes and silver loaded and then go and have a little lie-down." Wagging a huge meaty finger in Winfrey's face, he yelled. "Just make sure you are bright and shiny for breakfast; clean up, right?"

Winfrey answered. "For sure, Boss. I, I, I, I'm sorry Boss." Winfrey stuttered as he staggered out of the steamy wash-up area and, unbeknown to his Boss, headed for Harrison's suite. He had brought a bag containing the listening and tracking devices and a long-billed cap, which he now retrieved from it. Pulling the cap low on his head, Winfrey kept his eyes on the multi-colour carpet to avoid the CCTVs. From the galley to the owner's suites was quite a distance, so he headed off. But first, he visited the crew change room and borrowed a cleaner's cabin entrance swipe card from a uniform hanging on a wall hook. He also threw on a white coat to cover his steam soaked uniform. Winfrey was banking on Harrison being out of his suite. However, just to be sure, he knocked on the cabin door and waited a few moments. Using the entry card, the C.I.A. Agent swiped it, and the door lock opened. He was in.

As Winfrey made a quick assessment of the stateroom, he thought, *this is a lot easier than my usual gig in some drug dealer's ten-bedroom home or some African Dictator's office suites. Sure, this is opulent and large compared to a typical cabin. But the cabin layout still contained enough to focus the devices where Harrison would spend most of his time.* He quickly installed the four separate listening devices without the danger of creating any dead zones. Happy with his work, the Agent opened the stateroom door, looked up and down the two-hundred-metre-long hallway and, finding it clear, slipped out of the room. Never one to waste an opportunity such as his temporary freedom from his dish washing duties, he decided to complete the second part of his mission instead of returning to his tiny cabin.

Once again, Winfrey pulled his cap down and headed for the cargo hold. Unknowingly, he retraced the same route Wallace had taken when he discovered the artefact-filled crates. Winfrey had read the C.I.A. report summarising everything the Australian Agent had passed on. He was impressed by this Aussie, who was clearly a good operator. The Op file had stated there were four wooden boxes all side by side and that Wallace had drilled a hole in each one to confirm the crate's contents. This suited the Agent as it saved him from searching the cargo hold and meant he wouldn't have to repeat the drilling process to insert the tracking devices. Wallace's work meant minimum time near the crates, and only one hole reduced the likelihood of discovery; luck favoured the well-prepared. He arrived at the storage area; it was precisely how Wallace's report had described it. Winfrey walked straight to Harrison's fenced area, and, using his pick set, he quickly opened the storage cage. Approaching the first crate, he moved to the rear of it and, after a short search, found the hole previously drilled by the Aussie. Winfrey inserted the small tracking device through this same hole. He repeated the process for each crate. The C.I.A. Agent looked around to ensure there was no sign of him being there. Satisfied, he re-locked the gate and climbed up the steel stairs. Smiling, he headed for his small cabin, knowing the Tech requirements of the mission were completed. He would contact Colonel Randolph to confirm the listening devices and the trackers were functioning successfully and then concentrate on looking after the Pricipal Mr Wallace / Mr Johnson.

CHAPTER 15

I was used to being more focused; here is your target: get close, do the hit and go home. This mission had been all over the place and had dragged on. Now, in a holding pattern, it was over for me. I was on a cruise ship with basically nothing to do. However, I had been in too many dangerous situations to be lulled into any false sense of safety. I wasn't about to relax and act like I was on holiday like my fellow passengers. But it was hard. I was treading water. I didn't know whether I was still hunting or bait for some other hunter.

I walked to the back bar on Deck 12, and the barman named Rushane smiled over the cocktail blender.

"Welcome Mr Rob the usual J.D. and Coke, marn?" he asked in his deep Jamaican tone. How yah goin marn, you still in trouble with your woman?

Keeping up the pretence that Ramone was OK, I made a joke and felt so shallow, but I had to be consistent.

"You know how it is Rushy, 'no woman no cry', I am still in trouble, only the depth varies."

He laughed and handed me my drink.

"Ah, I miss Bob Marley marn, I really do. I loved that song." With that, he started singing. "No woman, no cry", repeating it in a slow reggae rhythm.

I wanted to do some thinking, so I wandered over to an empty table and, looked at the ship's huge wake and emptied half my glass in one pull.

In New York, Jonathan Sherwood was on the phone. His mind was anywhere but focused on his current call. His thirty-four-storied luxurious office suite window provided an ever-changing, ever-moving view of the harbour. And he was looking forward to the auction scheduled the following day. He figured it should clear him close to half a million. He smiled and thought, Amazing, *I still make that sort of money, and everything on the programme was legit.* He loved that he could weave his legitimate business in amongst his shady antiquities trade. If all goes well, his next auction will include both. Sherwood had more money than he could ever spend but still wanted more. It was only natural. The money was important. But deep down, even having to deal with either dumb scum like Harrison or people who were threateningly dangerous was a nice change from the predictable, mundane world he usually operated in. He enjoyed the buzz.

Still only half listening to Harrison phoning from the cruise ship, Sherwood was thinking; U*sing these amateurs was worth a try, but it had sure proven to be a high-maintenance exercise. It could still work, but never again with Harrison, who continued to whine.*

"Yeah, well, like I was saying, when will I get some support with this guy Johnson? He knows too much. None of us want any disruption when we arrive at your end."

This business had corrupted the New York society businessman. He had become a ruthless smuggler, even though he would never dirty his own manicured hands with murderer. Sherwood had seriously contemplated having Harrison taken out at the same time as this Johnson character. He decided killing the annoying cruiser was necessary, but it would only happen after the cargo arrived. As it was, the antique dealer had concerns about the number of bodies or missing people already accumulated on this cruise. He was still amazed that numerous deaths or disappearances could be so readily accepted due to 'incidents' being common on these huge floating hotels. He'd had enough of this guy.

"OK, Harrison, just sit tight; we have to assume whoever this nuisance Johnson is or whatever his real name is has reported to someone. We have time, but we must eliminate him and make some changes to ensure a smooth delivery. As we speak, I have a man on board, so just continue as normal, and we will be in touch."

"OK, Mr Sherwood sounds good. Will the new guy contact me? Maybe I can help?"

The New York Dealer smirked and thought; *Yeah, sure, that would be the last thing the new hitman would need or want.* Sherwood worked hard to stifle a scoffing tone. "He may contact you, but no, he will scrape through alone thanks. OK, I have to go, but like I said, just sit tight, hey?"

Harrison started to respond and then realised Sherwood had already hung up. He made a face and placed the phone in its cradle.

The days went by, and I started thinking that, living in luxury, I should keep up my fitness. I decided to do miles around the walking/running track, which was too much exposure for me. Fewer people would see me in the gym if I went late at night when most people would be busy elsewhere having fun. Meantime, unbeknown to me Winfrey was keeping up his cover and had settled into his dish washing role. He could not believe how many plates, knives and forks these passengers went through. Even though he was super fit, his back still ached, his arms were cramping, and every shift, he sweated so much he figured he shed a few pounds of water. And then breakfast was over, a break, well, at least until lunch. This entire Op would never have worked with a civilian principal to protect, but Johnson was a hard-experienced warrior. Winfrey had to pray that Wallace/Johnson would be OK without his over-watch while he washed dishes instead.

Winfrey was totally frustrated and more than a little concerned about being unable to cover him full-time. He had noticed Johnson had started going to the gym at night. Johnston's exercise regime matched well with Winfrey's dish washing duties, which made things easier. Winfrey's shift being over in time allowed him to keep an eye on Johnson at the gym. He figured the lowest profile way to shadow the principal instead of lurking around the door to the gym was to work out at the gym at the same time as Wallace. It was hard to lay low in the gym because it was less mobile and less crowded, but the Delta Force Officer still avoided being too close to the Aussie Agent by being flexible in his choice of equipment.

Wearing his Apple earbuds, Winfrey looked out to sea, peddling away on a Lifespan Spin exercise bike. He could see the reflection of Johnson in the sizeable sloping window. He was on a rowing machine over on the opposite corner of the gym. They had acknowledged each other with a friendly nod as they passed each other between machines and had the gym to themselves, except for an older man doing light weights. To maintain his covert existence, Winfrey avoided being obvious about keeping an eye on the Australian. This was the third gym session they had 'shared' without knowing each other. Winfrey hoped Johnson would think their virtually identical training schedule was purely coincidental. After wiping his balding head, the elderly passenger finished his last set and slowly shuffled out of the gym.

Winfrey slowed the bike and dismounted. Bending down, he picked up a water bottle and drained it in one swallow. He thought Johnson was about to finish, so he sat down as though he was catching his breath to wait for him to leave. This meant Johnson was hidden behind a bank of exercise machines and weights. Winfrey stood up, stretched, and covertly noticed Johnson had gone over to the weight bench and was setting for some bench presses. The Delta Force Officer thought; *Surely, he'll be safe for a few minutes while he finishes his routine.* Showing the self-discipline gained only by extensive surveillance ops, he left the gym without glancing in Johnson's direction. A few minutes later, Winfrey arrived at his cabin, looking forward to a long hot shower. He tapped his pocket and swore when he realised his door swipe card must have fallen out of his training shorts while he was on the exercise bike.

You usually need two people to do bench presses, one lifting and the other to spot. I had to be careful; I could get hurt if I dropped the bar on myself or became too heavy to lift back in the cradle. To reduce the risk, I kept it lighter than usual and concentrated on doing more repetitions. I wondered why I thought this was a good idea so late in my routine as I was puffing and sweating profusely. At home, I keep fit by walking for miles hunting feral animals, but pushing weights is different and boring. As I raised the bar above my chest, my thoughts turned to the Australian bush and my dog, Jake. I was sick of the excesses of the cruise, as wonderful as it was. I was tired of the endless pressure of undercover work, not to mention the dangers. I'd been away from home too long. After two sets of ten, I was just about to call it a day. I just started to push the bar up, intending to guide it back into the cradles on either side of the bench.

Suddenly, the bar weighed three times what it had seconds before. It crushed down on my chest and was forcing its way towards my throat. All I saw was a pair of bear-size black hands on either side of my own hands around the bar. As tired as my muscles were, my arms braced against the onslaught, understanding I would die soon after the bar touched my throat. My total being focused on a single goal to keep my windpipe from being crushed by the weight bar being forced downwards by this unseen giant. I felt my strength waning quickly, my legs screaming as I pushed them into the carpet, attempting to gain more power through my shoulders and arms. Everything in me pushed harder, although it was incredibly difficult for me to keep trying. I dug even deeper than I had ever dug before. I could tell I was losing; I was exhausted, and the relentless bar now felt many times heavier. The bar slid up my chest that last few inches and began to strangle me. I thought of home again. Then I stopped fighting as the world went black, the deepest black ever. A total silence. An absolute absence of stimuli of any kind. The giant had crushed my throat closed, and the enormous black arms remained a relentless weight pushing on my throat and chest. Then nothing.

Unbeknown to me, the big man who had just murdered me wanted to make sure. So he kept his total weight on the thick bar as he thought. He whispered to himself, his breath not even labouring after the struggle. "Well, that was easier than they had warned me it would be. I'm starving."

In Winfrey's business, you didn't lose things or leave things behind. This was why Winfrey was so damned annoyed with himself for having to return to the gym for his cabin swipe card. As he entered the gym room, he could see the crew member who had joined the ship at the same time as he had. Winfrey had a little joke to himself; *The guy's so friggin big you wouldn't think he needed any gym time.* Funnily enough, their paths had never crossed since they climbed the gangplank back in Venice. The man was huge; he had a V-shaped back to him, and initially, Winfrey thought he was performing some weight exercise. As Delta Force Operative continued further into the gym, he saw the man bend forward and suddenly understood what he was up to. Winfrey flew across the room. Attacking from the rear, he cupped both hands, slamming them over the giant's ears.

The huge assailant let out a blood-curdling scream as his eardrums shattered. The giant spun on Winfrey. His huge hands grabbed Winfrey's shoulders and hurtled him into a stand of dumbbells and weights. There was a whoosh as all the wind was knocked out of the smaller man's lungs. As his body hit the floor, knowing what was coming, he inhaled deeply in preparation for the giant's next attack. Black arms like tree branches surrounded him, threatening to drive out the little air he had recovered. The man was a one-trick pony, massive, strong, and fearless but with no technique or speed. He was so big Winfrey was like a child held in his arms face to face, but the Delta Force Officer's feet were still a good foot off the ground. Winfrey knew although the assailant's weapons were limited, they were still highly dangerous and lethal. Dangling in the giant's thick arms, he could feel his bones and cartilage being slowly crushed. Perfectly positioned, hanging in front of the enormous black man, Winfrey brought his leg back and kicked him with all his strength. There was a satisfying contact as he felt the man's balls squash against his groin. A high-pitched scream immediately followed this.

Falling onto his back, the giant let go as he flailed his arms wide in pain. He then bent forward to clutch his wounded testicles and glared at Winfrey. The black assassin rolled to his left and, using his immense arm strength effortlessly pushed himself to his feet. Once again, he attacked Winfrey unmercifully with bear-like strikes, cuffing him left and then right with fists the size of dinner plates. Winfrey had no choice but to attempt to deflect the blows and move away from the thrashing giant of a man. One blow landed hard on the side of Winfrey's head, sending him reeling backwards, eventually falling across a rack holding weight discs. Sensing another victory, the giant moved in for the kill, thinking Winfrey was done for. In a single motion, the smaller man swiped up a small five-pound weight and swung it using both hands. A sickening crack accompanied the appearance of a deep red furrow across the assassin's flat black forehead. There was a slight hiatus, and then a waterfall of blood fell down the giant's face under the weight disc and down his surprised face. The man's eyes glazed over. Then Goliath fell face down on the floor, never to move under his own power again.

Winfrey collapsed to the carpet and rolled onto his back, feeling grateful to be alive. He lay there for a while trying to recover; every joint ached, and breathing was both painful and shallow. His hammered body, now in the early stages of shock, and oxygen deprivation was falling into unconsciousness, blessed freedom and rest. However, deep within him, he was plagued with a nagging, demanding thought: *Wallace, where is Wallace? I don't remember seeing him. Is he OK?* Winfrey ignores his own physical needs and near-overwhelming desires. Now acting on nothing but his disciplined mental strength, further fuelled by adrenalin, he resurfaced from near unconsciousness. Winfrey slowly looked around through a drunken-like blur and saw something over to his right. Crawling on all fours, the Delta Force Operative clambered around the small hill that was the dead assassin. His heart sank when he saw the Australian's supine body draped over the weight bench, pale and lifeless. His chest was still pinned by the bench press bar that had choked him. He hurried as much as he could, ignoring his limbs and joints, screaming for him to slow down if not stop.

As he reached the body, Winfrey reached down and, lifting the weight bar, placed it in the cradles. He then put two fingers on the dead Aussie's pale neck, searching for any sign of the carotid pulse. Nothing. Winfrey cursed how long he had taken to dispatch the big man, thinking; M*aybe if I'd got back to this guy earlier, he would have made it; shit, what a mess.* There was no time, no choice. Winfrey was only starting to breathe normally himself. Wallace was dead. "Oh fuck, fuck." He had to try something, anything. He then put his aching arms under the Aussie's shoulders and dragged him to the floor. He laid Wallace on his back, arched his head back, extending his throat.

Winfrey had done plenty of first aid training but had never had to do C.P.R. on anything but a practice dummy. He started the routine by pressing the heart and pushing breaths into the inert lungs of the dead Australian. He knew it was nothing like the movies where, after three compressions, the patient splutters and then jumps up. Statistically, C.P.R. hardly ever worked, but it always had to be worth a try, didn't it? The stats didn't matter to Winfrey; he would keep trying to retrieve Wallace until he collapsed, unable to compress the victim's chest.

Not that it crossed his mind, but due to how late it was. Fortunately, no other passengers entered the gym. Winfrey continued to rhythmically push on the Australian's chest and puff breaths into the dead man's mouth and lungs again and again. All the time he was performing C.P.R., he was praying to see Wallace's chest rise of its own accord. Winfrey was extremely fit, but the fight and the time spent compressing this powerful chest, combined with the emotional energy of attempting to resuscitate this ally, was taking its toll. He would continue until something broke or gave way. This was non-negotiable on so many levels.

But still nothing. The young American's shoulders sagged from emotional as well as physical exhaustion. This Aussie hero, whom he hadn't ever met, was dead. **Steve Wallace was dead.**

CHAPTER 16

Winfrey stopped everything and looked up. There on the wall near the entrance was a DEFIBRILLATOR LIFEPACK CR2. He flew to it, dragging the case from its wall hooks and ran back to Wallace's body. He had been trained on the DEFIBs and felt stupid for not looking for the device from the get-go. After another five chest compressions, Winfrey sensed rather than saw a slight change, some small reaction. He checked for breath, still nothing. Rechecking the carotid pulse, he was rewarded with the faintest drum. Back on the chest, five more, then another breath and Wallace was back. He was Fuckin Back! Delta Force hardman Winfrey had a small tear in the corner of his eye. He wasn't sure if it was emotion or effort, probably both. The American remembered the Aussie agent's real name from the file and had figured he may not respond to his cover identity.

Winfrey screamed. "Wallace, can you hear me? Steve, you're OK, you're OK."

From somewhere deep, deep down, I could hear my father calling me. I was lost in the bush overnight after getting separated while we were hunting. I was cold, wet, hungry and very scared; it was the darkest, longest night I had ever seen. I felt totally disconnected, and I had no answers for where I was or what had just happened. I wasn't even capable of formulating a question. I had a feint realisation of being somewhere, but I had no idea where that was. After a few minutes, I slowly opened my eyes; they were sluggish and heavy. The overhead lights glared down at me. My tongue stuck to the roof of my mouthing, and for some reason, each breath seemed to hurt my entire throat, incredible pain. I could hear someone breathing softly over to my left.

Winfrey had never experienced this return-to-life scenario before, so he just sat back and let his muscles and lungs recover. After a few minutes of silence, the revived Aussie Agent tried to talk.

"Who are you? Where the hell am I?" This request evoked laughter from somewhere beside me. I still couldn't see anyone, but I knew they were there. An American accent, I didn't recognise the voice.

"Take it easy, buddy; I'm on your side. Just rest for now, and I'll get you back to your cabin as soon as possible. Just take it easy now."

I felt shaky and exhausted but still needed answers, so I repeated my original question. "Who are you? Where the hell am I? How come my throat hurts so much?"

Another annoying giggle.

"OK, just take it easy; you've been through some serious shit. You're still on the cruise ship. Goliath over there nearly succeeded in choking you under that weight bar. The good news is your alive, he's screwed, you might be feeling a bit sore, but he ain't feelin anything."

I felt like I was on a battery charger and slowly gaining power.

"OK, it's all coming back slowly, but I still don't know who you are. What did you call me before?"

Winfrey had already formed a high opinion of Wallace, and the Aussie's quick recovery and astuteness confirmed that it was not misplaced.

"Yeah, well, I had to use your real name to get into you deep. I figured you were so far out of it that yelling Robert Johnson wouldn't crack it. I am Lieutenant Ben Winfrey Delta Force."

Modestly, he said while offering his hand to me.

"Not all that 'Special', Agent Monroe, through my boss, requested our support, and here I am. I was inserted on this cruise at Venice to look after you and do some techo surveillance on the Tango Harrison.

I was still very groggy, holding my throat in an attempt to lessen the pain. I croaked. "So, what happened here?"

Winfrey looked a bit hesitant before he responded.

"I'm really sorry, man; I thought you'd be OK for a few minutes without me. I had only left the gym five or so minutes, and it all happened. Obviously, I was frigging wrong **big time**. He must have been waiting for you to be alone before he struck. Anyway, I returned to the gym to find this big prick choking you with a weight bar. Coincidentally, he came on board with me; who would have known, hey? Anyway, I took him out, and after a while, I dragged you back from wherever you went."

Rubbing my bruised chest, I said. "OK, so this is from CPR. I guess I owe you my life, Winfrey. At the moment, I can't do anything to repay you, mate, but if you ever need me, I'm there, OK."

"Can I call you Steve?" I nodded, and he continued.

"Well, Steve, my mission was to protect you, and I did a friggin terrible job of it, so we are probably even."

Looking over at the dead bison on the floor of the gym, I smiled at my good fortune. "Alright, Ben, we will call it quits for now, but thanks again, mate. He's a biggin, alright, you did well to topple him."

Nodding, Winfrey agreed. "He went close to killing both of us, Steve, but it looks like God wasn't ready for either of us today, hey?"

The Delta Force Operative wanted to get away from the crime scene as soon as possible and hoped Wallace was up to moving. But first, he needed to clean things up a little. Winfrey walked over to the dead assassin, grabbing his ham-like hands and struggling with every step. He slowly dragged the giant corpse over to the bench press. I watched him struggle with the huge carcass, but even though I wanted to help, I was weak as a kitten, so I just sat there, regaining a little strength.

The irony was not lost on either Agent as Winfrey draped the dead body on the bench. He hoped that this would give the appearance that there had been a terrible accident while the dead giant had been doing bench presses. The American Agent removed the weight disc still embedded in the giant's forehead, ending his reign of terror and the fight of his life. He wiped it clean and placed it back in the weight rack. Winfrey then loaded the long bar with three twenty-pound plates retained by a collar on each side. The Operative set the bar in the bloody groove in the assassin's forehead. Grisly as it was, he had to ensure the accident looked feasible under any scrutiny. He pushed down on the bar directly above the wound across the blood-covered forehead and was happy the bar fitted nicely into the linear wound in the dead man's skull. Satisfied with his work, he wiped the bar and weights for fingerprints and returned to me. I was still dizzy and disoriented after my ordeal and only vaguely understood what I had just seen Winfrey do.

Turning to me, Winfrey asked. "Steve, how you going, buddy? You up to bugging out of here?"

I wasn't sure I could walk without collapsing. "Yeah, sure, but I feel about as sharp as a bowling ball."

"Sorry mate, I really think we've pushed our luck being here this long. The after-show gym junkies will be here soon. We've gotta be gone so they can find him and not us."

Of course, I knew he was right. "OK, let's head to my cabin.

"Normally, I would avoid us being seen together. But mate, you need a hand. I guess if anyone sees me falling or leaning against the wall, they'll just think you've had one too many." Winfrey said. "Yeah, it should look pretty normal cruise ship fun. I'll stay close to make sure you're OK."

Our luck held with no one else coming into the gym and neither of us passing anyone as we left the area. By the time I reached my cabin, I was exhausted and staggered inside and collapsed onto the bed. Ten minutes later, I was awoken by Winfrey knocking on my cabin door. I dragged myself up to let him in. I was starting to feel less confused, and I noticed he was wearing a long bill fishing cap pulled down low and immediately recognised the quality of his field craft by avoiding the CCTVs. I felt much better except for a sore chest and a tender throat.

"Welcome, Ben. I don't know about you, but I need a drink. What do you think?" "You're not wrong, Steve; I'll have whatever you got."

I poured two good JDs and handed one to Winfrey. "Here's to dead giants and new friends." Clinking our glasses, we both took large pulls and let the smoky liquor confirm we were still alive. For me, it was easy to feel alive because the bourbon burnt my injured throat like acid. But it was worth it.

Looking at the glass of smoky whiskey, I asked. "Now, where are we with all this, Ben? Does Monroe actually have a plan?"

"Well, Steve, he may have, but I've already changed the original plan. I had no choice about that. I was ordered to carry out my mission without ever meeting you. I've been doing pretty good until today. But I didn't really have time to work out a way to save you from the big fella without you seeing me."

Suddenly, it dawned on me I knew this guy Winfrey was familiar.

"I'm sure happy you didn't hesitate for that reason. Ah, I never thought anything of it, but now you say it, I remember seeing you around. I figured seeing you so often, it must have been the only time you could get to do those things like go to the gym." Ben smiled. "Yeah, well, I just tried to be with you without you knowing. As well as babysitting you, a big part of my being here was to plant some listening devices in Harrison's suite and trackers on the cargo you found. That's all done, and they're all working well."

I hadn't completely recovered from the attack, but someone had just tried to kill me. I was angry and wanted someone to pay. Talking with my new ally was at least making me feel like I was doing something towards revenge. I had been thinking about the situation we now found ourselves in. Someone had ordered my death for the second time and gone to the trouble of importing a hitman. I was hurting and angry enough to want to kill Harrison on sight. But I was also starting to see a way we might be able to benefit from the attack. It seemed like a great idea, but feeling the way I was, I thought it best to sleep on it and allow my mind and body to recover more. We arranged for Winfrey to come back to my cabin when his breakfast shift ended.

A bit after 1000 Hrs, Winfrey knocked on my cabin door, and I let him in. I ordered Cabin Service because we had yet to eat something. While we waited for the food and, more importantly, the coffee to arrive, we continued our war council. Slowly, I could feel myself recovering from my brush with death. Winfrey had also received a battering and was enjoying the medicinal effects of a night's sleep even though he had an early morning start for work.

"Winfrey, I've been thinking; I would bet Harrison never met that big guy you downed. The fact he came on board with you means he couldn't have been like the others, recruited on board by Harrison. What are your thoughts about you contacting the target, our Mr Harrison?"

He smiled and shook his head. "First of all, my friends call me Oprah for obvious reasons. Secondly, sorry you're breaking up real bad; I can't hear you." Winfrey said in a sarcastic radio voice. he was six feet away from me.

I understood his viewpoint, but I persisted.

"No, come on, Oprah, I'm still not on my game. Let me explain it a bit better for you. Firstly, like I said, Harrison doesn't know what the assassin looks like. You take the giant's place, and you're in; maybe privy to discussions, dates and times, who knows. Secondly, you can report to him that you have successfully eliminated me.

Harrison will welcome you as a hero and trust you immediately. It all makes sense to me anyway."

I could see Winfrey was beginning to like my idea.

"Well, Steve, I can't really argue with your logic. I guess the only flaw is there is no way we can know what that big fella was supposed to do after he killed you. Was he to report back to some unknown boss or just stay on board until the next port and then disappear?"

I was impressed with Ben's assessment.

"You're spot on, Ben, but I think you can get around that. As the assassin, you might get a slight rocket up the ass from our unknown boss for contacting Harrison if you weren't s'posed to. But my best guess is Harrison's boss or contact is the assassin's boss, too. If you can bluff your way in and get Harrison to report on your behalf, you successfully taking me out; all the worries are gone in one go."

I could tell Winfrey was a warrior. He might look like a Surfie pretty boy, but he had proven himself against the odds back in the gym. And he had told me about his Military service, a Marine and then Delta Force put right up there with any elite unit in the world. He was used to making changes halfway through a plan and understood battle was fluid. However, he knew he must gain approval from Special Agent Monroe for this plan deviation.

"Oprah. Oh, that takes some getting used to. Anyway, if you get close to Harrison, I am unsure where I'll fit in being dead. I'll be hiding here; it's only a matter of time before someone springs me. And, of course, we are still making out that poor old Ramone is still with me, so we can't hope to keep this charade going much longer. Having said that, too much effort and blood has been spilled for me to bail now. I need to stick with it. Before they tried to kill me again I'd had enough, but, now I want to see this through. It's not my style to leave an Op half-executed."

"OK, I'll go for it all, Steve, but I've gotta get approval from my boss back at Delta HQ. I will sell it as good as I can; I reckon he'll buy it. Of course, the hard part will be that he has to pass it by Agent Monroe."

My frustration boiled over. "Ben, for fucks sake, it's starting to feel like a friggin school P& C committee meeting. I don't think we have that much time. Sorry, mate, I've been in the Military long enough to know you have to do what you're saying. It's just after the couple of days we've had, I got to tell you these pricks need hitting and hittin' hard."

Nodding, Winfrey responded. "Steve, I hear you, but the back-room boys know the time constraints. My gut feeling is they'll think it's a great plan. I'll phone it through straight away and let you know."

They may have known the time constraints, but it still took two days and several calls between Winfrey, his superiors and the CIA minders. Winfrey was either caring or clever in that he didn't keep me posted regarding the progress. He was shielding me from the bureaucracy I'd predicted.

Even so, I was still frustrated by all this, but deep down, I was grateful I didn't have to deal with them. I knew what it was like. Often enough back in Afghanistan, I had battled the same shit face to face enough times. Maybe I was getting too old for the patience and diplomacy it demanded. To ensure Harrison or his helpers, if they existed, didn't see me anywhere, I stayed in my cabin. Room service food was fine, and Winfrey ensured I didn't run short of JD. I had kept the room attendant away by leaving the do not disturb sign out, but I knew this couldn't go on much longer. He would worry that he was going to get a kick in the ass from his supervisor if he didn't get to change the linen.

Finally, Winfrey knocked on my cabin door. I let him in quickly so he was kept from standing in the hall too long. Winfrey looked happy as he pushed past me into my cabin. Putting on his best Aussie accent.

"Hey mate, how's life 'confined to barracks'?"

Sitting on the end of the bed, I got the Army joke. But I was going stir-crazy.

"Yeah, very funny. At least when you get CTB in the Army, it's usually because you've had enough of good a time to get into trouble and deserve it."

Smiling, the Delta Force Officer asked. "Well, do you want the news, or do you want to keep complaining?"

I jumped off the bed and demanded. "What did they say? What's the go?"

Winfrey smiled again and nodded. "Firstly, don't shoot the messenger. Steve, OK, I know how you feel about sticking this out to the bitter end. Between all the work and Ramone and everything, I totally get that. However, things have pushed it another way. They approved the plan, all of it. Well, except for your part from here on in. They decided you are to remain dead. Which means they want you to disembark at Mykonos and head home. Of course, there will be a debrief, and they both asked me to pass on their thanks on how well you have done. Basically, the mission is over for you, buddy. For what it's worth, without getting too soppy I would love you to watch my back. I think we could make a lethal team. But deep down, I think we both know they're right. You being around might compromise the whole plan. If Harrison believes you dead and then finds out some way that you're not, then we would probably both be really dead."

I heard his words but found it hard to comprehend at first. My mind was overwhelmed with memories of the mission. I was thinking, How can I just walk away from all this after all my involvement? But it looks like I have no choice. I can't hide in my cabin indefinitely. To keep Winfrey safe and help his entry to Harrison's inner sanctum, he must claim he killed me. I have been all over the world chasing this Hawala wind wherever it took me. I feel like I have been on this mission for an eternity. The operation had taken me all over the world: Thailand, Egypt, Jordan, Dubai, Italy and now Greece. I thought of Ramone and her sacrifice that had been part of this battle. I made my decision. The mission was bigger than my need for a feeling of completion.

"I can't handle Oprah, mate. So Ben, except for watching your back, I can see I am no longer needed. And, if I am honest, I can't really over-watch you if I am supposed to be dead and trying to keep a low profile. I'll never forget you saved my life, mate, and although I prefer to work alone, I think you're right; we would make a good team. So, Ben, what's the plan? I get off at Mykonos like I am going on a shore excursion and then disappear?

Nodding, Winfrey replied.

"Yeah, that's what they cooked up. I know it seems a bit cold and abrupt, but it's all being done on the run. Of course, they will check Mr Johnson off the ship as usual. Not returning to the ship will activate a red flag and spark a search. They will go to inform your wife only to find her gone as well. We believe they will devise several possible scenarios but never find a definitive solution. The embark/ disembark check system is very efficient. But, we hope they come to think somehow you and Mrs Johnson / Ramone got off the ship and disappeared without explanation. I need you to buy two tickets for the Mykonos shore excursion."

When someone disappears, they follow standard procedure. After a physical search fails to find the two of you; they will post a public announcement several times. We expect Harrison to eventually hear this; in his eyes, the ship's announcement will make your disappearance official to him. We believe, ultimately, the ship's crew will assume that you and Ramone have met with foul play somewhere on the island. This rumour will spread throughout the ship, and I will ensure Harrison hears about it when I meet him. If my infiltration is successful, I will infer that it was me who took you out on the island. That should work."

Smiling, I accepted my lot. "That seems like a damn good plan especially accounting for Ramone and my disappearance. That's pure genius. Or about the best anyone could come up with, considering the quality of the ship's systems. But all systems fail somehow and inevitably."

Winfrey was relieved I had worked through my removal from the operation and the ship and had accepted it. "Steve, it was your idea for me to infiltrate Harrison's set-up; the brass back in the States thought it was a great idea."

"Mate, you didn't have to do that, but thanks. Ben, I can't make any demands, but I would really appreciate it if you or someone could let me know how it all goes when it gets rounded up if it's not too much bother."

Except for sharing another few drinks and a bit more discussion, that was the last time I ever saw Ben Winfrey, a man I owed my life to, a real hero.

In preparation for my disappearing onto Mykonos, I focused on setting up as many props that supported 'our' disappearance and tidied up any loose ends. I had ordered two dinners from Cabin Service the night before we reached the idyllic island. Most of one meal, I cut up finely and flushed down the toilet. But the dirty plates suggested two people ate in our cabin that night. I threw all Ramone's spy gear and burglar devices overboard during the night, leaving only everyday passenger items in the cabin. The morning of the Mykonos excursion, I left all our bags and gear in the cabin, taking a bare minimum in a backpack for my trip home. This was to ensure that everything would look entirely normal during any search after we failed to return to the ship.

I disembarked, knowing I would not return to the ship and casually headed away from the docks. I had decided it was impossible to hide with so many cruise passengers discovering all the sights, shops, and tavernas. So I found a little bar that was away from the water and all the cruise ship tourists. I took my time drinking Ouzo brought to my table in a tall glass along with another with ice only in it. The clear spirit turns milky white when poured over the ice. This was my first chance to relax in weeks and I snacked on Greek style octopus and calamari. There, I kept out of sight until the cruise ship left beautiful Mykonos Island. Once I saw the last tender take the passengers back to the ship I took the first steps on my journey home. After many flights and airports, I finally landed in Canberra, Australia and after a quick phone call, I was picked up by a car from the National Security Centre (NSC).

By the time I arrived, I was exhausted and jet-lagged to a standstill.

A Warrant Officer Williams, who was Duty Officer for the night, welcomed me back and explained that Colonel Goodrich had gone home for the night. The Colonel had left orders that I was to be taken to a nearby hotel to catch up on a well-deserved rest, his words, not mine. WO Williams smirked a little as he continued.

"Sir, the Colonel did say that. Then he said have the Major back here in front of me at 0600 Hrs. Obviously, not a real long, well-deserved rest, hey, Sir?"

Lying in the hotel bed, I was conscious of the lack of the ship's movements and noises I had grown so accustomed to. However, I was so tired it didn't stop me from immediately falling into a deep, uninterrupted sleep. I was too tired to dream, and when my alarm went off at 0500 hours, I awoke still not feeling terrific but certainly a lot better than the previous night.

0600Hrs saw me carry a mug of strong black coffee into Colonel Goodrich's office. I wasn't in uniform, but as required, I came to attention instead of a full salute. He jumped up, acknowledged my respectful gesture and then shook hands.

"Thanks, Steve, welcome back. You've certainly had an incredible adventure. I know you can fill in all the blanks, but Steve the Intel outcomes have been nothing short of outstanding. Speaking of which, before we get onto the current debrief, that Intel you brought back from the Timor mission was so rich we are still mining it. All over the region, missions are being planned and executed as a direct result. We had no idea that troublemaker of a mayor was so involved in the terrorism network all over Indonesia."

I realised I was still pretty knocked around by the last few days and all the travel. And even though I had only been sitting there for half an hour, I was already feeling pretty tired. A lengthy debrief followed with Colonel Goodrich that would be added to the reports I had already filed. These would then be passed on to Special Agent Monroe for synchronisation with what he already had.

When we got to the part where the giant hitman had choked me to the point that I had technically died, and Winfrey had brought me back using CPR, the Colonel looked pail.

"Steve, we had no idea. Are you OK? Were you injured? I can't begin to tell you how glad I am you made it."

"Sir, I'm fine; my throat is still very sore, and my chest is covered in bruises from the assailant and then from Ben Winfrey pounding on it. But yeah, I'm fine, still drained, though. And that, thank God, means I'm alive."

I continued. "We have learned a great deal about antiquities smuggling. However, except for Harrison on board the Southern Star, we weren't any closer to knowing the Management end of the supply chain. As far as I know, we still didn't know any details of any fund distribution system, the famous Hawala."

Colonel Goodrich was a class act when it came to leadership. He must have understood where I was coming from.

"Steve, don't be too hard on yourself. You're exhausted, and you've been in a highly stressful and continuously dangerous environment for an extended period. In addition to that, the pressure on a person to maintain an assumed identity is immense. And all combined with whatever degree of grieving you're battling with to do with your CIA partner. Well, Steve, it may take a few months to recover both physically and mentally. And as you can imagine, I have no idea what lasting effects actually dying has, but you'd think there must be some."

"I'm OK, Sir; just like you said, I'm exhausted." Suddenly, I felt a wave of emotion flow over me, and I knew I needed to be alone.

The Colonel went into caring mode again, dropping Rank. "Absolutely, mate, and I'm not putting anything onto you. I just want you to be OK and maybe have a full check-up before heading home. Will you do that for my peace of mind? Of course, get some solid rest first."

"Roger that, Sir, can it be in-house? I would prefer that if possible?"

"Sergeant Winatong will arrange it all," Goodrich said with a smile.

Colonel Goodrich continued. "Steve, just quickly, everyone is carefully optimistic that between the Intel you captured and the follow-up work, it will all result in a devastating blow to ISIS and several other terrorist groups. It all depends on the listening and tracking devices your mate Ben Winfrey planted and whether he could successfully infiltrate Harrison's circle. For security reasons, it's gone very quiet. Agent Monroe has dived for cover, so all we can do is wait and hope your blood, sweat and tears pay off. We assume the last phase of the operation will be after the crates of stolen treasures finally land in the USA. We expect the contraband would be followed to the group or individual receiving the shipment, resulting in raids and seizures. These, in turn, would reap a harvest of more Intel from computers and files along with prisoners that may provide further Intel under interrogation."

Even though this info was exciting to me, I was so whacked my reply probably sounded disinterested. "Sir, that is great; I'll certainly be interested in the final wash-up."

"The Colonel could see me wilting. "Steve, you look beat; let's call it a day. We've got you booked into a nice hotel close by. We will let you know about your Med/Psych check. But what you need most is about forty hours of solid sleep."

Emotion, again, this is common for me and lots of other soldiers. You keep it together when you're out there, but when you come home, you fall apart.

"I'm sorry, Sir, I did everything that was needed, all I could, but now I am out of that pressure cooker...... I can feel exhaustion climbing over me, weighing me down in every way. Sir, can you please let me know how it all goes?"

"For sure, Steve, I'll pass on whatever I get. But for now, please try and rest and look after yourself."

A short ride to the hotel, one drink, and I crashed.

CHAPTER 17

Aboard the Southern Star, en route to New York, Harrison was on the phone again. And not for the first time, Sherwood rolled his eyes as he suffered Ian Harrison's bleating. The antique dealer interrupted him again, moving the conversation onto more critical issues. Glad that his Tech had provided so much comms security that enabled him to speak without concern.

"Now, Harrison, the main reason I called was to fix your screw-up yet again. Don't worry about Johnson.

Harrison broke in. "It's easy for you to say, sitting in your New York office, I'm here, and Johnson is trouble."

Sherwood was thinking how much he hated having to talk to this idiot. "OK, OK, let me be even clearer. By now, he should be history, no longer anyone's problem." Pushing on before the cruising buffoon could interrupt. "However, we must accept that Johnson has done us some harm. He must have reported to someone, and we still don't even know who he worked for. It's unlikely he discovered much about our cargo, but just in case, I need you to do something. When you get to New York, I want to be sure there is nothing to see, that is, if someone is waiting for you. We are as safe as we can make it, YES? No way can I lose another shipment like last time, you hear me?

"I wasn't even involved in that I...."

Sherwood's blood pressure rose to new heights along with the volume of his normally quiet voice. "Look, I know you weren't involved. Shut up and listen. I know you weren't, but I still took the hit, and it won't happen again."

Harrison cringed under the tirade; he wasn't used to anyone talking to him like that. Back in the day, if anyone had tried it, the person wouldn't have seen the next sunrise. Things were different, but he stored it away for a later date.

Sherwood, controlling himself as best as possible, quietly continued. "Now, I've been thinking, I need you to move those crates out of your storage and into another area. I'm sure all the full-time cruisers don't use every space. Once the crates have been moved, the current markings must be blacked out and relabelled with new addresses." He went on to tell Harrison the details of the new markings.

Still smarting from Sherwood's lack of respect, Harrison knew familiarity annoyed the fancy-pants antique dealer.

"OK, I'll get that organised. John, I'm not complaining. I just need to know what's going on. This Johnson character has rattled me. He's got more lives than a friggin cat. They were a top team he took out on Burano Island." He could hear Sherwood's laboured breathing and pressed on. "And although we don't know for sure, he must have been involved in Sal's disappearance."

Sherwood resented this nuisance, using his first name like they were friends, and his voice dripped with his anger and dismissive tone.

"Yeah, yeah, don't get your panties in a wad Harrison. I already told you Johnson is not a problem. I have it all under control, OK? As soon as I hear something, I'll let you know."

Harrison knew when to stop pushing. He had felt the hot wrath of this arrogant antique dealer before and figured it was time to be a little more deferential.

"Sure, Mr Sherwood, I'll.........."

Looking at the handset, he realised he was talking to himself. "Nothing, he's hung up on me again! The fuckin arrogant New York prick, the sooner this cruise is over, and they unload that contra-fucking-band, the better."

Winfrey was a highly experienced operator. His success and survival had always depended on being as prepared as possible. Applying this to his infiltration of Harrison's team, he had found out the on-board name the hitman had used. This was easy as the discovery of the dead giant's body lead to the crew talking about him and as time went by details such as his name emerged. So, at least when Harrison reported to Sherwood, he would have the correct name. Winfrey was sitting in his cabin rehearsing a script of what he had planned to say to Harrison. He must convince him he was the hitman the New York antique dealer dispatched. The existence of Sherwood was fresh Intel captured by the listening devices installed by Winfrey just days ago. The CIA knew little about him, but that was changing by the hour.

His Sat-phone chirped. Winfrey could see it was Colonel Randolph, his Delta Force contact.

"Hello, Sir, what's new?"

"Lots, Winfrey; first, can you give me an update on our two missing passengers?"

"Well, Sir, good news on that front: Mr. and Mrs. Johnson are believed to have met with some tragic accident or foul play on Mykonos. The ship's Officers followed the missing passenger procedure as we expected. Harrison couldn't have missed the numerous public announcements requesting help or information regarding the couple."

Winfrey continued. "Scuttlebutt is that a Security Officer has had an official warning for somehow letting Mrs Johnson off the ship without scanning her card. There is a digital record of Mr. Johnson disembarking, and the two shore excursion tickets worked exactly how we had hoped. So it appears that Wallace's escape from the ship has been successful."

The Colonel was pleased by this report. "Great news, Winfrey, overall, but especially because it will support your next move. I'll pass on a SITREP to Munroe straight away."

"Winfrey's fortune undoubtedly favours the well-prepared. You haven't attempted to contact Tango 1, have you?

"No sir, just giving it some final prep when you called."

"Great. Our friends in high places just listened into a call between Harrison and Sherwood. Harrison is worried about what

Wallace/Johnson might try next. Sherwood hasn't heard from his man, so he couldn't confirm Johnson's demise, but clearly, he expected it to either have happened or was imminent. Of course, we know he hasn't heard anything because you took out his hitman. Both Harrison and Sherwood are hanging out for a report." Winfrey didn't need a diagram.

One of the keys to Delta Force's worldwide operations was seizing the initiative and adapting to the fluid nature of battle. Winfrey wanted to grab this opportunity. "It seems like a perfect opportunity for me to approach Harrison. I'm hot to trot if you say so."

The Colonel had one hundred per cent confidence in his operators and Lieutenant Winfrey, who had an impressive track record. Randolph knew this was too good a chance to waste, and more importantly, it offered Winfrey a much safer entrée to the Tango. Tapping Harrison's phone and room had answered all the scary questions.

"Winfrey, go for it, son. It seems that Sherwood has ordered Harrison to move those crates, so if you mention that to him, it will sound like you're on the team. By the way, they can't stand each other. When the last call finished, Harrison had a bit of a meltdown about Sherwood. We heard it all thanks to your bugs. Harrison hates Sherwood; your Tango thinks he is, and I quote an 'arrogant New York prick.'"

Winfrey appreciated the near live Intel; it might prove to be gold. The fact his control understood that such a seemingly small thing's value when attempting to establish rapport inspired confidence in his leadership. Winfrey thought; *it just gets better and better. I love dissension between crims or terrorists.* Harrison hating his New York contact could be capitalised during that first contact.

The Delta Force Officer decided to strike while the iron was hot and headed towards Harrison's suite as soon as the call with Colonel

Randolph finished. He was confident before the call; but experience told him this sort of thing could quickly go sideways. But now he felt the barriers may have been removed, and establishing a quick rapport with Harrison should be much easier using this bonus Intel. It was mid-afternoon, so the wealthy suite owner should be in. After three knocks, the older man, whose face appeared, looked like someone's grandpa. It was hard to believe he was a smuggler who had played some part in several murders.

"Oh, hello, I thought that was my afternoon tea. How can I help you, son?"

Winfrey had to get inside that suite quickly. The last thing he wanted was to have a long discussion standing in the hallway.

"Mr. Harrison, Sherwood sent me. Can I come inside, please?"

Harrison's tanned features paled before Winfrey's eyes, and there was a moment where he looked like he wanted to slam the door in the young man's face. The suite owner may well have assumed that he was dispensable to Sherwood, let alone an irritant requiring removal. Winfrey had seen that look before and thought; *this guy thinks I am here to kill him.*

Recovering quickly, Winfrey spat the words.

"That arrogant prick, I'm so glad he's not on board, Sir. I really need to get out of this hall."

That worked like punching in a four-digit entry code. Harrison turned and then staggered towards the bar, eventually clinging to the highly polished bench, still looking like he would collapse without its support. He recovered slightly and poured himself a big scotch, swallowing it in two gulps. Winfrey was taken aback by Harrison's response to his arrival. Winfrey allowed Harrison to remain scared and unsure for a while longer. He is terrified of me. Winfrey had to reassure the old man while still not alluding to understanding what was scaring Harrison.

"Mr. Harrison, I'm Moses Bishop." With that, he thrust his hand out to be met by the clammy palm of the terrified man.

Winfrey didn't want to lose any momentum.

"I wasn't supposed to contact you, but I figured it would make more sense if we could work together. Now, Sir, the good news is Mr. Johnson won't bother you ever again."

The older man visibly relaxed, Harrison interrupted Winfrey. "You killed him, did you kill him?"

The beginnings of an evil smile replaced the older man's initial look of fear.

Winfrey thought to himself; *so much for benign grandpa, this guy's bad news.*

"Settle down, Mr. Harrison. It's what I do, but you don't have to shout about it."

"I'm sorry, Moses, you don't realise how happy you've made me."

The Delta Force Officer was on a roll. "Now, Mr. Harrison, I heard you had to move some crates or something. Have you got plenty of labour for that?" Winfrey could see the seed take straight away.

"No, Moses, part of why I am so happy about Johnson's demise I've got no help left because he has eliminated all my on-board team. Can you give me a hand moving the gear?"

"Sure, no problemo, but can you do me a favour? You can tell I can't stand Sherwood, and I know I will get a rocket up the ass for talking to you direct." Capitalising on Harrison's fear of Sherwood ordering his death, Winfrey encouraged him to be even more scared. The younger man continued. "Sherwood didn't want me to talk to you for some reason. I'm not sure why. Mr. Harrison, can you do me a favour?"

Winfrey could see Harrison would do anything to stay on the right side of the supposed hitman. "Could you call Sherwood and tell him about Johnson. And that I am helping you now."

Harrison smiled and nodded. And Winfrey knew he was in deep. For the sake of the CIA Agents listening, Winfrey knew a nod didn't work.

"Oh, that's great, Mr. Harrison. I really appreciate not having to talk to Sherwood, he's such a smart ass."

The next day, they met again in the smuggler's luxury suite. Harrison was keen to complete the moving job in the owner's cargo hold. "Moses, when is your next shift?"

Winfrey could see Harrison was utterly relaxed and trusting of his new team member. "I don't start for close on three hours; what's on your mind?"

"Could we have a look at the crates and see if we can find a new home for them?"

Nodding, Winfrey responded. "Sounds OK, but let's not go down there together. You take off, and I'll make my way there in a little while later."

The Delta Officer acted as though he did not know about the owner's storage area.

"Mr Harrison, how do I get there? Do I need a special security card?"

Harrison explained where the area was and what Winfrey needed to access it. The two men met an hour later near the suite owner's storage area entrance. The two new partners walked around the wired-off corridors until they had identified a suitable unoccupied enclosure. Harrison and Winfrey arranged to meet back in the cargo hold the following day at the same time.

Returning to his room, Winfrey made a quick call to Colonel Randolph at Delta Force HQ. "Sir, I'm in clean and strong. That Intel you gave me, and the fact that Harrison wanted Wallace dead so badly opened the doors wide."

Winfrey continued. "I am unsure how much Intel from the listening devices the CIA boys are passing through, but I have infiltrated Harrison's team.

In fact, I **am** Harrison's team. It looks like our Aussie friend has wiped out Harrison's on-board team, so now I'm it. This time tomorrow, I'll send through all the new locations and identification details on the crates. It couldn't be going better, but I tell you, Harrison is a cold fish, or maybe more correctly, shark. Even though, as far as we know, he has no criminal record and is supposedly new to all this, he seems ruthless and experienced. I had to stop him doing friggin cartwheels when I told him I'd killed our Mr Johnson/ Wallace."

His control continued. "Great work, Oprah. It must have been difficult to hide your anger at him carrying on like that."

"Yeah, but I figure one way or another, he'll get his. I just hope I'm there to see it."

"That's for sure, Lieutenant; I'll be in touch; keep that pretty blond head down, hey?"

Winfrey smiled and pushed the end button.

The next day, Winfrey met Harrison down in the owner's storage area. Initially, Winfrey thought he had gotten there before the old smuggler. However, Harrison swaggered around the corner of a welded steel wall in the cargo hold.

He pointed over his shoulder and said, "Moses, good to see you. Just behind that bulkhead, there's an area with nothing in it. The nameplate says it belongs to Tom Carter in Suite 2208. It's empty now, so there is no chance he will use it this side of New York."

"Fine, Mr. Harrison, what's the plan?" Winfrey had to be careful not to reveal that he knew more than he should have without the benefit of the listening device.

Harrison looked at Winfrey. "I'm so delighted to have you helping, Moses."

Winfrey immediately thought, *What a surprise. Harrison wasn't the labourer type due to age and wealth; little wonder he's happy for me to be here.*

Harrison took on his best Management tone.

"OK, first we black out all the existing markings, then we put on all the new names and addresses. We'll put poor old Tom's name on everything, and anyone seeing the boxes in his storage area won't give them a second thought. Harrison unlocked the padlock, holding the chain and wire fence together using his owner's key. The couple moved into the storage area, Winfrey carrying the paint and equipment.

As Winfrey had assumed, he did most of the work with Harrison acting as director. In no time, the old markings were blacked out and replaced with new ones. After some pushing and sliding, the crates were in their new home, looking like they had been there forever. Moses/Winfrey was wet with sweat, and Harrison looked cool, calm and happy.

Winfrey was talented at collecting Intel without appearing nosy.

"Mr. Harrison, I get changing the markings on the crates, but surely the freight documents are still in your name?"

As Harrison put his padlock and chain around the new compound, he replied. "That's not a problem, Moses. Now we know these boxes are freight in every sense of the word. However, to anyone who sees them, they are my property, stored until I need the contents at a later date. They could be full of overflow items from when I downsized to move into my suite. Some fellow owners have push bikes or sporting gear; who knows? I can leave it here forever or take it off the ship whenever I want."

Winfrey was quite impressed by the simplicity of this owner's system. It sidestepped customs inspections and duties on both ends of the journey.

When the items came on board, they were taken straight to the suite owner's storage unit. No one considered them actual freight in transit. Winfrey headed back to the crew's accommodation, thinking; *well, Harrison,*

we did all that, but it meant nothing with those trackers still in place; changing the markings won't hide them.

The library-like peace of the New York antique dealer's office was shattered when one of Sherwood's burn phones rang. He quickly walked over to pick it up, hoping it was his ISIS contact, and was disappointed to see it was that dumb ass, Harrison.

"Yes." His elegant yet still New York accent instantly conveyed his disappointment and annoyance at his day being interrupted by the call.

"Mr Sherwood, just thought I would let you know we have moved the items; all good. Moses helped me."

Sherwood thought; *at least that little objective had been achieved, then a realisation hit him.*

"What the fuck do you mean Moses helped you, do you mean Moses Bishop?

"Y.....yes, he asked me to let you know that the 'other' problem has been permanently solved and that he is giving me a hand until we get to New York."

"You two have got it all worked out, haven't you."

He lost it, screaming into the phone. "Tell that fuckwit, Moses, I'll catch up with him face to face. When was fucking initiative one of his strong suits?"

Harrison had expected praise and could only manage an unintelligible stutter in response.

Annoyed at this break in his plans, Sherwood became even more angry to see that his hand was visibly shaking due to the anger. He hated lowlifes having such an effect on him. Sherwood quickly figured they were too far away from him to intervene, and his idea of Bishop eventually eliminating Harrison was still possible.

He started thinking, *It might work out when I'm ready. Bishop will sort Harrison, and I'll have Bishop dealt with here in New York for disobeying me. Harrison was still on the line.*

Calming himself, Sherwood continued. "OK, OK, I suppose you have both done well in the long run. Tell Moses to keep going that way; I'll let you know the details for getting those crates off the ship. I'll talk to you in two days. Keep your heads down. We are nearly home, yes?"

"Great Mr. Sherwood……." Harrison was stunned to silence; the antique dealer had terminated the call again without the smallest gesture of civility. Harrison smiled to himself. Maybe one or two more calls with that pig, and then I'll get to retire yet again. I'll sell my suite and disappear forever.

CHAPTER 18

It was cold and misty in Langley, Virginia, as Director Dave Myers looked at the latest listening device transcripts from Harrison's suite. He oversaw the entire Hawala operation, driving and approving the various decisions and changes this operation had demanded. He had lost his wife and teenage son on 9/11. Myers had become committed, if not obsessed, with shutting down this terrorist financial system Hawala ever since they identified that it paid for some or all of the attack on the Twin Towers and Pentagon buildings. Flicking to another screen, he was staring at a digital nautical map of the world with the route of the Southern Star marked on it. Just like the old World War Two movies but digital. There was a flashing black star moving slowly along this red line. This cruise ship's location had just been updated automatically by the satellite tracking devices inside the crates of stolen antiquities. Opposite him, chewing on his third doughnut, was Special Agent Munroe. He wasn't fit; you could call him a slob and not get too many arguments, even from him.

But he got things done; Myers had worked with him before and knew he was way sharper than he dressed. And on what turned out to be a very complicated Op, he had done an outstanding job. He had been the late Agent Ramone's Control, and losing one of your team was always tough. Then, after Ramone's murder, he had become Wallace's Control by default. This command structure was made more challenging by Wallace being an Aussie. Munroe was now in constant contact with Delta Force Officer Colonel Randolph. Who, in turn, was the conduit to their undercover Operative Lieutenant Ben Winfrey. This chain of command was both an acknowledged strength and weakness to the CIA Management. Munroe sprayed icing sugar as he spoke. "You know, Director Myers, it's always this part of an Op that worries me the most. Like a winning relay team stumbling or dropping the baton in the final fifty yards of the gold medal finals."

Myers tried to ignore his subordinate's lack of table manners. "Yeah, I know what you mean; that Aussie has given us more than we could have ever hoped for. Ramone gave it all; we all agree with that. And now it seems to have come together better than we could have dreamt. This Delta Force Op Winfrey couldn't have done any better, either. He saved the Wallace's life and successfully set those listening devices and trackers, three hits out of three mission targets. Now he is entrenched just where we wanted him and when we need it most."

Munroe knew his boss would have already thought of it but asked just in case. "We should try to recruit that Winfrey guy ASAP; like most DF guys, he's top-shelf in any man's war. Would you like me to handle it?"

"Good thinking, Munroe, yeah, you have a try, tread gently though, but don't go upsetting Colonel Randolph by stealing his Operatives, or at least being too obvious about it."

Munroe smiled at his boss assigning such a political task. "So, Sir, how do you see the next few days?"

Myers couldn't help smiling for a different reason; few operations went this well. Munroe wondered what had caused a shadow of sadness to pass over his Director but ignored it. Myers was thinking of Ramone as the smile faded, he responded. "The Assault Team is assembled and on standby. The ETA for the Star is thirty-three hours from now. We have a small team on surveillance of Sherwood's home and another on his office. We don't expect him to get his hands dirty, but you never know who he might meet, so it's all worth a go. You're good to go, yes?"

Munroe's part of the final phase was that he was responsible for the IT geeks who would be invaluable immediately after the raid.

"Yeah, the geeks are hot to trot, but you know what they're like. It's like herding cats but worse because they're all near genius level. They are all smarter than me and yet as dumb as a bag full of hammers with everything else other than computers. I'll have them in that antique dealer's office as soon as he's in 'cuffs'. I have briefed the Assault Team Leader, and he knows that Sherwood is to be pushed into a corner away from every electrical device as soon as they enter. He may have a one-stroke deletion or warning program set up, so we need to keep him away from any phones or keyboards. They must crack all his contacts and data before word can get out about his arrest and the latest antiquities' seizure. If his customers, bankers, and especially the Hawala agents and masters know he's gone, they will shut down their addresses and accounts within an hour."

Agent Myers knew Munroe was a top Agent, and his plans confirmed it.

"Good work, Munroe; sounds like you've got everything covered. You go in behind the Assault Squad. Get in there as soon as the raid is executed, and make sure the cutouts close Sherwood down."

Relaxing a little, Assistant Director Myers opened his bottom drawer and withdrew two glasses and a bottle of American sipping Whiskey. He poured two good shots of the smoky liquor. Moving on to a more general discussion, they were both looking forward to this extended operation ending and the high-value expected outcomes.

"Pouring another drink for both men, Myers raised his glass in a toast.

"Credit where credit is due, Munroe. You know, we wouldn't be in such a great position if it wasn't for our partners in this op. We may not have got anywhere without that Australian Steve Wallace. He came through when push came to shove. I don't think it would be premature for us to update our friends down under at the National Security Centre at this point. And, of course,we need to pass on our sincere gratitude for their contribution. He pushed a button on his phone and asked his admin to get the National Security Centre on the line.

Thousands of miles away at the National Security Centre, Canberra, Australia, Major General Watson and Brigadier Dodds sat at the dark mahogany board table. The usually sunny view of a stand of gum trees and grassed lunch area had been replaced by cold fog filling the wall of glass running along one side of the meeting room. Dodds leaned forward and pressed the disconnect on the speakerphone in front of the two old warriors. They appreciated the thanks the Director and Agent in Charge expressed regarding the massive contribution to the operation that Major Wallace had made. The Senior Officers raised their glasses in a toast on hearing the operation had been successful. They both knew anything that takes finances away from ISIS would translate into saved lives.

Once their glasses were finished, Brigadier Dodds picked up the phone again, turning to the Major General. "Colonel Goodrich has been the contact for us with all this. I know we were all worried about Steve Wallace. He's a wonderful Soldier, but this Op was way too James Bond for his skill set. And I know you were the same as me, Sir, all this sharing men and Intel is not to our liking."

Colonel Paul Goodrich answered his phone after one ring. The Brig gave him an abridged version of the CIA call they had just completed.

"Paul, we are delighted with the way this has turned out. Good work on your part, and the Yanks are eternally grateful for our cooperation and Steve Wallace's outstanding performance. That's about it for now. Can you pass on our congratulations and thanks to Major Wallace. And let him know how the Op is going. I know he was upset about being pulled out of the game at half-time after such a committed effort."

"Thanks, yes, Sir, I'll let Steve know how it's all going. And I'll pass on the Americans and your appreciation as well."

The Brigadier was an experienced manager of men and always tried to show a personal interest. "How's that wonderful family of yours going, Paul? You're not spending too much time here, are you?"

After the argument he had left his home on this morning, Colonel Goodrich was glad this was a phone call. The Brig couldn't see the face he had just pulled regarding the time that he needed to spend in his office. Smiling to soften his voice, he replied.

"Thank you for enquiring, Sir. They are fine, and we have all settled into Canberra well."

"Good to hear, Paul. You take care and say hello and thanks to Major Wallace from us." A loud click signified the call had been terminated.

After filling his coffee cup, the Colonel, knowing how his Operative was sweating on learning how the Op was going, punched in Steve Wallace's number.

My phone vibrated, and seeing who it was, I immediately went to our pre-arranged position for non-encrypted comms. We knew my phone wasn't secure, so our conversation had to be cryptic and ambiguous, as well as the content we dispensed with rank and titles, attempting not to sound official or Military. Having a friend in Canberra was OK, but we were always 'short and sweet'.

"Good morning; how's it going down there in our great nation's capital where all the big decisions are made?"

"Why is it when anyone from here phones anyone in some part of Australia, the call is always answered with sarcasm? I know the answer; I suppose we deserve it by association."

"Sorry about that, you're right, it seems to be nearly obligatory. What can I do for you?"

"Relax, Steve; we don't have any work for you just yet. I just got off the phone talking about your last holiday. From what they said, it sounded like you had such a great time; everybody is interested in it. Thought I'd let you know how your new friends are going."

Laughing at the jibe, I bit. "I will never live that cruise down, will I?"

We were always careful about what we discussed on an unsecured line, especially this close to the sharp end of the final phase of an op.

"Yeah, I only wish I could have afforded to stay on board, but I had to come back and earn some money to pay off my holiday. I guess the lucky ones who stayed on must be near the end of the cruise by now?"

"Yeah, you're right, only a day or so. Your new cruise friends are going to be so happy when they dock. They don't know it, of course, it's a big surprise, but lots of our friends will meet the ship and make them feel welcome when they get home. The man I spoke to said how grateful they all were for all the fun they had when you were with them. Of course, that made everyone over this side of the pond very happy, especially the two grandpas. Anyway, I just thought you'd like to know how they were going. Of course, I'm glad how it all turned out because it was me who gave you the idea to travel in the first place."

"Yeah, you're right. I wouldn't have thought of it without you. OK, thanks for all that; please let me know if you hear how the welcome party goes, and as usual if I can help in any way, let me know."

"For sure, Steve," switching to another casual code, he continued. "I nearly forgot that Doctor you had some tests with somehow didn't have your contacts, so he asked me to pass on this report. He said you were fine but very run down and that you should take a holiday. But he said avoid cruises if that's how you came back from them; some time in the bush was his recommendation."

"Hilarious Paul, what he's really saying is ease up on the grog, too many on-board parties, hey? Anyway, thanks again, talk soon. Bye"

Even though the coded conversation had been painful for both of us working within the constraints security demanded, I had got the news. I hung up.

Roma Queensland

My military career and probably my personality meant I enjoyed spending plenty of time alone. In the Military, it was always' hurry up and wait'. Unlike in the movies, Helos, trucks, or even the enemy walking into an ambush hardly ever arrived on time. You always have lots of time to fill in. Some of the boys sleep, some gamble with a three dice on a game called Crown & Anchor, but me, well, I think. I have always filled in the time thinking things through. I was constantly re-running thoughts and conversations, analysing their meanings. Probably too much, but that's me. I was deep in thought, thinking about how crazy my life had become. I'd only been home a few days, and it already felt like I had never been away. When you get home, you're back to reality, whatever you do, whether exotic, exciting, dangerous or downright mundane. There is a Bible verse that says: 'a prophet is not known in his own hometown or home.' Man, this is so true. Deep down, I knew this was a good thing; Chris had a way of keeping me grounded, keeping it real.

One minute, I'm living in luxury with the addition of a life-threatening adventure on a major Op and the next thing. Well, I'm doing the washing up. I was enjoying the view from the kitchen window, watching my dog Jake looking for non-existent sheep in the garden. Daydreaming, my thoughts wandered back to the cruise; *I wondered how my old mate, the cruise ship barman Rushane, was going, the Jamaican accent. "Dah usual Sah?"*

The Princess speaks. "Steve, the rubbish bin needs to go out, please." My daydream went straight from the penthouse to the outhouse. After finishing my domestic chores, I walked into our sunny little kitchen. I knew this was coming, I was surprised how long Chris had waited.

"OK, Steve, you haven't said much about your mission, and I know you can't tell me details. But what happened, big man?" Chris had been thoughtful enough to take a few days off from her local

Police Officer job to be with me on my return. And I appreciated it and was sensitive to these 'adjustments' brought on by the growth of a serious relationship. I loved this woman and appreciated everything that made her who she was.

I figured I needed to keep her involved, if not fully informed. I answered her question, avoiding anything classified and giving only minimal details. Demonstrating my depth of wisdom when it comes to women, I told her the parts I thought she would enjoy. For the life of me, I couldn't understand why Chris wasn't impressed when I told her I had been married to a good-looking American. And how my 'wife' and I were forced to share flashy hotel rooms and cruise cabins. Chris seemed to settle down quickly when I explained what happened to poor old Ramone. I explained to Chris that Ramone was an excellent agent and a top person and how, sadly, my cover wife had been murdered by the smugglers. Being a copper, Chris knew the risks and felt the loss even of a complete stranger. But I could still tell she had concerns, probably wondering if the marriage had ever been consummated. I was smart enough not to attempt to say anything about couches and beds.

Hiding her fears well, Chris must have figured a diversion would work and asked. "Steve, are you keen to go out for some Chinese tonight?"

I didn't answer; I had drifted away again.

"STEVE." She shouted. Where are you, Hon? You haven't really been here all day; what's on your mind?"

"I'm sorry, Hon. I was just thinking; it's been two days since Colonel Goodrich phoned me. The Southern Star must have arrived in New York by now. What was happening? Have they made some arrests? Had anyone been killed or injured? I hope I'm wrong, but there must have been some shooting when this much money is involved?"

I loved this woman too much to shut her out, and it helped to share my worries with someone other than Jake.

"Like I said, that cruise ship must have docked, which means the baddies will try to unload their cargo. If or when they do, it will start a chain reaction of seizures, arrests and hopefully an absolute ton of new Intel. You know what it's like, no different to a Police Operation. This stage is always the scary period."

Chris nodded as she got us both a beer from the fridge.

I continued. "The smugglers might not know who I really am or who I work for. But they know I was on the ship, which may have spooked them. After all this work, they might leave it where it is and disappear. That's doubtful guessing the cargo's value, but maybe. There's been a heap of great Intel captured along the way, but the high-value targets on the mainland are the ones I want to see put out of business."

I could see Chris understood the importance of this and asked.

"I thought the Americans knew where those things were headed, who the players were and who the antique dealer was."

"I'm sure they do, Hon, probably a fancy guy with flash set up, Auction House apparently on the surface all legit. Hopefully, the Feds will get him, he's history already. He just doesn't know it yet. It's the bankers and the agents spreading the money around to the terrorists and the terrorists themselves we are looking for. I should say they are looking for."

At first, talking about it made me feel a little better, but now, I was more worried.

"See Chris, I feel like I was there for everything but the end play. I know deep down it was the right thing, but it's still hard to handle. I feel like I should be there to clean up the mess I made."

She was a copper, which meant she had 'some' understanding of this stuff and where I was coming from. But, more importantly, she loved me. I tried to pull myself out of the hole I was in. I put my arms around her and drew her in tight.

"Chris, I know Goodrich is a good bloke. He'll let me know as soon as he knows. How's Mongolian lamb sound good?"

We headed over to the local Chinese, and like always, the food was excellent. Throughout dinner, Chris and I talked about nothing serious, which was terrific. Chris and I enjoyed each other's company like any couple in love. However, like when you sense a storm coming, I have an uncomfortable feeling that I should be doing something. There was unfinished business, and things were happening, and here I was enjoying the food. I wouldn't try to suggest I have any supernatural powers or some spiritual connection with our counterparts in America, but somehow, I was sure they must have been working. We finished our meal and returned home; both of us had eaten too much, but it sure was good. Chris was doing all the talking about maybe a holiday to the Northern Territory.

Sincerely interested, I was doing my best to listen. The truth was I was totally distracted. It turned out my gut feeling was on target because as Chris and I walked home, the Feds and a unit of Marines in New York were preparing for the final assault that afternoon.

CHAPTER 19

As planned, the American Feds held fire by keeping a very loose surveillance on the cruise ship, Harrison, and the crates now stored in another passenger's storage enclosure. The tracking devices Winfrey had planted allowed the Feds to stay away from the cruise terminal while knowing their exact location at all times. Winfrey was still on board and in contact with Harrison on an as-needed basis, but he wasn't needed much at this stage. Usually, the Southern Star had only a three-day turnaround before it set sail again. However, there was a problem with their huge Garbage Mastication Unit. This machine reduced tons of food and other material that were then jetsamed into the wake during the night. Being mostly biodegradable, this was a successful ecological and financial solution to the incredible wastage generated daily by such a cruise ship. This breakdown stretched the usual port stay into four and a half days.

Special Agent Munroe hadn't slept for close on a week. Everything was organised, checked and re-checked in preparation for the target cruise ship's arrival in New York. The ship had been moored to the pier for three days, and still nothing. He knew that nearly all the passengers disembarked here, returning home or continuing on to their next adventure. He had been dreading phoning Director Myers, everyone was on edge; no one was sleeping well, including Dave Myers. The call went through.

"Munroe, I sure hope you have good news for me. Have our crates been moved?"

"Ah, sorry, no news at all. I'm starting to get a sinking feeling that our honeymooning agents may have well and truly spooked them. They'll take a big hit by leaving the antiquities on board, but maybe they figure it's not worth the risk now they know we know."

Myers was tired and stressed more than he could remember; he handled multiple high-risk ops all day long, but this one dragged on and exhausted everyone involved. He was used to acting as the shield between his Ops people and the higher CIA echelons. And, of course, due to the elements of terrorism and finance, Homeland Security, Treasury, and all the alphabet agencies and services demanded SITREPS every few hours. “OK, the situation dictates we sit on our hands, and so we will. But you know there is a whole choir asking for how long? I assume that Delta Force guy is keeping an eye on Tango 1.”

Munroe was grateful that Myers was his next up. The AD had been there, done that, so he wasn’t stupidly demanding and certainly no drama queen. The Special Agent knew his boss shielded him from them all, thank God. In turn, he wanted to help Myers as much as possible.

“Yes, Sir, Winfrey is staying in place. After his great undercover work, he’s all set to arrest Tango 1 as soon as he’s given the Go. Timing-wise, we’ve confirmed that the ship’s maintenance should be completed tomorrow at 1200 Hrs. The ship will be gone within minutes of the engineers finishing their work.”

Myers rubbed his temples, wondering if his head was going to explode.

“Buddy, I’m sure you’ve thought of it, and I hope and pray this doesn’t happen. But what will you do if those crates stay on board? We may have to keep following them to another port until they get unloaded.”

“Sir, let’s hope they are only bluffing, waiting for us to blink first. Either way, this time tomorrow, we will know what’s going on. I know we all want this to end, for all our sakes, but also to finally get some solid outcomes.”

Myers could hear the fear in Munroe’s voice and knew he was one of the bravest men he had served with. “It’ll work out; you and your team have done a great job, the results have to come. Keep in touch and try to get some sleep." The call was done.

As arranged at precisely 10.00 Hrs the following day, a white sign written moving van with a hydraulic tailgate lift pulled up at the wharf security checkpoint. Sherwood had informed Harrison of the name of the transport company and the time he had arranged for the pickup. Harrison didn't have to do anything. The delivery instructions were once the crates were off the cruise ship, he had no further part to play.

As instructed, Harrison had warned the ship's Security staff of the upcoming event and that he would personally meet the contractors on their arrival shipside. To ensure seamless service, they informed wharf security to expect the truck. The transport contractors hired to pick up the crates didn't have a clue what was inside the wooden crates. And, of course, they didn't care. Sherwood had arranged the paperwork to be a simple transport order for household goods to be picked up and delivered without any fuss.

10.05Hrs the white moving van pulled alongside the ship's loading door, typically used for loading supplies for hungry and thirsty passengers. The driver had the correct paperwork; he dropped his window and handed the clipboard to the Southern Star Security Officer. The ship's freight foreman directed one of the ship's forklift drivers to pick up the crates from the secure area Harrison unlocked and stood beside. The forklift driver headed for Harrison's storage unit. He was surprised to see the elderly passenger standing outside a storage area assigned to another passenger. What did he know? He was just a forklift operator; Harrison had just unlocked it so who cares. The gate wall pulled aside, so he took the crates one at a time out to the waiting truck. Once loaded, the truck was waved through the wharf checkpoint. From there, the crates were taken unceremoniously to an anonymous, empty warehouse in the old Meat Packer's District. The delivery instructions had informed the moving van driver that no one would be at the warehouse.

Using the still active tracking devices installed by the Delta Force Operative, Munroe's teams sat in unmarked vans and monitored the smuggled artefacts. Once the truck delivered the crates to the warehouse, the Agents were confident that they would sit there for some time. They had no intention of rushing in and tipping their hand. While necessary, these crates had nearly served their purpose by exposing previously hidden layers of this multi-tiered organisation. An Assault Team was in position but out of sight to close all connecting roads and surrounded the warehouse once Agents completed all the other phases of the operation. Hope for the best—plan for the worst. The threat assessment was low; they expected to breach the building and seize the crates without a single shot being fired or facing any real resistance.

The threat assessment proved correct as they found it unmanned, the containers sitting on the dirty concrete floor in the otherwise empty warehouse. The smugglers had assigned no security to the crates. This strategy was probably an attempt to suggest that the boxes were just personal items of little value.

That was fine with Munroe and his team; he could now hand over the evidence to the Feds awaiting trial if needed. The Feds took control of the crates. One of their Techs approached the little group of well-travelled boxes and opened his tool kit. He swept each box and quickly located the tracking devices. He returned to his SUV and came back with a battery-operated jigsaw. He cut a square hole big enough for a hand to fit through and adjacent to each device. He then removed them one by one. Turning to the CIA Operatives, who didn't hide what they were feeling, looked between shock and anger and smiled. "Sorry guys, nothin personal, even I don't know where this stuff is going, and now you won't either. Then, the crates were loaded into unmarked Government vehicles, ready for the three-hour trip to the secret destination.

As with the previous seizure, the Federal Officers took these crates under heavy but covert guard to their Top-Secret warehouse, the Federal Secured Storage Facility (FSSF), where it joined every large quantity criminal seizure made in the last five years. A Platoon of US Marines supported the facility, monitored by a dense grid of CCTV cameras, Detection Motion Plates and sensors and Body Heat sensors. Two five-metre high razor-topped fences surround the FSSF perimeter. Coils of more razor wire were crammed in the gap between the two wire fences. The physical and electronic systems guaranteed getting in was nigh impossible, but if anyone did infiltrate this facility, they would be detected within seconds. Special security clearance was the only way to access work or visit the facility. They didn't have visitors.

This facility was such a high-security sector that only a handful of Senior Federal Agents even knew of its existence, let alone its location. Several cleverly developed physical deceptions and protocols were designed to misdirect anyone attempting to track a seizure. Those Federal Agents who were not actually cleared to work in the high-security facility but were involved in the initial transport and administration of these seizures were not privy to the final destination. After delivering the seized goods at a bogus destination, the original drivers would dismount and be ferried home again in a blanked-out van. Then, Agents and Marines assigned to the Top-Secret Warehouse would transport the seized shipment into the Federal Secured Storage Facility (FSSF).

Several distinct sections were evident within the gigantic building. The eastern side of the facility was highly regulated and sectioned off by high-tensile fenced units. There were pallets of high-value drugs covered with black plastic wrapping. These bins didn't hold the odd deal here and there, not even the odd key (Kilo).

These were the colossal quantity busts you saw on the evening news. This section contained millions of dollars worth of illegal drugs stored like chicken feed on multiple pallets. The place was like a scene from Pablo Escobar's life story.

To uninformed observers, the hundreds of pallets of illegal drugs stored in the hi-tech warehouse would question the wisdom of keeping such large quantities rather than destroying the product soon after the seizure. However, there was an unavoidable reason for this. The illegal drugs were managed using an incredibly rigid administrative system that ensured no error or loss in the strict evidence chain occurred.

When these vast drug seizures occur, the eventual court case may happen up to three years after the initial arrests and associated search warrants. In such events involving unimaginable amounts of money, the accused would typically have been refused bail as a flight risk.

However, the evidence must be securely stored, the physical product must be available for inspection by the court. And in significant seizure cases, the courts always demand to see the evidence, unable to rely solely on the DEA's records. Once the court case finishes, the incarceration of the felon triggers the destruction of the drugs in the facility's industrial incinerator.

Several other designated areas within the building accommodate large-scale, high-value contraband seizures. The exact requirements apply to the secure storage of illegal arms seizures and the resulting court cases. All seized weapons are stored in another fenced unit on the northern end of the aircraft hangar-like warehouse. Once the relevant court case has ended, this evidence will then be approved for destruction. The guns are crushed in a specially designed hammer mill, reducing the weapons to coin-size fragments. The exact processes are applied when destroying heavy munitions such as explosive items, rockets, grenades, and even missiles. This protocol provides a 'live' practice for the Bomb Disposal Officers at the

Federal Secured Storage Facility (FSSF) purpose-built demolition range.

A comparatively small unit exists behind high tensile wire containing crates whose contents would never be destroyed, that of smuggled historical artefacts or art work. The seized containers and crates contain the artefacts laid out in the consignments in which they had arrived. Like the other more lethal and contemporary contraband, these items are stored as evidence in preparation for upcoming court appearances. This contraband was challenging to Law Enforcement; was it tainted stolen property, or did it belong to the world community? Many high-level discussions had occurred in preparation for the post-court phase, thinking about the eventual fate of these incredibly culturally priceless antiquities. Regarding the first seizure, the Feds hadn't been able to identify the smugglers, the owners or even the recipients. Hence, these crates have been sitting in limbo ever since.

With no accused, there was no court case and no verdict that would typically initiate the removal of the items from the FSSF. And in any case, where would they send them? Senior Management of several Federal Agencies had met with representatives from The American Alliance of Museums and legal experts specialising in The Code of Federal Regulations of the United States of America. Of course, there were also international implications overreaching these antiquities due to their country of origin. The outcomes of these talks were that specialist curators were to inspect every item, whether a six-foot statue or a small brooch.

These specialists would confirm authenticity, source, and provenance, if any. Team Members destroyed in the incinerator any confirmed counterfeit items. The expert curators would then carry out the necessary processes to clean, restore and preserve the antiquities, including an ongoing maintenance schedule. Scientists installed the special controlled atmosphere tent used commonly during chemical or bacterial attacks.

Here, experts continually monitored humidity and temperatures and regulated as required. The item's final resting place was for Diplomats and others to resolve; however, the precious items would finally be safe. It was a goal that the ancient artefacts would eventually become available to all of humanity generally, in the sense of their beauty and history, displayed publicly in museums and libraries. No longer would the ancient treasures only be appreciated for their monetary value, for the greed of a few and definitely not the terrorist attacks that greed was eventually funding.

CHAPTER 20

Jake, the Border Collie cross and I had just returned from visiting a mate who ran a cattle property West of Roma. It was next to this property where, the year before, all hell had broken loose when I stumbled upon a terrorist training camp. Jake and I had enjoyed being away from town again and promised Mike we would come out for a stay as soon as I got some leave. Even so, I was still fidgety, wondering what was happening in New York. I had trusted my life to Colonel Goodrich, so I knew he'd keep his promise to phone me with a SITREP when he had something to report. He called at 1008 Hrs. the following day. I raced to the phone and grabbed it up to my ear.

"Steve, how you goin?"

"Great Sir. Have you got a job for me or some news?"

"As promised, I wanted to let you know what's happened since the Southern Star has docked."

There was no longer any danger that our discussion could lead to the smugglers being tipped off, and we both knew the chances of them having the resources to listen to us were remote. However, old habits guaranteed security when it was required. Now, it was all over; we no longer needed to speak in cryptic terms; this was refreshing.

Colonel Goodrich proceeded to relay an abridged version of the New York-based operation.

"Steve, after the ship docked, the crates were left alone for as long as they could before the Star was ready to sail off again. Anyway, the Yanks weren't greatly concerned because of those trackers. At the last minute, the ship's crew unloaded the wooden boxes under the guise of Harrison's personal property.

The truckie's paperwork recorded the crates as full of garden furniture and household decorations. The Feds are sure the transport crew was just that, as in not involved. When questioned, the driver reported he had instructions to unload and leave the crates in the empty warehouse at that address. Which is precisely what he did."

My excitement grew as the Colonel continued, but strangely, I felt a peace instead of the unsettled feeling I'd been battling for the last week.

Goodrich calmly continued. "At 0700 Hrs. our time, which makes it 1600 Hrs. New York, an assault team entered the hallowed halls of Sherwood's Antiques Auctioneer's Rooms. As planned, he was bundled away from his desk, computers, and phones as soon as the door kickers got in. Agent Munroe told me that by the time they had handcuffed Sherwood, one of the most sophisticated and skilled I.T. teams had already started working on his computers. Good news is they didn't even have to work out his password. Our 'highly esteemed' antique dealer didn't have time to close his computers down before they swooped."

I raised my clenched fist in celebration. "Oh, that's great, Sir. Was there any resistance?"

"They had assessed him as a low potential violent threat, the guys a high flyer, old school auctioneer art expert; I'm sure the first ins would have been careful. But no fight at all."

I was glad of the result and always happy to hear there were no casualties.

"Steve, Sherwood's arrest triggered two other simultaneous actions. The first was the seizure of those crates you looked after for a while. Once again, this went off without a hitch."

The Colonel laughed. "Munroe told me, and I quote, 'the Jarheads' crept around the warehouse, eventually storming in. They couldn't believe their eyes; no opposition; in fact, nobody was even present in the warehouse. I guess the baddies wanted to leave the gear there to ensure it wasn't being watched. Probably planned to pick it up in the near future after everything cooled down. It looks like they decided the crates were safe, and it was better not to attract attention by having security around a supposedly empty warehouse. Like who would have armed guards securing garden furniture right?"

OK. Mentally, I was ticking off the three phases of this mop-up operation: Sherwood, the artefacts, and lastly, Harrison.

I was immediately worried about something I could hear in the Colonel's voice.

"Now, Steve, I'm sure you're thinking about Harrison. Well, Lieutenant Winfrey was assigned the pleasurable duty of arresting Tango 1, our friend Harrison. Winfrey was still on board, and his cover with Harrison was still solid."

I sensed that Goodrich was stalling, not much, but enough for me to notice.

"Anyway, Steve, Winfrey went to Harrison's suite, and like I said, Winfrey's cover was still firmly in place. There was no reason the wealthy smuggler wouldn't have let him in.

From what we can gather, Harrison was armed and not reluctant to use his weapon when his freedom was on the line. Winfrey's attempted to place the man under arrest, and somehow, there's been a gunfight. The excellent news is Winfrey got Harrison; he is now eternally retired. The bad news is Winfrey caught a slug from Harrison's 45 Cal. It did plenty of damage and is now resting on his spine. They think he's been unconscious since that moment, but they can't be sure without witnesses. This is good because it means he probably hasn't moved.

They have him stabilised with plans to move him up to Walter Reed Memorial in D.C. where if and when they will take out the piece of lead."

Well, it was too good to be true, an operation of this size and value without causalities in the closing stages. Even so, my heart broke for my new friend to whom I owed my own life.

"OK, Sir, I know you're always flat out with a dozen other things, but can you flick a signal to them requesting SITREPs if anything changes? As you know, we wouldn't be having this conversation if it wasn't for Winfrey."

"Sure, Steve, I'll do my best to keep you in the loop, mate, but you know what it's like."

With others around and within the Military system, he would never have called me mate. However, it showed his compassion and understanding of my sorrow about Winfrey's injuries. Goodrich was a good man and an excellent Officer.

"Steve, just back to the operation for a minute; the big fish terrorist-wise are yet to be caught. Munroe hopes to harvest the Hawala contacts worldwide by accessing Sherwood's computers and phones.

This worldwide finance guarantee system has been operating under the radar, and now we may have got behind the magic mirror. As well as that they should capture a truckload of Intel about terrorist groups, individuals, community fronts, public organisations and official bankers.

Of course, picking up any Hawala agents will have a long-term impact on the terrorist funding system. Munroe told me they plan to 'steal' back any funds they can hack into from the legitimate banks; our boys have already accessed Sherwood's accounts. Although they will act quickly, that part may take a little time. Munroe could only provide a few details, but I expect he'll let us know how it all went in the wash-up. He's typical CIA, but there's no doubt they're all very aware of the fact they wouldn't be where they are now without your contribution. You wreaked havoc globally, but eventually, the net result is nothing short of outstanding."

I appreciated the praise, but out of respect for those we lost, I couldn't help but count the cost. I started thinking of Almahdi, the good-hearted smuggler from Petra, and Maria, the lovely young Filipino bartender. And, of course, Ramone, who, while she died in the line of duty, was still a terrible waste of a beautiful human being. I wasn't ready to include Winfrey, but deep down, I knew he would probably never be the same, whatever the outcome of his wounds.

"Well, Steve, that's all for now; like I said, I'll check on Winfrey's progress and let you know what cascades out of the Intel."

"Thanks, Sir, I appreciate your call; any news about the mission, please phone me any time, day or night."

Walking back into the kitchen, Chris must have seen the worry on my face. "What's happened, baby?"

I explained the Colonel's call and especially Winfrey's injuries. I had kept my own death from her, but she understood the bond that forms between soldiers in battle. She understood how upset I was for Winfrey.

Three days later, my phone vibrated; seeing it was Colonel Goodrich, my stomach sunk worrying about Winfrey's condition. I put on my best front and answered the call.

"Morning, Sir, what's new?"

"Steve, I've only got good news for you. Firstly, Winfrey came out of his coma and was stable enough to be choppered up to D.C. Your new best friend must be a tough guy because he's hung in there. Munroe said a team of five surgeons took nearly six hours to remove that bullet. It's early days, but all signs are positive, so it seems he's out of the woods."

Like an excited kid, I blurted out. "Thank God. That's wonderful news, Sir. He's a top bloke, and being Delta Force, even without saving my life, we had an instant bond."

The Colonel agreed. "Yeah, I'm sure there's been a lot of prayer for that young man on both sides of the Pacific."

"That's great news, Sir, I'm so relieved."

"Steve, just to business for a moment. The Yanks are over the moon. As expected, Munroe didn't or couldn't furnish a lot of detail, but I could tell from his excitement they picked up more than they could've ever wished for. I got the impression Munroe could talk to us all day and still leave out some of the results."

Colonel Goodrich must have taken notes while talking to Agent Munroe to provide this level of detail. He would have done this knowing he would have to give the Brigadiers a written report within twenty-four hours. Goodrich continued.

"He said Sherwood had access to no less than twenty-eight separate ordinary-type bank accounts worldwide. The 'biggie' for the CIA was the Intel identified eleven Hawala agents, or whatever they are called. He didn't say it, but I'm sure a team will monitor these individuals until the CIA know everything they can harvest. Then they'll be closed down permanently. I'm no expert on it, but this Hawala has been operating for thousands of years. And it's all about honouring a promise. I reckon that has to be a family business. So, it stands to reason that these eleven are probably tenth or whatever generation. Shutting them down has to be a devastating blow to terrorism worldwide. The contacts on Sherwood's phone and computers provided a mountain of Intel. Munroe said the Agency would be kept busy for months following up the new Intel.

A lot of people already known to them and a heap of new faces. He was excited about some terrorists the CIA had been keeping tabs on but had yet to be confirmed as threats. However, with this new Intel, there were definite targets. He didn't enlarge too much. It took them by surprise to some degree; he said there was a group of Americans involved, some relatively high profiles. The email trail they discovered identified some people who were neck-deep in laundering or banking the blood money. Some well-known entertainment industry characters were even donating money to supposed charities that, after some sleight of hand, eventually ended up for terrorist organisations. Munroe alluded to recouping a large amount of money from these suspect accounts. This success was a double whammy, taking the resource from the enemy and eventually using it to fund the fight against them."

"What about ISIS or other known groups?"

"Once again, Steve, he didn't provide much detail, but I asked the same question. Agent Munroe reckons he has the names and locations of the key players, the conduits to ISIS and others. He was so excited he even made a joke and I quote; 'Goodrich, I've got more leads than a professional dog walker.' " We both laughed and the Colonel continued. "He will be busy for weeks planning and mounting so many operations running at the same time to follow all these leads. Let's hope they all pay high dividends; they should. We all know it's gotta happen fast before everyone disappears into their holes."

I could hear the excitement in the Colonel's voice. Like Agent Munroe, I was excited and happy about the mission's success. More importantly, that this would hit worldwide terrorism hard the operations fuelled by this new Intel.

"OK, Steve, I'd better move on; keep in touch. I'll call you when I hear something. Bye now."

"Thanks for letting me know all that, Sir; like you said, let's hope they get all the way to the top. Thanks, Sir, bye."

And that was that. Great news about Winfrey: he was tough. I was sure he would pull through now. And I was confident the Americans would maximise the returns on all the captured Intel. It was all up to them; it had always been their mission, and for now, except for more news, I could relax.

I had been outside on the patio talking to Colonel Goodrich and was surprised at how long the call had taken. When I went back inside, I was still smiling.

"Great news so far: Winfrey came through the surgery. They got the bullet, so he should be OK."

"That's terrific, thank God. We both owe him for looking after the man I love."

I hadn't told her I had actually died, and what she had just said was an understatement as he had saved my life in the most absolute sense. I wanted to build our relationship with honesty, and Chris knew how dangerous my life could get. But I didn't want to worry her more than necessary by telling her any specifics about my last mission.

As happy as I was, Chris must have figured I needed encouragement; she attempted to summarise the outcomes. "I'm sure the payoff from all the sacrifices and effort will save hundreds of lives, even more. And by closing terrorist funding systems and taking out as many key players as possible, we are hitting them from all directions."

I decided we both needed a break. My' overseas holiday' was undoubtedly a fantastic adventure, but it was no break. I was glad it was all over. I was home. Chris and I decided to open a bottle of wine, and we headed out to the BBQ table in the shade of the patio. After opening a second bottle, we enjoyed the Queensland weather and each other's company. I had decided not to think about the mission from which I had just returned. However, something reminded me of my time with Ramone at the Shangri La. I had forgotten that for Chris, this meant stirring up all the questions about my cover marriage—big mistake. I shouldn't have mentioned anything to do with it again, damned wine. The smile that had been on Chris' face all afternoon was replaced with a mix of anger and worry. I did say I wasn't that smart when it came to women.

I thought about what had happened in my spare time at the incredible shopping centre in Dubai might distract her. I described the shops and entertainment in the vast shopping city. I then recounted what had happened from watching the men chasing the little boy, my intervention and the eventual outcome. It didn't change my beloved's opinion when I confessed that the amazing episode was unrelated to the mission. She was a country girl and a copper to boot; her awestruck romantic response was, "You, Steven are a shit magnet of the highest order, aren't you?"

I shook my head, lost for words, of course. I was met with further discouragement as I continued, eventually mentioning Royalty and extravagant wealth. Of course, she was right; the story was totally unbelievable.

"Steve, I know when a man is attempting to distract me. Now, even though I am only a girl from the bush, do you really think I am going to believe that fairy tale seriously?

I went to get some more wine.

Shouting, Chris yelled. "Hey, Steve, why is there a tow truck unloading a yellow Lamborghini on our driveway?"

THE END

TO MY READERS.

Thank you for reading TERROR IN PARADISE, my second book in the Action Thriller Steve Wallace sagas.

I really hope you enjoyed it.

Reviews help other readers find books they may like and assist me to strive for excellence in my writing. I really appreciate reviews, whether positive or negative. Please take a couple of minutes to post your review where you purchased my book.

Thank you so much.

Dave.

ABOUT THE AUTHOR

David Adams spends as much time as possible in the Australian bush, living off the land, gold, treasure fossicking, and hunting feral animals throughout Australia. He served as an Officer in the Australian Army Reserve during the post-Vietnam era. Dave has trained alongside members of the United States Marine Corps and Special Air Services SAS personnel. Serving his last two years in the A.D.F as a Platoon Commander Military Police provided him with exposure to law enforcement working closely with his civilian counterparts in the Queensland Police Service. Dave relies on this real-life experience to provide him with authentic characters, settings, and a knowledge of military equipment and procedures. He continues to travel the world in search of exciting settings and characters that he hopes will transport his readers to these exotic places while adding a reality to his books.

About the Author

ABOUT THE AUTHORDavid Adams served as an Officer in the Australian Army Reserve during the post-Vietnam era. Dave has trained alongside members of the United States Marine Corps and Special Air Services SAS personnel. Serving his last two years in the A.D.F as a Platoon Commander Military Police provided him with exposure to law enforcement working closely with his civilian counterparts in the Queensland Police Service. Dave relies on this real-life experience to provide him with authentic characters, settings, and knowledge of military equipment and procedures. He continues to travel the world in search of exciting settings and characters that he hopes will transport his readers to these exotic places while adding a reality to his books.

www.ingramcontent.com/pod-product-compliance
Lightning Source LLC
LaVergne TN
LVHW091031080826
845145LV00002B/445